# ZOMBIE TEAM ALPHA

## STEVE R. YEAGER

SEVERED PRESS
HOBART TASMANIA

Rating 4

# ZOMBIE TEAM ALPHA

# ~1~
## *FROM RUSSIA WITH LOVE*

Yuri Stakhanov limped along the mineshaft, occasionally ducking to avoid the thick timbers supporting the massive weight of the mountain above him. Years in various deep-shaft mines had left him with a permanent bend to his back and a hitch to his step. No longer could he stand as tall as he once had when he'd been a proud member of Spetsnaz—Russia's Special Forces. He'd been a soldier then and battled the fanatics in Afghanistan, but an incompetent fool of an officer and a lost temper had seen him banished from his beloved outfit forever. Now, his daily labors went into supporting his wife and extended family the only way he knew how—by digging deep into the earth for the elusive gold buried beneath.

After stopping to mop hot sweat from his brow, he resumed his shuffling gait, ever wheezing, ever coughing. The dim lamp on his helmet cast a narrow beam into the gloom, barely lighting the way ahead. In one hand, he held a small metal tin containing his mid-shift meal and, like all his mid-shift meals, had arrived by train earlier in the day. It had been made by his dutiful wife and was one small concession the company allowed to keep him connected to home.

He stopped again, this time to cough into his fist and spit out what came up, and when the fit subsided, he bent forward and rested his hands on his knees for a moment to let the pain in his swollen joints subside. As he straightened, he checked the aging Vostok watch on his wrist and grimaced. He had only twenty-five minutes left to eat his meal before he would need to return to work.

*Far too little time.*

Yuri lived a hard life, but he was no complainer, nor was he bitter over the typical injustices of life. He was approaching fifty and would soon leave deep-shaft mining to the young. He would become a pensioner, able to sit on his front porch, drink vodka, and smoke the smooth cigarettes of the American imperialists, who, much to his small pleasures, had their own troubles with the fanatics in Afghanistan.

With fingers calloused by years of hard labor, he unlatched the small metal tin that protected his meager meal from the rats and probed inside, searching for the buried treasure he knew was there.

"Ah," he said when he found it, nodding to himself proudly as he sat down on an outcropping of rock. His prize was a single piece of dark chocolate that his wife had wrapped in foil along with a sliver of ice meant to keep the chocolate cool so deep in the hot mine where the temperatures could reach 40 Celsius or higher.

With care, he balanced the tiny treasure on a jutting rock beside him and dug for more treats, but there were none to be found. What he did find were twin slices of a crusty brown bread and a link of pork sausage spiced with sage. They were not the delicious meatballs his wife often made and that he had hoped for, but it would do. Yes, it would do. All too often, she'd packed pickled cabbage. He hated pickled cabbage. It tasted too much like wet newspaper.

He chewed the bread slowly and deliberately while listening to the distant echoes of the pneumatic drills pounding away at the rock face. The drills never stopped, except when work had to be halted to blast with explosives. The sounds they made told him much about what progress was being achieved. By listening carefully, he could fathom the hardness of the stone into which they bored, and minutes ago, their pitch had shifted higher, informing Yuri that the bits had penetrated the thin vertical ore deposit and would soon need to be repositioned to alter the course downward and ever deeper into the earth. Which meant that the next few hours were going to be even more challenging.

Letting go of a weary breath, he glanced down the shaft the way he had come, knowing the minutes he had left before returning to work were ticking away fast and becoming even more precious.

He picked up the link of sausage and bit into it, watching as a light bobbed out of the gloom toward him. Despite the glare, he knew from the familiar movements of the headlamp that it was his crew mate, Petrov. The man was ten years his junior and already showing signs he would not make it as a miner much longer. Few ever survived long enough to become pensioners like Yuri, and

Petrov was not nearly so tough. He was never a soldier. He was never Spetsnaz. The man had gone to an institute to learn how to mine. *An institute,* Yuri had often thought, *to learn how to mine? To stand behind a drill and to not let go? How difficult was that? A brainless* chudovishe *could do the same job.*

Yuri shifted slightly to let Petrov sit next to him. The man let out a chest-rattling wheeze as he came to rest. Yuri kept a close watch on the man and caught where Petrov was staring—at the shiny piece of dark chocolate wrapped in foil. He casually scooted it out of the man's reach. While he enjoyed Petrov's company well enough, he did not trust the man with his beloved chocolate.

"Six days," Petrov stated proudly, which meant the following day would be a rest day spent back in the village and away from the mine. He then glanced both directions and drew out an aluminum flask from a pocket on his mud-stained overalls. He raised the flask in salute and stole a drink.

Yuri said nothing.

The man offered the flask, but Yuri refused to touch it. To drink while in the mine was a suspendable offense, which Yuri could not afford right now, even though the *svolochi* who ran the mine often would glance the other way when the men drank. The courage that came from a bottle was often of use to those who worked the mines—as long as production did not suffer and the strict quotas were met.

Another bobbing headlamp appeared out of the darkness. Petrov turned away from it and slipped the silver flask into his pocket, stood, and pressed himself against the far wall.

The new man who arrived, Daynov, held his hand out to block the glare of Petrov's helmet lamp as he came to a stop. Daynov was the youngest in Yuri's work crew. The kid was often brash but always respectful of his elders, so Yuri took special care to make sure Daynov knew how to remain alive and counseled him not to expend himself too greatly or too quickly. Yuri had often warned the young man to stay away from mining. *Find another profession,* he had often said, *you were never Spetsnaz. You are not tough like me.* It was an argument they'd frequently had.

Daynov waved away the light dismissively, but not before Yuri had seen the glint of something metallic in the man's hands.

"Six days," Petrov boasted again as Daynov came fully into the cone of light from Yuri's own headlamp. Daynov was twisting the metal object he held between his fingers, causing it to shimmer in the light. Yuri could not immediately tell what it was. It sparkled, but it was not gold nor silver nor tin nor platinum. And when exposed to the light, it gave off a shimmering iridescent gleam of reds and blues and greens. Faint, ghostly patterns shifted along its edges, giving the object the appearance of the disk movies Yuri had often watched in the recreation rooms after his shift. But it was certainly not one of those.

"What…is that?" Petrov asked.

Daynov bit the tip of his finger and tugged his worn gloves off. He ran a fingertip over the fragment, tracing along the sharp edges. "I do not know. I found it sticking from the ceiling. Perhaps it is a tool of some kind?"

"I have never seen anything like it before," Petrov said. "Yuri?"

Yuri pursed his lips and considered. He was the oldest of the three, and the implied expectation was that he must be the wisest. He drew a sharp intake of breath and scratched the whiskers on his chin. Exhaling, he said, "Yes, I have seen before." But that was a lie. To smooth it over, he took a bite of sausage and chewed while considering further.

"It's…very cold," Daynov said, turning the object over in his hands and running his fingertips back and forth across the pitted surface.

"Let me see," Petrov said. "Give here."

"No. Is mine. I found it. You can't—"

As Daynov looked up, Yuri saw confusion clouding the young man's eyes. Daynov suddenly went unnaturally stiff, as if he'd been shocked. His eyes became even more vacant and glossy. Yuri stopped chewing and set the remains of his meal onto the creased paper that had once wrapped it and wiped his lips with his fingertips.

Petrov hovered before Daynov, bobbing left and right and examining the man from different angles. He waved a hand in front of Daynov's eyes to summon a response then drew back in confusion when the younger man did not even blink.

Normally, it was difficult to get Daynov to stop talking. He was always telling anyone who would listen about a new woman, a new conquest, or how he had a new plan that would make him enough money to escape the drudgery of the mines once and for all.

But he was frozen solid, unable to speak.

Then Yuri noticed something else. He sniffed the air. It had a metallic tinge to it, as if the very air around him had become charged with electricity. Like after a lightning storm.

"Give to me." Yuri pushed away from his resting place and reached for the metal object in Daynov's hands. Daynov held on to it tightly, clutching it in a white-knuckled grip. Yuri tugged harder and, using his superior strength, was able to snatch it away. Petrov then helped the younger man sit on the mineshaft floor, and Daynov came out of his daze and started muttering incoherently. His lips moved slower and slower, until finally, he stopped making any noise at all.

Yuri stared down at the metal object in his hands. It was cold and growing colder against his skin. The object's surface was rough and pitted but strangely uniform, maybe even manmade. Squinting at it in the dim light, he brought it closer to his eyes to examine the strange surface pitting in more detail. He ran his index finger along one edge. The pits on the object were not random but somehow ordered into thin, precise rows.

Over his many years below ground, he'd seen every type of metal that could be found by mining. Most were locked in ores and had to be extracted before they could be processed. But there were a few rare specimens of naturally occurring metals that had been discovered accidentally—nuggets of gold locked in quartz, or the even rarer lumps of natural aluminum. But he had never in his life seen anything like what he held in the palm of his hand. It could not be natural. It had to have been manmade. But made from what? And by whom? And for what purpose?

He pressed his thumb against the cold metal. Through his thick callouses, he felt nothing except for a slight chill emanating from the object. Somehow, it was colder than the air around it.

*Impossible.*

After he had lifted his thumb away, his other fingers began to tingle. Curiously, he stared at them as he flexed each—one by one. They were all moving slower and slower, as if they had been stiffened by the cold. Soon, he had to fight just to bend his fingers even a fraction of a centimeter. A bitter coldness was growing rapidly in him as well.

It was then that he realized the terrible mistake he had made. He instantly wanted to drop the metal object and get as far away from it as he possibly could. But he could not let it go. He could only stare at the object while the coldness crept downward, deeper into his arms, into his elbows, into his shoulders, and finally into his chest. The icy tentacles felt as if they were reaching inside him and probing deeper and deeper, seeking, searching for something. Only the mental training he'd had as a soldier kept him from panicking. But his growing fear was beginning to win.

He could sense the foreign presence as it took control. It was something evil, wicked, and it was attempting to bore into his mind. His eyes involuntarily flicked to Daynov, showing the man on the mineshaft floor, only a few feet away. Though, to Yuri, the young man could have been a million miles away because he no longer had control over his own body. Not even his eyes.

Daynov grew more and more distant and indistinct by the second. Petrov hovered over the younger man and shouted down at him while alternately casting terror-filled glances at Yuri.

Yuri knew he should be able to hear what Petrov was saying. He could hear the sounds that were being made, but he could not understand the words being said. His body was starting to shiver, and his arms lifted not of his own volition. Then those arms went limp, and his right foot jerked and scratched at the dirt. He almost fell forward.

At his feet, Daynov began to convulse as his eyes went fully white and rolled back in his head. The young man's entire body was trembling and bucking wildly. Froth formed on Daynov's lips. He slammed down hard against the solid rock floor, and his back arched unnaturally, lifting him onto his head and heels.

The part of Yuri's brain still containing his own consciousness wondered if what was happening to Daynov would soon happen to him as well. *No.* He decided it would not. *I will resist whatever is invading my mind. I will hold out. I am strong. I am soldier.*

Petrov retreated from them both, raising a hand to his mouth and shouting unintelligible gibberish in both directions down the mineshaft. Then he tripped and fell onto his backside and frantically kicked away from the convulsing Daynov as his eyes went even wider with fear and his boots dug twin furrows in the dirt. Somehow, he was able to regain his feet. He stumbled in front of Yuri and shouted something. Yuri could not understand what Petrov was yelling but could see the man's lips moving and could hear the muffled cries, but the words were frustratingly not making any sense.

Frothy spittle foamed on Petrov's quivering lips, and each drop that hit Yuri's exposed skin felt like tiny pieces of red-hot shrapnel slicing deeply into his flesh. Then the coldness that had been growing inside him fled rapidly and was replaced with an intense heat, a searing heat, becoming hotter and hotter by the second. Through it all, Yuri could not move a millimeter on his own. He could no longer even blink. He could only stand there and take it while the horror that was invading his mind set every one of his nerves afire and caused him to wonder if those same fires were crisping and melting the very flesh from his bones.

He was panicking on the inside. He wanted to move. Wanted to so badly. More than anything in his life. But his limbs would not budge a millimeter.

Petrov's eyes opened wide, and he shouted nonsense at Yuri again. Then, stumbling, the younger man fell to the ground once more and struggled to lift himself. When he did, he twisted heels to toes and bolted away. Yuri wanted to call his friend back, wanted to tell him just what was happening. He wanted to make the pain stop. Whatever it took, he would endure it and overcome it. His eyes moved, but he was no longer in control of them. They followed the disappearing Petrov, who was quickly swallowed by the darkness of the mineshaft, leaving Yuri all alone with Daynov.

Yuri could still see, could still hear, and could still feel, but he could do nothing to control his actions. He was like a marionette hanging on a string and waiting for someone to take control. He wanted to let go of the object in his grip, but he could not command his fingers to loosen.

Time passed. How much time, he did not know, but the intense, burning pain slackened somewhat when he stopped fighting it. Then Petrov was returning, waving men closer to Yuri. Crisscrossing beams of yellow light filled the shaft and reflected off facets of the black stone walls. *Perhaps they can free me. Perhaps they can take this from me. Perhaps they can help.* As he wished for this small boon, he trembled with effort and was momentarily able to battle back against the invading paralysis.

Then the pain regrew to unbearable levels.

*Spetsnaz. I am strong. Spetsnaz tough. A true warrior never succumbs.*

Through teeth-grinding pain, he found he could move his eyes again. He could move his head. But it hurt so much to do so.

*I. Will. Not. Give. In.*

More men arrived. Their headlamps bathed Daynov in a flood of light. The young man was still at Yuri's feet, jerking about and trying to rise. Daynov's mouth was opening and closing. Bloody foam dribbled from his lips, and he had bitten off much of his tongue. Blood also streamed from his nose and ears, and his eyes were white orbs staring skyward. While he trembled spasmodically, his fingers flexed into claws and tore away the heavy cloth of his overalls and raked the flesh of his chest into angry red gashes as his fingernails bent and folded back.

The terrible, searing heat that held Yuri in its firm grip intensified.

*No.*

His lips moved involuntarily, or so he thought. His gums receded, and his teeth exposed and were being prepared for something terrible. He was not sure for what, or why. The heat inside him was intense and unrelenting. His entire body was trembling violently, uncontrollably, and for the first time in years, he was straightening to his full height. His spine cracked and popped, and his joints dislocated and shifted out of place.

*No.*

But with a growing dread, he realized he could no longer fight back against the invading presence. Whatever will he could raise to fight back against it would never be enough.

*It* was winning.

The shakes redoubled, and he lost all control over his body again and knew that his bowels had loosened, and he had wet himself like an invalid. The world around him became a hazy, streaking, crystalline blur. Unable to balance himself any longer, he toppled over. It seemed to take forever to hit the ground. Though, when he landed, he landed hard, striking his forehead against a rock and experiencing every bit of the amplified and distorted pain from the blow.

Around him, the world slowly shrank into a darkening circle tinged by red. Then the pain slackened for a moment, and Yuri was certain that Death was coming to claim him.

*I am Spetsnaz.*

Yes, he was once Spetsnaz, but even that had not been enough. He relinquished all control, hoping to hasten his death. His breathing slowed, and his body calmed as the pain vanished.

*Am I dead?*

Somehow, he realized he wasn't dead. He was conscious and aware of what was going on around him. He could still feel all the aches and injuries he'd suffered over his lifetime, but they were now intensified as if his brain had been rewired to shunt all pain to his consciousness.

*Such terrible pain.*

He knew that he was no longer alive, but he was not dead either. He was just a passenger trapped inside his own body. He sensed that the new presence in his mind with him had almost no understanding of the world that surrounded it. It was a newborn babe in the woods.

But it did have one savage desire—*to feed.*

# ~2~
## CUTTER

Jackson Cutter opened his eyes. Then he closed them. The sunlight streaming through the round porthole window above his head was entirely too vivid. His head hurt. Really hurt. But that was nothing new, at least for the past year. Today, he just wanted to lie in bed, wanted very much to sleep for another score of hours—but nature, being something even he couldn't ignore, begged to differ.

*Damn.*

Grunting, he fell out of bed and stumbled naked past piles of clothing littering the gritty fiberglass floor of his Catalina 445, stopping briefly to grab a white terrycloth robe he'd swiped from the nearby two-star hotel. As he continued to stoop to avoid bumping his head on the low ceiling, he searched for something else to wear. Through the blur, nothing other than a pair of slippers caught his eye, so he slid his feet into their fuzzy coolness and stumbled his way out of the forward stateroom.

*What was that?* In the narrow connecting hallway, he paused for a beat, closing his eyes and resting one hand on the bulkhead while running his fingers through his unruly hair. All wasn't right with the world, and it took a moment for his foggy brain to work up enough steam to understand exactly what that was. There had been another shape on the bed beside him. One that was familiar, and yet not so familiar, all at the same time.

He returned to his bed and peeled the sheets away slowly, exposing a tanned, completely nude, well-proportioned woman.

And that was partly a problem. *Who are you?* He drew a deep breath and let it out slowly, almost wishing he hadn't inhaled so deeply. He placed a closed fist against his forehead. The competing drummers playing fills in his mind went into overdrive, playing cymbal after crashing cymbal. He rubbed his temples to relieve the nagging pressure while continuing to work on figuring out who in the hell the woman might be.

*Still breathing. Good.* She was his type. Maybe not his type a year ago. But, yes, based on her generous curves, she was definitely his type. In all honesty, though, he couldn't remember a damn thing about the night he'd spent with her.

And that was a real shame.

With a sigh of resignation, he shuffled to his nightstand next to the bed and located a roll of twenties he kept hidden inside a fake beer can. Peeling off six bills, he grunted, then peeled off another three for good measure, folded them neatly, and stuck them between the woman's fingers. She moaned and rolled over, covering her mouth with the back of her hand, yawning. She continued to turn until she was lying on her stomach with one arm dangling limply over the side of the bed and the money clamped professionally between her slender fingers.

For a moment, Cutter stared at the tattoo above her apple-shaped derrière. The inked lines seemed to have all bled together, and he couldn't tell if it was his vision that had gone bad or the ink job had been subpar. He blinked to clear his eyes and pinched the bridge of his nose. *Ink.* It had to be the ink job. He was still far too young for his vision to already be going.

"Great," he whispered to himself. "Now, who the hell are you?"

Figuring the answer would come to him eventually, he let her sleep and headed topside, ascending the short ladder in fuzzy slippers while tying his robe closed. On deck, he grabbed his Marlboro Reds from a shelf next to the helm, tapped out a single soldier, and lit it in his cupped palm. He let the cigarette dangle from the corner of his mouth while blinking furiously and making his way forward along the deck. The sunlight was still entirely too vivid, and the ocean sparkled like a million tiny diamonds, or in his case, a million tiny shards of broken glass.

Arms up for balance, he stopped long enough to take a satisfying drag from the cigarette, savoring the way the hot smoke rolled on his tongue, then closed his eyes and waited for the quick burst of nicotine to jump start his alcohol-saturated system back to life. That burst never came. But he had committed himself already. He'd endure. It wasn't as if he had a choice.

Once he made it to the bow, he lifted himself up on tiptoe and opened his robe. Leaning back, he relieved himself over the port side of the boat, watching as the dark yellow stream came out in an almost perfect laminar flow and arched gracefully through the air before splashing into the clear blue waters of the bay.

*Vivid.*

A tourist couple happened to pick that moment to stroll past on the docks. Both were dressed keenly in white cotton sailing outfits and ready for a daylong excursion on some of the very best waters in the entire world. Behind the couple was a small blond-haired kid. The little guy was quickly clutched closer as the trio scurried along a bit faster. Cigarette dangling from his lips, Cutter nodded his friendliest hello and good morning, and took another puff from one side of his mouth and blew it out the other.

The wife and husband ignored him, but the kid looked back and giggled.

Finished and feeling slightly better, he laced his robe shut and stumbled back to the bridge to begin one of his other daily rituals. After turning over bottle after bottle of rum and tequila—all empties—he swore a few choice words to anyone who would listen. But then he realized there was still hope. A half-filled beer bottle was sitting amongst the dead. He lifted it and shook it and heard sloshing liquid and didn't see anything moving about through the cloudy brown glass, so he took a swig.

Other than warm beer, he tasted gritty cigarette ash. Nasty, gritty cigarette ash. With a flick of the wrist, he tossed the bottle over the side of the boat and looked for another as he worked to get the awful taste out of his mouth. Choking into his closed fist, he stuck his other hand in the pocket of his robe, and his fingers brushed against the roll of twenties. They were his only saving grace. But, with annoyance, he glanced at the path he would need to take to get to what his body required most.

Sighing, he remembered a song from childhood. *Just put one foot in front of the other, and soon you'll be walking out the door.* And with a belabored groan, he tossed his nearly-to-filter cigarette and jumped from the boat to the dock. A bad landing forced him to his knees, and he had to grab a metal pole and recover against it for a couple of beats of the drummers in his head. Then he let go and set off on the long journey up the slatted pier to his ultimate destination.

Andy's Bar & Grill.

He sidled up next to the NO SMOKING sign located beside the PLEASE WAIT TO BE SEATED sign and paused to light another cigarette before continuing into the outdoor seating area. As he went, his robe fell partially open, exposing him to the early morning crowd already there and breaking their fasts. With a grunt, he cinched his belt tight again just before reaching the bar under the eaves of the restaurant.

*Dignity matters.*

The man behind the six-stool bar was a native of the islands he liked to call "Kiki." It probably wasn't the guy's real name, but it worked well enough. Kiki threw him a pained look, shaking his head from side to side while grinning with a huge set of perfectly white teeth. Cutter slid onto a barstool and took one more puff from his cigarette before stamping it out on the scratched wood of the outdoor bar. He blew a stream of smoke above his head and held up four fingers and pointed at the bottle of tequila just over Kiki's left shoulder—the expensive stuff.

"No, sir, Mr. Cutter. It's breakfast time, sir. Bar's closed. Just like always." Kiki wiped at the bar with a rag, concentrating on what he was doing.

Cutter spun on the barstool and eyed the crop of morning patrons, widening his legs a little to let in a cooling breeze. Plates of eggs and ham and bacon and sausage and pancakes were being consumed by fat tourists, which at the moment didn't look very appetizing. Only a few of the locals were awake at this hour. They usually slept in late unless they had a charter to run, or a group of beer-swilling fishermen to corral and snap pictures for. Among all the trappings of the hearty American-style breakfasts, Cutter picked out a few in the crowd daintily probing at fruit cups or slurping down oatmeal or granola or whatever the hell that crap was. He'd always figured that life was too short to spend it eating granola or fruit, or even vegetables. Not when God provided thick juicy steaks and good whiskey to all His blessed children.

He spun around and raised three fingers and pointed to the tequila bottle again, this time pulling his wad of crumpled twenties from his pocket and slapping them all on the bar, thereby igniting a new fire under Kiki and completing their daily dance.

"Yes, sir. Right away, sir, Mr. Cutter," said a smiling Kiki.

Cutter downed the tequila in two swallows before wiping his mouth clean on the sleeve of his robe.

Kiki, bucking for his usual large tip, engaged, saying, "It's going to be hot today, Mr. Cutter. Real hot. Need anything else, sir?"

Cutter ignored the man's weather report and obvious pandering. *Hot? It was always hot here.* That's why he had come to the God-forsaken place in the first place.

Barbados reminded him of Hell—but with a nicer view.

He glanced at Kiki and smiled. The man smiled back. Then Kiki's eyes refocused on something just past Cutter's shoulder.

"You look terrible, Jack," a woman's voice said.

# ~3~
## *AMERICAN BREAKFAST*

Cutter swiveled on his barstool to face the new arrival. *Morgan.* The woman's full name was Morgan Crow, and he had known her ever since she was twelve years old. She was the daughter of one of his best friends, Zen "Shouting Bear" Crow, who had been responsible for introducing Cutter to his wife, Sharon. Morgan also happened to be one of the co-owners of the search, recovery, and private security business he had all but abandoned a year ago, way back in the great state of Texas.

Cutter eyed her suspiciously. It was still difficult to focus on her, partly because she was backlit by the sun reflecting off the glassy waters of the bay and partly because his vision was still a bit blurred.

He squinted at her. "You cut your hair."

"You like it?"

He considered for a brief moment. "Nope."

She shook her head as he pivoted back to the drink Kiki had refilled. She then climbed onto the barstool to his left. A large man took the barstool to his right. That man was Kyle Gauge, another surviving member of Cutter's company of thieves and miscreants. He glared at each in turn, then raised his glass to them both, drained it, and indicated to Kiki that he wanted another.

"Jesus, Jack," Morgan said. "It's eight o'clock in the morning. Go easy on that stuff."

"You want one too?" he asked.

Morgan shook her head no.

"Coffee," Gauge said from his right then grunted and set his meaty fists on the bar. LOVE was tattooed on his right set of knuckles and HATE on his left. The ink was a souvenir from a stretch he spent in prison for "accidentally" killing a guy in a bar fight.

Kiki returned with the half-empty bottle and started to refill Cutter's glass, but Morgan put her hand over it to shield it before he could.

"Hey," Cutter said.

"Hey, yourself, Jack. We came a long way to find you and…well, you should at least be a little happier to see us, don't you think?"

*Go away, Morgan*, he thought, but said nothing.

"Still haven't taken it off yet," Gauge commented.

Cutter stared down at his glass, shifting his fingers to hide his white-gold wedding ring. He had a strong desire to strike the man. But he held back. He'd done so once before and had busted two of his knuckles on the granite rock that served as the man's a jaw. And the bigger problem with Gauge was that the man liked to hit back. Hard. The guy had a right haymaker that tended to leave anyone in its wake feeling as though they'd been run down by a battleship—or dead.

He glanced back at the wedding band on his finger. *No, of course I haven't taken it off. They'll have to cut it from my cold, dead finger.*

Morgan cleared her throat. "It's been what, Jack? A whole year?" She leaned forward and placed her elbows on the bar.

Cutter stabbed out his cigarette and tapped another free from the pack in his pocket. Morgan snatched the smoke from his lips before he could light it and crushed it between her fingers and let the flakes of tobacco fall away. "Don't you know those things will kill you?" When he didn't respond, she continued. "You are a hard man to track down, Jackson Cutter."

Gauge let out a one breath grunt that could often be confused with a laugh.

Morgan shook her head. "It took me almost an hour this time to locate you, and then about four more for us to get down here. You are not very well hidden, Jack. Only slightly better than when you tried to play ostrich in the Keys. You've got to watch it, boss."

"You're slipping," Cutter said. "And I'm not your boss. Not anymore."

Morgan shrugged. "No forwarding address. No contact since the funeral. No nothing. Not even a postcard telling us what a great time you are having. We were all a little disappointed back at the shop. Gauge and I think you are…a real jerk."

Cutter shrugged. "The word is 'asshole,' Morgan. Just say it."

"No," she replied with a trace of disgust.

"Another round, Kiki," Cutter said as he pointed to his glass. Kiki glanced from Morgan to Gauge before shaking his head no and setting the bottle on the shelf behind the bar.

"Ok—ay then," Cutter growled. "I'll go somewhere that appreciates a real man like me and takes this." He held up his roll of twenties and peeled one off and dropped it on the bar before getting up, intending to walk out.

Gauge slid from his barstool and blocked Cutter's path.

"Out of my way, Schwarzenegger," Cutter warned.

Gauge did not budge. He became an immovable object being met by an unstoppable force.

"Come on, Jack," Morgan said. "We just want to talk to you. Be friendly about it. Don't you want to know what we've been up to over this past year? After all, you are the one who abandoned us. We figured you could—at the very least—carve out maybe a few precious minutes from your busy laze-about schedule for us. It's important."

*Pfffff. No way.* But the way she was looking at him told him it would be better to just shut the hell up and listen. Then he changed his mind again.

"Out of my way," he told Gauge and stepped around him.

Gauge pivoted, and Morgan ran interference, blocking his path yet again.

"No," she said. "You will stay here and listen to me and hear what I have to say. Trust me when I tell you that it will be well worth your while."

"Whatever," he grumbled. The two drinks and cigarettes were already having the desired effect on the pounding in his head. The single drummer had backed into to a steady four-four beat and might even be willing to take a fiver soon. He raked his fingers through his hair to pull it back from where it had flopped over his eyes.

"I'm hungry," Gauge said.

"You are always hungry," Morgan quipped, taking Cutter by the arm. "Go find a waitress and order something. We'll take that table over there." She shook him lightly. "Can he get you anything to eat, Jack? Something healthy for a change?"

"*No.*"

"Fine," she said right back to him, mimicking his childish tone. To Gauge, she said, "Get me an egg-white omelet with spinach, cheese, shallots, and a dash of rosemary. Got that?"

"Two eggs, scrambled," Gauge replied. "Check."

Shaking her head, Morgan led Cutter to a table set next to the railing separating the eating area from the lapping water of the bay. She checked the surrounding patrons. *Morgan being Morgan—cautious to the extreme.* He'd lived where he had long enough not to care that much anymore. No one was after him. Not anymore. He just wasn't worth it.

Cutter sat in one of the padded chairs by the railing. "What's so goddamned important for you to ruin my vacation?"

"Normal people's vacations don't last a year, Jack." She scanned the dock area. "I like your slippers, you know. But why bunnies?"

He lifted and glanced at his fuzzy, bunny-eared slippers then dug in his pocket for his cigarettes and lighter. He drew another smoke out, daring Morgan with his eyes before igniting it. She let it slide, so he inhaled and leaned back and blew out a stream of gray.

He displayed the cigarette to her, wrist bouncing. "You have until I finish this to tell me why in the hell you are down here bugging me."

"Just wait," she said, crossing her arms.

Cutter shook his head. "Whatever."

Gauge arrived and scooted a chair out with his foot. The wooden legs clattered against the rough concrete flooring. He sat in the chair and folded his arms across his exceptionally large chest.

Eyeing him, Cutter wondered if the man had gotten even bigger since the last time he had seen him. *Maybe.* Gauge was an interesting specimen of humanity, and Cutter had always admired the guy. He was a series of odd contrasts. He'd come from Seattle, which usually didn't produce such large examples of masculinity. And Gauge was no dummy either, though he often played one for effect.

Morgan sighed, unfolded her arms, and rested her forearm on the table. With her, half of what she said, she normally said with her hands doing half the talking. "Jack, we've been worried sick about you for a long time."

*Bullshit.* He said nothing. It had been a year, which meant it must have been a very long sickness for them not to have attempted to contact him any sooner.

"When you left us," she said. "No, when you *abandoned* us, all the good business dried up. Nothing has worked right ever since. It's like the wheels fell off the bus and nobody wants to hire us anymore. Not for any sized job, no matter how small or insignificant, and certainly not without the great and wise Jackson Cutter in charge of the operation. You know how much that sucks for us? We may even need to go get jobs in the real world soon. Maybe that will lead to us having to push papers from one desk to another. Imagine the horror in that?"

Gauge nodded along.

"And," Morgan continued, "it also means the company is almost bankrupt."

Cutter waited for a long moment, or about another four bars of drumming in his head. *Lying, obviously. With Morgan around, the company would never go bankrupt.* He took another puff from his cigarette and blew it out the corner of his mouth. He leaned forward in his chair and rested both elbows on the tabletop, causing it to wobble.

"So...what?" he said, shrugging. "I don't care."

"*So what—?*" Morgan repeated in an agitated tone. She leaned in even closer to him. "You started this business from nothing, Jack. You recruited me. You brought on Lumpy"—her nickname for Gauge—"and we used to all work so well together. Don't you remember that? Now—? Now—? Well, are you just too self-absorbed in your own misery and pity-party that you can't recognize that others might be depending on you? I hate to say this, Jack, but...we need you. Sharon would have wanted you to come back by now."

At first, Cutter just sat there, seething inside. *A little too close to home, Morgan.* He scanned the vacationers and the few locals sitting quietly nearby and eating. Not a single damn one of them gave a shit if he lived or died.

And, in point and fact, neither did he.

"No thanks," he said and stabbed out what remained of his cigarette while preparing to stand and get the hell out of there.

Morgan yanked on the loose fabric of his robe and pinned his arm against the tabletop.

"Let go," he said in warning.

"We got a job offer, Jack. A big, fat, juicy one."

"Not interested."

"Really, it's a big one. Biggest score we've ever had."

"Still not interested."

"What if I were to tell you that you are broke too? Completely broke."

"You'd be lying."

"Am I?"

*She had to be.* Then Cutter thought about it for a moment, looking from her to Gauge. The big man nodded. Among her many talents, Morgan Crow was a computer security expert, a hacker extraordinaire, and a whiz with electronic gadgets of all shapes and sizes. She was one part German, one part African, one part American Indian, and a whole shitload of trouble if you ever got on the wrong side of her.

"You wouldn't dare," he said.

She kept quiet. She just continued to pin the arm of his robe against the tabletop staring daggers at him until he sank back into his chair.

"It's already done, Jack. You are flat broke. Even the Cayman accounts. And if you do not agree to come along with us today, your little 'vacation' here will come to an abrupt end."

Cutter reached into his robe's right pocket and felt the roll of twenties. They were probably all he had left other than the boat. He massaged the bills between his nicotine-stained fingers.

*Not yet.*

He stood. "Screw you, Morgan," he groused as he retightened the belt on his robe. Then he headed for the exit with his bunny slippers scuffing loudly against the rough concrete.

# ~4~
## THAT ATLANTA BUSINESS

Cutter didn't like the look of the two men sitting across the conference room table from him. *Assholes.* Something about them rubbed him entirely the wrong way. While he was not opposed to being rubbed the right way, or even the right way when it was oh-so-wrong, these guys would not be his first choice to do it. And for that matter, they would not even be on the list.

Perhaps it had been the four-hour flight he'd just endured, mixed with an hour-long taxi ride into the heart of the city that had set him on edge. Perhaps it was his anger with himself over his final capitulation to Morgan and Gauge that had allowed the trip to begin in the first place. Or, it could just be that the last time he'd worked with the guy directly across the table from him, the mission to locate a mysterious artifact deep in a mine in Ecuador had been a complete and utter Charlie Foxtrot. Whatever it was the was prickling him, he was already nearing the getting-ready-to-walk-out-of-the-room mode, catch the next flight back to where the sun shined brightest, find a fat bottle and a native girl, and crawl inside both.

But he owed it to Morgan to listen to these guys—*for a little bit, anyway.*

Her arguments had persuaded him to go to Atlanta and hear these guys out. *Hell no* had he made it easy on her, but she basically had put his balls in a vise when she had drained his bank accounts. So, while she fully deserved his righteous wrath, he had to play nice, for now—*which sucked.*

*Damn her.*

While they had flown to Atlanta, she'd briefed him on the operation and the similarities with the Ecuadorian job—the one that had gone south and led the death of his wife, Sharon. Morgan had also dangled the validation of Sharon's theories in front of him, too, but he questioned how that could possibly be, given the vastly different geographic locations in which these similar artifacts they'd been discussing had been discovered.

*Maybe, though, just maybe, she had a point—a small one.*

Gauge had returned to Texas to begin preparations in anticipation of them taking the new gig. Which to Gauge, meant purchasing and assembling the biggest guns and explosives and other armaments that a large advance payment would allow for. *Morgan is betting big on this one*, he'd thought on the plane ride. He didn't quite have the same certainty of purpose, as he hadn't yet decided if he would even take the job. So, in his mind, Gauge was already acting a bit prematurely. But that was Gauge. The man just liked guns—the bigger, the badder, the better. And, although he still wasn't committed yet to the cause, Cutter was suspicious that both Morgan and Gauge were thinking the briefing in Atlanta was more of a formality than a necessity. Those two were planning to take the gig no matter what. Maybe even if he refused, as well.

*Let's see about that.*

He still had serious doubts that he could go through with it and wondered if he'd freeze up and lose his focus like he had in Ecuador. He didn't want to make another bad decision that would get more people kill. Hell, he wondered if he even would be able to step into the darkness of another mineshaft ever again. Regardless of all that, he wanted to meet whomever it was that was bankrolling the little adventure—if only to look him or her or them in the eyes and figure out why in the hell they wanted one of those damned artifacts in the first place. It all seemed a little reckless, considering what he had encountered in Ecuador.

Those same reckless souls who wanted Cutter and his team to take this mission were the same ones at the table. They consisted of one man in a suit, and one flunky Cutter had worked with before. The flunky he respected about as much as he respected television evangelists and product pitchmen, who were just slightly more respectable than network TV news anchors.

"Mr. Cutter," the flunky across from him, said.

The man was called John Wayland. He was the same guy who had hired Cutter to take on the failed the mission in Ecuador. Cutter had to admit to himself that it took guts for Wayland to face him again, and he let him know it with the way that he sat with his arms folded across his chest, thumbs pointing upward, chin lowered.

Wayland laced his fingers together on the tabletop and began rubbing his thumbs against one another. A bead of oily sweat had formed just under the hairline of his slicked-back hair. It sparkled in the harsh light from the spotlights above and did not want to roll off his forehead. It seemed glued in place. The man wet his lips and cast a quick glance at the woman sitting next to him.

The woman was a chiseled-faced beauty about thirty-five years old, Cutter guessed. She could have easily passed for being in her late twenties, though. His guess to the higher side came from the tiny crow's feet surrounding her eyes that she'd attempted to hide behind a pair of oversized, dark-framed glasses. She had rich, well-toned skin and did not seem the type to let vanity drive her to hide behind a painted-up face. That gave her a natural beauty which made Cutter very much wish to see her completely naked one day. *I've seen her before.* He was certain he had, but couldn't place where that had been. And unfortunately, when he had seen her then, she had not been naked at the time. He was fairly sure of it. He would have remembered. But he couldn't recall where it was that he'd seen her, which bothered him to the point of distraction.

"This is Dr. Reyna Martinez," John Wayland said. "She teaches graduate classes at Columbia University and is the best there is in the field of speculative biology and evolution. And she has... Well, she will be accompanying you on this expedition."

*Like hell she will.* It was then that his brain connected all the dots. He knew her by reputation and by a single photograph. He'd seen her profile picture on the dust jacket of a book he'd once noticed lying open on his wife's desk. It was all about evolution and the future of mankind, that sort of bullshit, but he could not recall what the title was. Sharon was always reading one textbook or another, and he still had not cleared them out of the home they once shared. The task still waited for him back in Texas. Whether or not he would ever go back there, he did not know. Nor did he care. Sharon was an anthropologist by trade, specifically an expert in the field of Bronze-Age man. And it was something, of which, she constantly reminded him just how well he fit in with her chosen subject matter's knuckle-dragging ways. She used to tease him about being a direct descendant of the missing link in the chain of evolution. He rather enjoyed proving her right, too, and he continued to prove her right by licking his lips and giving Dr. Martinez a leering wink.

She glanced away with the subtle wrinkling of her nose showing her disgust.

"We work alone," Cutter said, hiding a private smile. He interlocked his fingers behind his head and tilted back in his chair.

"That is not at all possible," Wayland said as he scratched his neck, just under his jawline.

Leaning forward, Cutter pulled back his hair and let his hands slip off his head and come crashing down hard on the tabletop. Water in the tall glass next to him splashed out and spattered on the conference room table. He glanced down at the mess and wiped the stippled droplets with his middle finger, smearing the water around and creating an annoying low-pitched stuttering noise on the polished surface of the mahogany tabletop.

"If we do this," he said, "we do it alone and our way this time, Mr. Wayland."

"I have been informed—" Wayland stopped. He glanced at the man seated at the head of the conference table. The man was someone Cutter had not met until today. The guy had a round face with protruding cheekbones, which Cutter thought made the guy look a little like a chimpanzee in an expensive suit. That made sitting there and taking Wayland seriously a real challenge. Chimp-man was obviously in charge and pulling Wayland's strings, which was a bit of a mindset shift. Cutter had always thought that John Wayland had been the man in charge all along, given his exclusive involvement in their past dealings. But it appeared, Cutter realized, that he might have been wrong in that assessment. He had seen Chimp-man before on cable TV. The guy had been on a business channel, but Cutter knew little else other than the man had thought of himself as a player on Wall Street. Gold was what he remembered the guy being into. There was something about gold mining in the guy's background, but what that was, he did not know. Given that the failed mission to Ecuador had been to retrieve an artifact from inside a gold mine— a real Indiana Jones kind of job—it all had to be connected somehow.

*Who are you?* Cutter had asked himself, and no matter how hard he flogged his brain, he couldn't recall the Chimp-man's name or where the connections all lined up. Pieces were missing from the puzzle. Partly, that intrigued him as well as watching Wayland squirm a little.

Chimp-man nodded, and Wayland started to say again, "I have been informed—"

Cutter held up a hand and glanced at Chimp-man. "I'm going to cut things short here and assume that, by bringing us this far, you are not planning on taking 'no' for our final answer. So, if you can pay the freight, the girl can come along for the ride, much as that troubles me." He winked at her again, and she sneered. "But she takes all her orders from me, okay? I'm not going to compromise there. So are we all going to be all right with that?"

He smirked at her, and she frowned back, letting him know just how easily he could get under her skin anytime he wanted to—*or she is bright enough to let me pretend I can.* Cutter figured if they actually took the gig, he'd have to sort it out somewhere down the road.

"But not him." Cutter waggled a finger at John Wayland. "That guy stays here. He is not to be involved in any shape, form, no how, and no way. Got it?"

Cutter set his hands down on the tabletop and stared down Wayland, wondering again if the last mission they had been involved in together had been a setup from the beginning. That mission had ended with Sharon's death and no goddamned artifact. *Or had it? Could that little weasel have hidden the success from him somehow?* Cutter had never quite figured that out. He'd had other far more pressing things on his mind at the time. His wife. Who'd just died. And yet, here he was, back at the negotiating table being asked to do it all over again.

There was an old adage about enemies and how close they should be kept, but Cutter also knew that whatever he said next, Wayland would get involved somehow—worm his way in, so to speak. It was just how that guy seemed to operate. So whatever was going on, or going to go on, Cutter would make sure to extract a little payback from the man before this was all said and done.

And that would be much easier to do if he had cause to do so. If not, he'd trump something up.

"Agreed," John Wayland said, nodding almost a bit too easily.

*Really?* Cutter suppressed the surprise he felt, or thought he did. He glanced at the tabletop and back up again.

"Your fee, Mr. Cutter, will be two million US. Half on acceptance of our arrangement, the rest payable when the artifact is safely returned and in our possession. This is to be a simple transaction for us all, and you are expected to cover all incurred expenses related to this little…adventure. Including, of course, any transportation costs. Are we clear on that?"

Cutter glanced at Chimp-man, who remained enigmatic. *Who are you really?* The payout was far more than he had ever been offered for any job like this, so it made him extremely apprehensive to take it. The amount was about three times what they were paid up front for the failed job in Ecuador. It was tempting. Perhaps too much so. Money was talking.

*What do I have to lose?*

"Okay," Cutter said without any further consideration. He sensed surprise from Morgan at his easy and rapid acceptance of the first offer. His usual play was to hold out for at least one or two more rounds. Often, he would walk out of a deal just to see if they'd come chase him down. The desperate ones did. Which was just about every job he'd been offered.

"Good," Wayland said with just a brief hint of nervous release.

Cutter figured the guy would make an excellent mark at the poker table. He would welcome pitting himself against Wayland anytime the guy wished to play because, right now, Cutter knew that he held the winning hand and had not yet placed his final bet down on the table.

*One more round. Just for kicks.*

Wayland opened a thick manila folder stuffed with papers. "We have arranged papers and passage for you and your team. Your arrival will be marked as a corporate flight inbound to our mining operations in Koni. This is assuming your travel means are by private jet, which I assume you have been briefed on by Ms. Crow along with where it is you will be landing?"

*Right.* Cutter nodded an affirmative. He actually did not know. She hadn't told him yet.

Wayland glanced at Chimp-man. "But—to maintain the operation's complete secrecy, we will be unable to supply the proper official travel visas necessary for entry into Russia. Although, I assure you, the appropriate people have already been contacted, so your entry and exit should not be an issue for a team with your…shall we say, unique abilities?"

*Not good.* Heading into Russia uninvited was not the best way to make friends there. But these clowns were spending a whole bunch of US dollars to make things happen quickly. Those same greasy skids could lead to a whole mess of new troubles, or they could make him some new friends. He'd been to Russia once before and found that the appropriate paperwork only mattered in the larger cities or when one got too near the sensitive military sites. All other places were under the control of local bureaucrats, who were usually out to line their own pockets and didn't much care about official protocol, which he'd learned was a relic of those raised in the former Soviet Union.

Wayland tapped the folder in front of him with a pen. "You will have full use of one of our company planes and its pilots if you wish."

Cutter watched the man carefully. It all was supposed to seem like a simple shoot and scoot mission to retrieve the artifact. *A little too easy.* That was exactly what he had thought the last time before everything had gone south. So, there were probably a million glaring reasons not to accept the job. But on the table were a couple of million other reasons to take it. And, if he could somehow prove once and for all that his wife had been right about the origins of the artifact? That what she had told him was indeed true? Well, then, that might just be the single good reason for going.

It was a calculated gamble, certainly, and he really had nothing to lose by taking it. His own life didn't matter so much anymore. It hadn't been going all that well lately.

He held up two fingers. "Two million, up front. Two more when the good doctor is returned safe and sound along with your artifact. And we supply our own transportation."

Wayland closed the manila folder. "But you have already agreed to our deal, Mr. Cutter."

Cutter feigned disinterest. "I changed my mind, Skippy. Sorry. Happens sometimes. There are just too many unknowns and too many risks for what you want to pay us. We wouldn't want a repeat of last time, would we?"

He continued watching the man carefully to see just how far the guy would bend. He also wanted to get a read on what might have happened the last time they'd crossed paths. Yeah, he'd just doubled the fee, too, which he didn't expect to get, but his earlier read on Wayland had told him that the guy would check with his boss in some way, fold the hand he held, and then agree to whatever was being asked for.

Wayland glanced at Chimp-man. *Bingo.* Almost on cue, the guy at the head of the table nodded just once as Cutter had predicted.

"Done," Wayland said, seeming relieved.

*Assholes. The very best kind—desperate assholes.*

Cutter nodded. "Okay, I'll get it done."

"*We* will get it done," Morgan corrected, placing her hand on top of his and patting it.

"Yes," Cutter said, correcting himself. He grinned at her, trying to make it genuine. "We will get it done." He had no intention of allowing Morgan or Gauge or anyone else to accompany him on this operation—other than the doctor. This was going to be a solo gig on his part. He'd slipped up in his wording and hoped Morgan hadn't caught his true meaning. He was just tired. *Won't happen again.*

Now that he was done screwing these guys, he wanted to lean back and have a smoke and four fingers of expensive single-malt Scotch, but part of Morgan's initial prodding involved him ditching his cigarettes at the airport before they'd left and drinking nothing but Diet Coke on the plane ride. If she wanted to mother him all the way back to Texas and until the wheels were up and he was on his way overseas without her—*then fine.* He owed her that much. He just needed to figure out how in the hell he was going to tell her and Gauge that they weren't coming along—and make it stick.

# ~5~
## *SIMPLY THE BEST*

Less than a minute after Jackson Cutter and Morgan Crow left the conference room, John Wayland adjusted his collar and turned to his boss, Anton Moray, while keeping one eye on Dr. Reyna Martinez, who was scribbling away on a yellow legal pad, seemingly minding her own business.

Wayland tapped a pen against the folder in front of him. "I know Mr. Cutter might seem a bit brash, sir. Quite frankly, many find him to be a real prick to deal with. But, I assure you, he and his team are the best at what they do. Definitely the best that our money can buy, I mean. At least on such short notice."

Mr. Moray said nothing.

"The failure that happened last time? They—I mean, we, were just unlucky, sir. That's all. But the story was contained, so no harm, no foul, right?"

When Mr. Moray blinked, Wayland chuckled nervously. Then Mr. Moray adjusted his cufflinks and stood. He walked to the large bank of windows and looked down.

"You have told me all of this before, Mr. Wayland. I certainly hope that what you have told me is the truth of the matter."

"It is, sir."

"Has everything else been prepared?"

"Yes, sir. They will have no trouble entering Russian airspace. But—well, we had planned to fly them in on one of our jets, so having them use their own method of transportation is a slight deviation from our initial plan and a loss of our direct control over them, but I can handle it. Rest assured. And—" Wayland hesitated. What he had to say next needed to be phrased with care since it could be interpreted in many ways. "Once their mission has been completed, I will personally see to it that they never bother us again."

The man at the window nodded only once and left the conference room.

# ~6~
## *GUN NUTS*

Ceramic mug filled with coffee in hand, Cutter strode up next to Morgan and Gauge, who were stacking and sorting items on a series of folding tables set up in the middle of their company's warehouse. Both glanced up at Cutter at the same time and nodded. Morgan then brushed a lock of her newly shortened hair over one ear while Gauge grunted and returned to his work.

"How long until go-time?" Cutter asked, and then slurped his coffee.

"I need at least another hour," Morgan answered. "There's a load of specialized equipment coming in on a charter. Should be here within the hour. I just heard that the G4 is already at the airfield, fueled and ready to go, but I had to make a slight adjustment to our normal crew. Hope that is okay with you."

*Of course.* Cutter trusted her with that and whomever she might have selected to fly him there. Hell, he trusted her with just about everything. He raised his mug and was just about to ask her what she meant by a crew adjustment when—

"We have one quick stop in Atlanta to pick up Dr. Martinez," she said before he could speak, "and it's overseas from there. Got your passport ready, Jack?"

"Which one?" He had collected quite a few over the years.

She smiled back, and he let the whole replacement crew matter drop. She knew what she was doing. Her smile quickly faded, and she headed off, typing away one-handed on her small tablet computer.

He found Gauge checking various weapons arrayed on one of the larger tables in the spacious warehouse. "How we set?"

The big man looked back and raised an eyebrow. "This is just a quick extraction mission, so I'm thinking we go light this time around. Just like you always say."

But Cutter knew that 'light' for Gauge held an entirely different meaning than it did for most normal people. But it did fit well with Cutter's own *go in light, get out fast* mentality.

Arrayed on the table before him were a plethora of legal, somewhat illegal, and *this-will-put-you-in-prison-for-a-long-long-time* weaponry.

Even as muscular as he was, Gauge struggled a bit to pick up the first of the weapons. "This is a GAU-2/A M134 Minigun. Got this baby made up especially for us. It's been lightened, and the fire rate has been tweaked down a bit to preserve ammo. But it's still plenty fast. I also had it fitted with a special battery pack that will—"

"Looks like it weighs as much as a Buick. You sure you can handle it?"

Gauge grinned broadly and set the big gun down next to the tripod mount for it. "You have to ask?"

"And when you pull the trigger the first time and are out of every bit of ammunition you can possibly carry for it in two seconds flat?"

Gauge shrugged. "Then we leave it with the vehicles."

They both moved to the next weapon.

"Recognize this?"

Cutter shook his head as if he didn't, which caused Gauge to smile again.

"This is a Milkor MGL grenade launcher. Six chambers of 40-millimeter goodness, here. We got a bunch of different projectiles for it—from smoke to flash to fireworks to tweaked-HEDPs, which come with a slightly larger kill radius."

"Define 'slightly larger.'"

"Oh, maybe seven to ten meters instead of five. Best not to use them at close range, though. They might just bounce around for a while and then go boom in a big way. But they are great for covering your ass in a retreat. Just remember not to fire them too closely and you'll be okay."

"Still seems a little heavy. Got anything more my size?"

Gauge frowned at that statement and set the shell he had picked up back down on the table next to a long line of others. He reached for the next weapon on the table and picked it up. "This is a Fostech Origin 12. When you want to clear out the room with a lot of boom, this is what I'd recommend. Chews through ammo, though."

"Again, a little bulky for me. What else?"

"Maybe these will do. They are a few of the newest additions." He picked one up and flipped it to Cutter.

Cutter caught the weapon and tested the weight. *Nice.* The assault rifle was light and compact, which he instantly took a liking to. He lifted it to his shoulder and looked down the barrel. He could imagine himself shooting it either up at his shoulder or slung low from a strap.

"Like it?" Gauge asked. "That's a Badger AA6 chambered in .300 Blackhawk. It's a mean little son of a bitch. We got these ones specially made up for us. Short barrel, suppressed. You won't go deaf shooting it. And it fires both subsonic and supersonic thirty-cals. I got these babies upgraded with SarPoint sights with tactical flashlights, green lasers, and 2 MOA dots." He paused to take a breath. "Then I had the shop strap on M203s launchers that will take the same loads as the MGL. These babies will make sure that whatever we go up against will soon be with God Almighty, and by the time they get there, they will be so thoroughly ass-fu—"

"They'll do," Cutter said approvingly. He tossed the weapon back to Gauge. "Can you strap night optics on them?"

Gauge blew out a sharp breath and rolled his eyes. "Wouldn't want do that."

"Why?"

"Headsets. Morgan's got new tech lined up for us."

"Okay, good," Cutter said. "What about sidearms?"

"I got that covered there too, boss."

Cutter grunted his approval. "You still planning on bringing Betty along?" Again, he was certain of the answer, but it was his little ritual he always went through with the man. It felt a little like putting on an old pair of board shorts.

Gauge beamed back enthusiastically. "I never leave home without her." He withdrew the custom nickel-plated Desert Eagle .50 that he kept in a shoulder holster located next to his heart. The massive handgun had been modified extensively, but the only visible evidence of those modifications was the extended magazine, which stuck out somewhat.

*Thirteen rounds always beat eight rounds*, Gauge had often said.

Cutter picked up his coffee mug and raised it in salute. "Add a couple of MP5Ks for good measure."

"What do you want with those puny things?" Gauge shook his head dismissively. "Too small. Not so good."

"For you," Cutter replied. "I'm also thinking Glocks. Some 19s for the ammo swap with the MP5s. I can carry a lot more extras then. And add in an additional complement of Glocks, including one for the doctor. A small 26 should do just fine for her."

Gauge continued to lovingly admire his Desert Eagle fifty-caliber beast. "What if she doesn't want it or doesn't know how to use it?"

"Then you show her the hell how to," Cutter replied as if the answer should have been obvious.

Morgan returned and lightly touched Cutter on the shoulder. "I hate all these guns. I really, really hate them. You do know that bringing all this firepower into a mine is a seriously stupid idea? There could be so much methane down there that your first shot could very well be your last."

Gauge grunted a wide smile he shared with Cutter, who was trying to ignore Morgan's mothering.

Cutter leaned in closer to Gauge. "That reminds me. Explosives. C4 packs, detonators, all the jazzy stuff."

"You two are crazy," Morgan said. "You guys know that? You are nothing but gun nuts. Little boys with big toys."

She thrust the tablet computer she held into Cutter's hand and patted his shoulder. "Still, Jack, I'm glad you're in a better mood. We've been seriously worried about you."

Cutter stared blankly at the manifest on the screen. He didn't have a clue what half the items on the list would ever be used for. But if it was on her list, then it was damn well indispensable. Except for guns. She always left out the guns.

She pointed the screen. "See those checkmarks?"

He did. Only about ten percent of the boxes were checked.

"Help us out then with all that, won't you? Go find some of those things in the bins over there. Or are you still thinking you are doing this job on your own?"

*Yes, I do plan to do this all on my own.* Somehow, though, she'd figured out his plan long before he had broached the subject with them.

She turned and walked away, toes crossing her centerline with each step. Much as he hated to admit it, he admired the way her hips swung as she moved. It was just too damn bad she played for the other team.

*Too damn bad.*

# ~7~
## *WALK OUT*

Cutter strolled across the concrete floor of the spacious warehouse and entered his office, meaning to get started on a few of the items he had recognized on Morgan's list, then deciding to see if he could find something to drink first. It had been hours since he'd had one.

He hadn't been inside the office in over a year. Nothing actually looked touched. Things were dusty, yes, but it was obvious that someone had cleaned up the rampant destruction he had left behind the last time he had been there. *Good.* They had put all the pieces back together neat and tidy, including a photograph of his wife that sat prominently on the scarred desk. They had even gone so far as to replace the broken glass in the picture frame.

Head shaking, he turned the photo over so he no longer had to see her image staring back at him and slid into the seat behind the desk. The plush leather squeaked as the chair adjusted to his weight. He needed a minute.

By the time he looked back up, Gauge filled the office doorway.

"What's this crazy story about us not coming with you? We found this job, and we found you. Near as I figure it, that entitles us to a share the spoils. Now you want to deal us out? That's goddamned horseshit, boss, and you know it."

*Great.* Somehow, Morgan had figured out his plans and had sent Gauge to lay the guilt trip on thick and heavy. She had been the smart one in that exchange, sending the big guy in first as a sapper. Still, Cutter didn't much care what either of them thought right now.

Gauge stepped into the office proper, closer to the desk. Cutter rubbed his shirt pocket searching for his cigarettes. Not finding them in the habitual place, he opened the bottommost desk drawer and peered inside. *Nothing.* Not even a single goddamned bottle or pack of smokes. *Damn you to hell, Morgan.*

Gauge scowled. "You listening to me?"

*No*, Cutter wanted to say. Instead, he rocked back and set his well-worn boots on the desktop. The rattlesnake-skin leather had felt strange when he had first slipped into them after spending almost a year of going barefoot or in flip-flops.

He laced his fingers behind his head and leaned back in his chair. *Might as well start in on him.* He figured Morgan would be along soon enough. "I don't need you two coming along with me and getting in my way." He stopped to examine his fingernails and rubbed them on his shirt.

Gauge just stood there, not saying a word, but his jaw was working hard, grinding back and forth on gum like a cow chewing cud. Finally, he shook his head and walked out of the office, saying nothing.

*Well, that was easy.*

Though, about a minute later, as predicted, Morgan came into the office with Gauge in tow. She was pissed. And when she was pissed—

He pulled his boots off the desk and hung his head low and waited for her lecture.

She folded her arms across her chest. "What the hell do you think you are doing?"

He said nothing and just absorbed the anger.

"Of course we are going with you. None of this silliness. Anything to the contrary is a joke. We landed this gig, Jack, so we will do our jobs, and we will get our cuts. We could have left you drowning in your own swill back on the Good Ship Lollypop. So—"

She wasn't done, and Cutter knew she was about to either fully unload on him or get to her point. He had but to wait.

"And that last job? Let me assure you, it wasn't your fault that Sharon was killed."

*Yeah, right.* He stroked his chin in mock thoughtfulness while she deflated a tiny bit and backed off. He could tell she really wanted to lay into him and couldn't decide whether or not she should.

It didn't take her all that long to decide.

She puffed up again. "Oh, and another thing. You think this is entirely your company? That you own it all by your lonesome?

You think we are here simply as your lackeys? You really think that?"

*Of course he didn't.* But he kept his mouth shut.

She stepped closer. "We built this business, Jack. Together. *WE*. Got it? I know things have not been so peachy for you, but it's time for your little pity party to be finally over."

*Oh, yeah?* His anger flared.

She stopped to draw a breath. "Why do you think we dragged your sorry rear end all the way back here? It wasn't your shining personality we wanted to see again. No, we did it because we knew we wouldn't be able to handle this job on our own. And if—"

*Blah, blah.* She went on for what seemed another few minutes. He tuned her out and stared at Gauge, watching the big man nod, cross his arms, nod again, uncross his arms, and then repeat the process, occasionally shifting his balance between his left and right leg. Even he wasn't fully buying her indignation. It was a bit too much.

When she finally finished, she was practically panting while staring forward with her mouth hanging slightly ajar. She had said her peace. She was done venting, and he knew it.

He said nothing in response. He just stared back.

She glanced down at his desk, head swiveling back and forth. "Jack. You. Just—" She landed on the overturned photo of his wife and stopped talking.

*Yeah, that.*

He got up from his chair and, without a word, walked past them both, out through his office door, out through the warehouse door leading into the midday sunshine, and ultimately, out through the chain-link fence topped with razor wire and security cameras that surrounded the entire property.

# ~8~
## *WHAT AN A-HOLE*

Because Cutter only had a thin roll of bills left in his pocket, Morgan found him halfway into a bottle of the cheapest whiskey that the bar down the street served.

He refilled his glass and raised a toast to her as she sidled up next to him, staring at his reflection in the mirror behind the bar. Gauge was with her and took the opposite side, just as he had two days ago in Barbados.

Morgan shook her head. "You're a big, fat loser, Jack. You know that?"

*Yeah.* He did know that. It was nothing new.

He tossed back the shot and one-gulped it then set the dirty glass on the bar and started to pour himself another. Morgan snatched the bottle out of his grip and set it out of his reach.

"Jackson Cutter, look at me."

He did, angrily, but said nothing.

She bunched her fists and set them on the bar. "We gave you plenty of space after Sharon's death. But she's gone for good. She is never coming back. Ever. You understand that?" She said the words as if she had rehearsed them a dozen times.

*Like I care what you think.* He rubbed one finger on the rim of his glass.

"Heck, Jack. You need to get your head out of your—"

"Ass," Gauge added.

"Yes, out of there. And get it back into the game. We've got a big job to do. And you need to take charge. It's finally a decent score for a change. We'll get a chance to get it right this time."

Cutter stretched for the bottle, and she slid it down the bar even farther out of his reach with the backside of her hand.

"It's not just you who was hurt by Sharon's death, Jack. She was our friend too. We loved her. But the company's gonna be flat broke soon. You have to face the hard truth."

Gauge grunted an affirmative, causing Cutter to swivel his bleary eyes toward the man. He suddenly wanted to hit the guy just to get him to hit him back and maybe break something.

She touched him on the elbow, and he flinched away.

"You know I'm right. Since you've been gone, all the good business has dried up. No one wants to do anything with us anymore. We're tainted goods, Jack. Tainted."

*Whatever.* He was done with the business anyway. *Flush it.* He didn't care.

She sighed. "We've almost closed up shop ten times already, but this latest job dropped in our laps and was tied up with a neat little million-plus dollar bow on it. We can do it, Jack. I know we can. We can do it and put Ecuador behind us."

He wasn't so sure. In fact, he would never be able to forgive himself for what happened there. He reached for the bottle again, and she blocked him.

"Believe you me, I've considered the heck out of leaving and getting a corporate gig on my own, but thanks to my record, I'll never be able to hold another security clearance again. No clearance in my line of work means no job. Unless, of course, I want to turn rogue again. You hear that, Jack? What you did when you abandoned us here affected more than just you, you selfish—"

"Prick," Gauge added

She nodded her approval.

Cutter remembered what she'd done. It had been done on his behalf well over two years ago. She'd been caught hacking into the Federal Reserve for him, a huge no-no. If it weren't for his prior governmental connections—thin and shaky as they were at the time—she would currently be spending a long stretch wearing nothing but orange, which, with her hair color, was not a shade that flattered her.

"So you found that doctor lady attractive, didn't you?" he asked. "And now you are looking to hookup with her then?"

Morgan shoved him hard, knocking him from the barstool to the grit-covered floor. He rolled sideways and curled up on the dirty linoleum floor. Holding his belly, he coughed, which turned slowly into a chuckle, then a full-blown laugh.

"Goddamnit, Jack! You really are an assho—a real jerk!"

Slipping off the barstool, she shifted until she was towering over him.

She glanced at Gauge. "Hold him down."

Gauge shifted positions and pinned Cutter against the floor with a knee to the chest. Morgan climbed on top him and grabbed his hand and tugged at his wedding ring. Cutter panicked and tried to snatch his hand away from her, but Gauge held him in place as she twisted and yanked to get his ring off. Finally, she got the white-gold ring off his finger and stood triumphantly, then staggered back on her heels.

"Give it back," he growled from the floor.

Gauge lifted his knee and Cutter attempted to rise, doing so unsteadily, wobbling on his feet. Tiny pieces of grit and broken peanut shells had stuck to his face. He wiped at them with the back of his hand.

Morgan frowned. "You'll get this back when you grow the heck up, Jack." Fetching Gauge by the arm, she added, "We'll be at the shop getting everything ready. We expect you to sober up and be there shortly."

*Like hell, I will.*

He watched Morgan and Gauge walk out of the bar and not look back. As the door closed behind them and shut out the light, he sank to the dirty floor, curled up, and buried his face in his knees.

"You gonna be all right there, pal?" the bartender asked.

# ~9~
## FBI-ED

By the time the plane touched down at Hartsfield-Jackson in Atlanta, Georgia, Cutter had managed to pull himself together to a reasonable degree. Reasonable for him, at least, which meant that he was not immediately planning to kill the next person who pissed him off.

*Well—maybe.*

He'd slept for a good, solid, four hours, which was also just enough time for the buzz to wear down to a nominal level and leave his mouth as dry as cotton in July and his head humming show tunes.

Morgan had returned to the bar and convinced him, finally. Yeah, he'd made it difficult for her. But she'd won out in the end. She was relentless and never seemed to give up no matter what, which was something he both admired and hated about her, often at the same time. She'd scooped him up off the floor and dusted him off and got him to the airport on time. He'd been a complete asshole about it, too, and had called her a *bitch*, which went so far beyond wrong that it left him feeling ashamed of himself. Perhaps that was why he caved in the end. That, and she'd given him back his white-gold wedding band.

Half of him appreciated the close friendship they had. The other half resented it. The argument over coming along for the ride was one he was in no mood to continue. It was too late and would be pointless to even bring it up, as he had nowhere else to go, and it was clear that she'd just keep chipping away at him until he eventually folded, no matter how big a tantrum he threw.

All he could do now was try to do better.

Gauge sat in the seat across the aisle from him, still bleary-eyed and half-dozing. The guy could sleep through a death-metal rock concert and wake up fully refreshed when the cleaning crew arrived to mop up all the blood.

Morgan closed her laptop and came to join them. Cutter glanced down at his hands. He didn't want to look her in the eyes just yet.

"Gentlemen," she said, "we've got company coming. And they don't appear to be friendly."

Cutter peeked out the porthole-sized window beside him on to see what had caught her interest. He saw flashing blue and red lights and men spilling out of shiny black sedans and SUVs. There was a lone woman shouting commands at the men, who appeared to be a whole host of suited-up seriousness. About half of them were cupping their hands over earpieces to hear each other over the roaring noise of the jet's twin Rolls-Royce engines. The group was moving quickly and importantly, all wearing dark blue windbreakers with three blocky white letters emblazoned on their backs.

FBI.

"Dang," Morgan said, shuffling back to her seat, muttering, "Not the best time for this." She swung into a chair before a tiny table and flipped open her laptop and began typing furiously. "Jack, can you do something about this? Maybe go and do a meet and greet with our guests?"

"No," he said. He wasn't ready yet.

She glanced up from her screen at him. "How about calling in a few quick favors from your contact list?"

Most of his governmental connections were no longer on speaking terms with him.

"Can't," he said.

"Okay," she breathed. She sighed and started typing even faster. "I just need a few minutes. Can you at least buy me that?"

Cutter sighed back at her. His head was pounding again, and he attempted to blink away the pain. It didn't help.

"Screw you, Jack."

Rubbing his temples, he tried to think. *This is just great. What in the hell do those government monkey-suits want this time?* It was always something with these statist types. Could hardly do business anymore in the US without some damn bureaucrat sticking their goddamned nose into it and wondering just how badly they could screw it up, and often doing it just out of spite.

America—the land of the free.

*Yeah, that.*

But it could be it was not any of his many pending legal issues they were going after. It could be related to Morgan. Though, he thought he'd cleared up those problems over a year ago after their last job had soured. It was the one good deed he'd done before heading south for his extended vacation. And all his favors had been used up on that one. *Where is this new hassle coming from?* Someone obviously still had a beef. He also figured that with all the guns and the half a ton of illegal high-tech they had tucked away in the plane's cargo hold, things could get real messy, real fast.

"Morgan?" he grunted in annoyance.

"Shhh, I'm working," she fired back, typing with a ferocity he'd rarely seen before.

Cutter grunted, deep and guttural, putting the pounding in his head out of mind. Then he collected Gauge and started to deplane. Gauge stopped him, and they shared a confused look, and then they both glanced over their shoulders at Morgan before stepping out into the cold. Cutter was still wondering what he was going to do and how far he was willing to go. He assumed Gauge was thinking along those same lines.

*All the way.*

No matter what, Gauge would have his back. The man always did, as did Morgan. Cutter made his decision right then. If this were just about him, then he'd play his role for all he was worth and give Morgan and Gauge the opportunity to continue the mission without him.

On the tarmac, the Gulfstream's engines continued to whine, slowly spinning toward a stop. He stepped down the jet's short stairway and sized up the not so friendly looking party of Feds.

A pale guy wearing a black jacket and narrow necktie stepped forward. "Hands up where we can see them, Mr. Cutter." The man was pushing fifty and also pushing a belly that was seriously threatening to tear the second button of his suit coat clean off if he inhaled too deeply.

Standing next to the guy was a very stern-looking woman in a dark pantsuit. She appeared to be the guy's boss. She had the face of someone who had not been properly laid in years. *Decade maybe?* Her face was screwed up so tight with self-righteous importance and indignation that it was amazing she could walk with that stick shoved so far up her—

"Where is she?" the woman asked.

Cutter halfheartedly raised his arms in surrender. Gauge stepped beside Cutter, who then rested his right hand on the man's shoulder, as if he were subtly restraining the larger man from attacking the FBI agents.

It did not have the desired effect. The smug look stayed a firm part of the woman's countenance. She showed not even a hint of fear at Cutter's rather mean-looking attack dog.

"Where is she?" the woman repeated. Wrinkles followed her every utterance, cracking her Spackle-job makeup.

"Who?" Cutter replied innocently.

"Don't get smart with me, Mr. Cutter. We know she is onboard with you. Harboring a fugitive and crossing state lines with said fugitive is a felony. Federal. I'm sure you are well aware of that."

"A fugitive?" Cutter asked with mock surprise while suppressing a hint of real surprise. He let go of Gauge. "I think you may have us confused with someone else."

The woman did not appear to buy his disjointed line of reasoning.

Cutter let his hands drop slowly. "Besides, isn't hunting down fugitives and bringing them to justice the purview of the U.S. Marshal Service?"

"Not if it has to do with a Homeland Security incident involving computer espionage."

"Sorry," Cutter said, head shaking. "I never have been able to figure out all that overlapping governmental responsibility bullshit out. There are just too many layers—if you ask me."

"We didn't ask you. Where is she?" the fat man beside the stern-looking woman asked.

"Where is who?" Cutter asked in return. "Or is it whom? I never could quite remember which is the rig—"

Two men with guns raised broke off and rushed forward to surround Cutter. Four others hastily surrounded and restrained Gauge.

"Easy," Cutter said as his arms were wrenched behind his back, and he was patted down for weapons.

One of the men tried to take Betty away from Gauge.

"I wouldn't recommend doing that," Cutter warned.

The man grunted and took the Desert Eagle .50 anyway. Gauge shrugged off the men surrounding him.

More guns were raised.

"Now's not the right time," Cutter said out of the side of his mouth. "You'll get it back. I promise."

The woman in charge stepped forward. "Doubtful. You know it is a felony to have a loaded weapon at an airport?"

"Is everything a felony now?" Cutter asked, figuring just about everything was except for paying taxes.

The woman sneered at him.

Two men entered the plane and returned with Morgan walking between them. Her head was bowed low. Both men held her by an arm so she could not twist free from their grips.

"*Mizz* Crow," the woman in charge buzzed. "You are under arrest."

"On what charges?" Cutter asked.

"You stay out of this," the lead agent snapped.

"She's with me," Cutter said, "and I'm afraid I can't let you just go arresting her without cause, can I?"

"You have no weight here, no pull here, Mr. Cutter. And your friends are not going to help you, either," she added with spiteful derision. "Should we also take you into custody?"

"On what trumped-up charges would you dare to do that?"

The woman said nothing.

Morgan glanced up, or someone who looked a lot like Morgan glanced up, only this one had long hair. Cutter suppressed a smile.

"Cuff her!" the lead agent spat.

The men who held Cutter dropped his arms and hurried over to fake-Morgan and wrapped her up tight, the first clipping on a pair of silver handcuffs, the second holding her still. They dragged her in front of the agent in charge and held her in place.

With lips held together tighter than a duck's butthole, the agent in charge raised a cellphone to Morgan's face and squinted as she went from picture to person.

A puffing grunt was all that escaped those overly taut lips.

"Take her away," she finally said.

"Not so fast." Cutter was already striding forward, but he was intercepted by two agents. He tried to bump them aside and continue, then four more joined the first two, forming a solid wall of windbreakers and suits.

"Don't worry," Cutter said to the woman who looked almost like Morgan. "Our lawyers will be on their way as soon as I can get to a phone. This is total bullshit. Trumped up bullshit, you know it."

Fake-Morgan nodded fearfully.

Dropping their arms and doing the monkey dance as they backed away, the agents peeled off one by one from Cutter and Gauge.

Cutter remained on the tarmac watching them escort fake-Morgan to a black SUV, duck her head inside, and shove her into the backseat. The SUV sped off, followed by the parade of shiny black vehicles decorated with blue and red lights.

*Jackasses.*

Cutter reentered the plane. "Who in the hell was that?"

Glancing up from her laptop, wearing the former pilot's jacket, Morgan grinned at him. "That was our pilot."

She began typing again on her laptop. "Time to get to work, Jack. The doctor will be here soon, and our friends will be back within the hour once they fingerprint her. So if you've got any shopping left to do in Atlanta, you had better get to it quick. You have maybe twenty minutes."

Cutter nodded. "The pilot, huh? So the copilot can fly us there?"

"Or you," she said.

*Me?* It had been a year since he'd flown any kind of aircraft, but he could do it—once he was completely sober. Though, going by their newly accelerated time schedule, it might have to be a bit sooner than that. He rubbed his temples again, hoping the headache would fade soon.

Before he sat, he drew Gauge's gun Betty out from where he had concealed it inside his over-shirt and handed it back to the man. It had been quite a feat, but he'd still managed to lift the weapon from the FBI agent who'd taken it when he'd fallen against the man. Cutter figured he probably deserved a reward. That gun was huge.

Gauge raised one corner of his mouth in a half-smile.

"Boys," Morgan said dismissively.

He gave her an affirmative nod as he watched Gauge crawl back into his former seat and make himself comfortable. The plush chair was probably still warm.

# ~10~
## DR. MARTINEZ, I PRESUME

Dr. Martinez showed up in the tiny terminal building precisely two minutes before she was expected to arrive, which was ten minutes after the FBI had left in their black SUVs. She was carrying two bags. Both were draped over her shoulders and were not weighing her down in the least, which gave Cutter a small glimpse into her abilities. She was not the helpless, babe-in-the-woods type, which he appreciated. She exuded confidence and strength just in the way that she stood so tall. Trailing behind her was a polished metal case much larger than her two shoulder bags combined. It probably contained some sort of instrumentation.

"Dr. Martinez, I presume," he said as he greeted her on the tarmac.

"Mr. Cutter." She rather formally inclined her head a smidgen. "Are you fully prepared for this assignment?"

"There's nothing we can't handle."

She grinned slightly and offloaded her bags onto him as if he were her personal manservant and stepped past him without uttering another word. He pivoted to watch her. *Hot damn.* She was wearing khaki cargo pants with plenty of pockets up and down the sides and a light-blue button-up shirt, sleeves rolled all the way to the elbows. The pants were tight in the butt and fit her generous curves, which was a trait Cutter both admired and appreciated. When his eyes made it down to her feet, he noticed she was wearing tan Timberline boots without a single scuff or scratch mark on them. That made him roll back a bit of his assessment of her as he realized that she'd probably just purchased the entire outfit off the rack at REI on her way to the airport. He was half-surprised that he hadn't seen dangling tags still attached somewhere. Regardless, he continued to observe her with muted admiration as she headed for the plane.

Gauge came shuffling down the short stairway near the cockpit, and she nodded to him once in passing as he set foot on the tarmac. She stepped around him and headed up and into the plane with a bounce to her step. Gauge twisted to keep watching her as she disappeared inside the G4.

"Stop gawking," Cutter said to the big man as he approached the plane.

"I am not gawking. Just making sure she gets safely onboard."

"Is that so?" Cutter said as he offloaded all her bags onto Gauge and followed the good doctor onto the plane.

# ~11~
## SLEEPING LIKE BABIES

*"Gulfstream seven-four-niner-two, you are ordered to return immediately to ATL-twenty-seven-L."*

Cutter sat in the pilot's seat and stared out the front windshield of the G4. He kept the plane on its current heading, which would take them northeast on a trajectory of zero-three-zero. His head still hurt, but it was down to a manageable hurt. And what made matters worse was finding out there were not going to be any in-flight cocktails available.

*"Gulfstream seven-four-niner-two. Final warning. Return immediately to—"*

"Fat chance," he said to the co-pilot over the headset before switching frequencies on the Honeywell TCAS II, fully intending to ignore any future warnings coming from those pesky US-based controllers.

He was in charge now, taking over piloting responsibilities from fake-Morgan, the former pilot who was currently in the hands of the FBI and probably being interrogated already. He almost wished he could see the lead interrogator's face when he or she found out they had the wrong suspect in custody, and he was also hoping that it was a she, specifically the duck-lipped woman agent. Normally, he had a great love for all women. It didn't matter if they were large or small, plump or thin, old or young. But every so often, he made exceptions.

The past few hours had been a big change for him. Being literally in the pilot's seat again left him in total control of the team's destiny after a year-long absence. If given half-a-chance, he would have relinquished that control already. It just felt wrong, and he wasn't ready for the responsibility.

While Morgan had managed to throw the FBI off their scent temporarily, it had also meant that the team needed someone else who could step up and pilot the plane. Morgan and Gauge had never done it, and Cutter was not about to approach Dr. Martinez and ask her as that might seem a tad inappropriate, all things considered. And as soon as he had queried the co-pilot concerning the man's abilities, he decided the guy was not the right one for the job. *Too skittish.* So, Cutter reluctantly had to assume that he was the right guy for the job, even with the lingering effects of alcohol poisoning dulling his reactions.

"Thought she said we had an hour?" he mumbled to himself as he checked their altitude and heading.

It hadn't quite been an hour since the FBI had left them. Maybe more like forty minutes. Morgan was almost never wrong in these matters of estimation, but he had to admire her thinking. She must have altered the official profile picture the FBI had of her, which was a lot harder than they made it look on TV. And he was doubly surprised they had not grounded the plane under the auspices of some other trumped-up charge.

The co-pilot touched the controls, and Cutter glanced over at the man. "We should turn back," the guy said over the headset. "They'll scramble out of McGuire and intercept us if we don't."

"And do exactly what?" Cutter asked. "We're okay. Don't worry about it. I hardly ever crash these things."

The co-pilot did not have an answer to that. The guy just swallowed thickly and stared ahead.

"Keep flying on this heading," Cutter told the co-pilot. "You can do that for me, right? I'll be back in a flash."

The man nodded his affirmative, but the gesture reminded Cutter of a scared rabbit just about ready to bolt to safety.

"Don't worry," Cutter said reassuringly. He put a hand on the man's shoulder and squeezed. "We do it like this all the time. We can fix it up good with the government types later." Which, of course, was utter bullshit. This was a first for him and his team. Usually, he had the well-greased palms of leveraged government officials backing him. It was going to touch and go for awhile, at least until he got his feet back under him and a little cash and could start greasing those old wrinkled palms once more.

The co-pilot re-checked the heading and made a few minor adjustments of his own as he seemed to settle in behind the wheel. When their course did not change, Cutter unbuckled himself from the pilot's seat and made his way back into the cabin area. Morgan shrugged at him and returned to typing on her keyboard.

He came to a stop next to her and squatted. "What've you got for me?"

She held up one finger to beg for a moment then went back to typing, keys clacking and rattling above the whine of the engines. He bounced on his heels and rolled his neck around in a circle to work out the kinks. When he moved it a little too far to the right, he winced. He'd somehow hurt himself falling off the barstool.

But that was only a small worry. The bigger one was his concern over the response to them leaving US airspace without a properly filed flight plan. In the day and age of overblown fears of terrorism combined with the silliness of political correctness, anything not under the thumb of government regulators could become a target. And even the slim possibility of getting blown out of the sky by an AMRAAM missile launched from one hundred miles away was not on his short list of planned accomplishments for the year.

"Morgan," he repeated—this time with a little more urgency.

She kept typing.

Cutter glanced at Gauge. *How the hell can he do that?* The man was sleeping like a baby.

"Have faith in my abilities," Morgan finally said. She finished typing and made a flourish of pressing the return key on her laptop. Cutter couldn't quite see the screen, but he did see the canary-eating grin that broke out on her face.

"What'd you do?"

She waited a beat. "Get back up there and keep flying, Captain Skyjack. I told you I would handle it. And I just did. Just flip the squawk over to eight-four-one-three and climb to forty-three-point-one on heading oh-seven-zero. We are now VIPs from Templar Investments in route to London, England."

Cutter didn't dare ask what was in store for the real 8413 designated aircraft.

# ~12~
## CAN WE TRUST HER?

Four hours into the flight, Cutter felt a hand land heavily on his shoulder, causing him to wake from his stupor.

Morgan pulled aside his headset and whispered in his ear, "We need to talk, Jack."

He rubbed the sleep from his eyes that he hadn't realized had gathered there and stifled a yawn. Sadly, he also realized that he was now perfectly sober because his mouth tasted as if a rat had slept on his tongue, and perhaps had died there as well.

"I don't think we can trust her," she whispered to him over the droning whine of the engines.

Cutter had made the same jump in logic the moment he had met the doctor, but it was nice to get Morgan's confirmation. Dr. Martinez was a very attractive woman, which didn't necessarily make her bad. It was just something about her attitude. Arrogance and condescension were two traits he found terribly unattractive, and she had them in spades.

"Why?" he prodded.

"She's got those eyes, you know? She's up to something."

"What eyes?"

"She's got eyes for you."

"Is that so bad?"

"Yes," Morgan said, nodding. "I figure she is either nearsighted or just plain stupid. But that's not what I wanted to speak to you about."

"Go on."

She hesitated. "I'm not sure we should even be doing this job."

Cutter narrowed his lips and set his hands on his thighs. He tried to pivot in his seat, but couldn't. He wanted to look at her and not have to stare up over his shoulder to do so.

*What? It's too late. How much more committed can we get? We can't back out now,* he wanted to say, but he figured she knew that already. *So what the hell is this about?* The whole damn gig had been on her and Gauge. He stared out the window at the blue sky and gray soup below them.

"Yeah, Jack, I know the money's good and all, but after doing a little more research, I'm getting an uneasy feeling about this. I mean, what do we really know about this artifact beyond what Sharon told us about it the first time around?"

At the mention of his wife, Sharon, he cringed a little. It still hurt to have others saying her name, especially now.

He ran his fingers through his hair and swept it back. "What we know is that we have four million on the line, and much as I appreciate your company, I could be back on the island curled up beside some—"

"I know that, Jack. But what I'm really wondering is—where did this new artifact come from? Is it going to be as dangerous to get to as the other one was?"

Cutter nodded in sympathy and shrugged. *Yeah, it probably was. So what?* "The money makes it easy to look past that. And it was you who insisted on coming."

"Yeah, I know. Still. We were searching for this same kind of thing in Ecuador for Pete's sake. How did another one just like it show up in Russia of all places? And how hard will this one be to find? Those things—the creatures we went up against? They were nasty. They reminded me of zombies, Jack. Like those Walking Dead brains, mmm brains, types."

*They weren't that bad. If I had only—*

She kept talking. "We know almost nothing about them too. Sharon was the expert. I just came along to handle the tech. And—"

She glanced out the front windscreen then back at him. "Why us, Jack? Why were we sent a second time and why now?"

*Why, because we failed the first time?* he wanted to say but held his tongue.

When he did not respond, she squatted lower, next to him. "Why us?" she repeated.

Cutter leaned sideways and checked on the co-pilot. The man was staring forward, pretending to ignore the very appealing woman crouched beside him, and was struggling to do so. Morgan was an extremely attractive woman in her own way, but she was not interested in men.

He glanced back down the length of the plane. Gauge was still comfortably asleep in his seat. In the seat in the row behind him, Dr. Martinez had her headphones on and was staring down at her laptop, stern-faced. The screen reflected off her glasses, making twin blue dots in the lenses.

Leaning closer toward Morgan, Cutter touched her on the knee and said directly into her ear, "I never said I wanted you to go along with me on this job. Remember? I said I could do it on my own."

When he pulled back and saw the hurt look his words had caused break out on Morgan's face, he withdrew his hand from her knee.

"It's just—" she started to say. "Why is it you always have to be so pigheaded about these things, you know? You've gotten worse at it too, Jack. You weren't like this before. You were—" She glanced out the window. "Why can't it be like it was back then?"

*Never again.* It would never be like it had been before he'd lost Sharon. *Never.* He clenched his jaw. The world owed him a little breather for what it had taken from him—*didn't it?*

He groaned a little. "So what is it that's really bothering you? Where are these negative impressions about Dr. Martinez coming from? Is it—maybe you find her attractive?"

"She's not my type," Morgan shot back. "Just so you know— the pilot. She and I—" She shook her head. "Never mind."

Cutter nodded back. *Okay, I get it.* He let go of his budding anger.

Morgan asked, "What do you think of her?"

"The pilot? I thought she was a little too old for me."

"She's twenty-four, you perv."

"A man has got needs, Morgan. A man has got needs."

She shoved him. "No, I meant her." She indicated toward Dr. Martinez with a tilt of her head.

"I think she's way too old for me. Plus, I don't think she likes me much either. But if you insist, I'll do my best. What do you think she looks like naked?"

"Jack, I'm being serious here. Do you think we can trust her? We know absolutely nothing about her. *Nothing.* I've been investigating her background. I've seen her university bio, her bank account records, even the results of her last pelvic exam. All were squeaky clean."

"Isn't she okay then?" he asked with a bit of hesitation.

"I don't know. I just have the creepy feeling we are being set up somehow, and that she is behind it."

# ~13~
## *TRUE DANGER*

They didn't land in London. Nor did they comply and divert when requested to by the EU controllers as they flew past Denmark and Sweden. Morgan had been able to stay one step ahead of everyone and keep up her game of swapping transponder signals to match the existing routes of other flights, up until the moment their Wi-Fi signal from the only satellite she could hack into disappeared over the horizon and went dark.

Now they'd have to make the rest of the flight to Russia on their last known course, hoping the appropriate administrators and commissars had indeed been notified and properly greased. And, given the currently strained relationships with Russia, any requested extradition back to the US would be scoffed at, perhaps even mocked.

Cutter smirked, thinking again of the stern-faced woman agent they'd left behind in Atlanta and what she must be thinking about all this. *She is probably apoplectic.*

He climbed from the pilot's seat and made his way past a snoring Gauge and back to the seat where Dr. Martinez was sitting. She was reading a book, something about genetically engineered dinosaurs made from chickens or something. *Looks kind of dumb.* He didn't even bother to check the name of the author. It wasn't his type of story.

He sat in the seat opposite her, and she set her book down and looked at him over her glasses, which were perched on her thin nose. She pushed them up slowly with her middle finger.

"That book any good?" he asked.

"What is it you want?"

"Right down to business, huh? No small talk? No, 'How are you doing today, Jack?'"

A tiny smile played at the corner of her lips, and she pulled off her glasses and bit on one of the tips.

*Damn that's hot.* Cutter squirmed in his seat a little. She had that school librarian look—smart with a touch of naughty underneath. He swallowed the small lump in his throat. "We are about an hour out from Vuktyl airfield—if you wanted to know." He leaned in closer. "Where is it exactly that you call home?"

Dr. Martinez put her glasses back on and picked up her book and opened it. She raised it slightly and started reading again.

"Just trying to make small talk," he said dismissively. "Don't you think we should get to know each other a little better before we land? Hell, I don't even know why I thought this job would make any sense in doing whatsoever. We probably should have passed." He did know a lot more than he was saying, really. Playing dumb worked such wonders on people and often got them to open up and talk freely. *But not always.*

She set her book in her lap again. *"And?* A little unprofessional, Mr. Cutter. Do you expect me to brief you and explain it all? Maybe at a level someone such as you can fully understand?"

*Bingo.* He had her thinking just like he wanted her to. The best way to deal with arrogance was to turn it into an advantage. It was a simple maxim of his.

He scratched at the two-day-old growth on his cheek. "Yeah, I kinda was thinking along those same lines."

She drew a deep breath. "Very well." She removed her glasses once more, folded them neatly, and set them on top of her book. "You are expected to do what I say, when I say it, and for how long I say it. Got that?"

*Really?* He pulled away and shrugged. "Is that all? Well, if you insist. Do I get to be the one on top at least?" He started to unbutton his pants as he watched her for reaction.

Her eyes widened a bit. "What the hell are you doing?"

"You don't want me to get undressed first? That's kind of impractical, but—"

She frowned at him and said nothing else, so he changed to a more serious tone. "No? I guess not then. So, given that we have some time to talk, is there anything we should be preparing for when we land? Any complications to consider when we go to fetch this—artifact? After what happened last time"—He became deadly serious—"I don't want to walk in unprepared."

"No," she replied, "you have to do nothing other than to protect me while I go to retrieve it." She rearranged her glasses on the back of the book. "I foresee no other complications."

"Then why the hell were we hired and paid a king's ransom to go get it? Why not someone else? And don't you think we should be playing a bigger role given our history? We've been through this before, and, last time, it got completely screwed up because we went in there with barely any information whatsoever. We were attacked by these…things…and my wife was—"

"Mr. Cutter," she said, speaking to him as if she were lecturing a small child. "You have been hired to escort *me* to the mine and help *me* retrieve the—" She paused. Her lips moved as if she were searching for the right word.

Cutter waited, hoping that she would describe it in such a way as to give him a better clue as to its real function. Even his wife had refused to tell him much about the artifact, preferring to keep it as one of her few secrets from him. She'd once said the origin of the thing was so crazy that he wouldn't believe her if she did tell him. And he believed in a lot of crazy shit.

Tantalizing him, Dr. Martinez opened her mouth to speak. Then she stopped herself and remained silent.

"Damn," he whispered, mostly to himself.

"I assure you," she said coldly, "I will be the only one allowed to go near it and touch it. *Am I clear?* We can't risk the recovery going wrong again and people getting hurt."

"Why is that?"

Again, she did not answer. She was hiding something. *What? What are you hiding?* He watched her for clues, but discovered nothing. She put her glasses back on and picked up her book.

*Whatever,* he finally thought as he made a fist and bumped it against his thigh. He'd had plenty of clients that wanted to keep things secret. He always made them pay for that privilege, just as he had now. Four million bought a lot of privacy. He was also certain that he'd find out soon enough what was going on. She couldn't hide it forever. And, thanks to Gauge, they had enough armaments to start a war if they wished to do so.

Instead of continuing his current line of questioning, he pivoted back to his original question. "Why us? There are scores of other private security teams out there who could have been hired to get you to Russia and back."

She lowered her glasses and looked him straight in the eyes. "Because I once knew your wife."

*Ah.* Everything began to click into place. He remembered her now from the book cover dust jacket on his wife's nightstand. There was an implied connection between these artifacts and primitive man at some level. It had been his wife's field of study. Dr. Martinez was apparently a professional colleague of Sharon's. But what was the ultimate connection between the two?

He slapped his hands against his thighs and stood. If Morgan got the Wi-Fi signal back up, he intended to do a little internet research on Dr. Martinez. Morgan had said earlier that she'd assembled a background report on her, but he still wanted to do a little research of his own. *Maybe I can find some nice nude selfies if I search hard enough.*

# ~14~
## *MAYDAY!*

*Sometimes I can be a damned fool.* Thankfully, Cutter also knew that God was well known for watching out for fools and small children. He had always figured he was more of the former and less of the latter, despite the fact that others often debated the point vigorously.

Right now, though, in all seriousness, he hoped that God had his back because if He didn't, Cutter and everyone else on board the plane were screwed.

It had started when they'd altered their route to skirt the final sliver of EU airspace just past Sweden. While they had taken on a splash of extra fuel in Atlanta just before scooting out of there in a hurry, their not-so-well-calculated flight plan that had called for an addition refueling stop in London before continuing into Russia had failed. Apparently, the US justice system really wanted him and his crew—*the bastards.* While Morgan had planned for reserves, just in case, those reserves hadn't quite been enough and were now completely depleted, which had caused the engines to quit.

*At least all the annoying whining noises were gone.*

Looking over at the co-pilot, Cutter asked, "Did you get confirmation we can land? It might also be good to check in with them and make sure they are not planning to shoot at us during our approach."

The co-pilot turned a lighter shade of pale.

Cutter tried to hold the wheel in a loose grip but with just enough firmness that he remained in full control of the aircraft. Coming over the mountains and descending below twenty-thousand feet had kicked up a great amount of turbulence and was causing everything to feel like a bad rollercoaster ride, doubly so, given that the aircraft was nothing more than a glider now—and a very poor one at that.

Keeping the G4 on the verge of a stall and making tradeoffs for distance was one of the most challenging ways possible to fly such a heavy jet. And, as much as he hated to admit it to himself, he was still gripping the controls just a little too tightly. *Loosen up there, partner.* He rolled his shoulders and glanced at the co-pilot. The guy said something over the radio in Russian then nodded to Cutter, who asked back, "Did you express to them the seriousness of our situation?"

The co-pilot, wide-eyed, nodded back.

Cutter had tried to contact the control tower in English, which was supposed to be recognized worldwide by all country's control towers, but this particular one apparently wanted to be different, or their grasp of the English language was about as good as his grasp of Russian, which consisted of maybe one or two words.

"Here we go," he said, rolling his shoulders again before withdrawing the plane's flaps a notch.

Ahead, he could see nothing other than a thick gray mass of clouds. Below the windscreen, lights were blinking incessantly on the instrument panel, and the artificial horizon indicator showed that their flight path was level. *Good.* But he could also tell that they were making an overly steep descent. *Not so good.*

Since the G4 did not make even a second-rate glider, added to the fact that it was also stuffed full of a heavy load of armaments in the cargo hold, it flew much like a pig with stubby little wings. But, fortunately, there was one small bit of additional good news—this wasn't the first time he'd made a landing on instruments alone, though he would have preferred to have had the engines running, and to have been able to actually see the ground. *Probably better I can't.*

Readjusting his sweat-slicked grip on the controls, he whispered to himself softly, "A nod for a wise man, and a rod for a fool," which seemed a far more appropriate thing for God to be doing than simply protecting fools. *Stupid should hurt.* But in this case, he could sure use that nod.

He turned to check on his passengers. Morgan was glancing at him nervously from her seat. She'd closed her laptop and stowed it away beneath her feet, but her hands kept fidgeting as if she still wanted to keep typing.

She mouthed, "We going to make it, right?"

"Of course," he mouthed back and punctuated it with a smirk.

Gauge was fully awake and staring out the window beside him. Even though he was feigning calm, Cutter could tell that the man was a little scared. Gauge was not the type would want to die in a fiery plane crash. He was more the type who would want to be taken out in a hail of gunfire while riding on the back of a shark and firing a bazooka.

Behind him, Dr. Martinez sat quietly, staring forward. Cutter had probed her a little further over her relationship with his deceased wife, but she had given up no additional details that connected all the various dots. Morgan hadn't been able to add much either, but at least he knew a smidgen more about those artifacts, at least enough to know not to touch one. Still, there was something important Dr. Martinez was holding back from him, and that bothered him to no end, but not quite as much as figuring out how in the hell he was going to land the aircraft.

With a sudden jolt, it felt like the bottom had dropped out from under him and he was falling. He went weightless for a brief second and rose from the seat. Then he smashed down hard in his seat and was rocked sideways as the entire aircraft shuddered and banked hard to the left. He jammed his foot into a corner and corrected right and was buffeted again by another patch of turbulence, then was thrown forward and hit the control yoke, causing the air in his lungs to rush out all at once.

Unexpectedly, the plane smoothed and leveled out all on its own, but still continued to buck in smaller and smaller staccato waves as it settled.

Gasping, Cutter took a few quick breaths and refocused on what the hell he was doing. Alarms in the cockpit were going off incessantly as even more buttons started flashing in a dizzying, chaotic display, like some madman's dream. He quickly refastened his harness and cinched it tight. He realized he'd been far too casual about everything. It was time to get serious.

"I'm trained to fly," Cutter said through the headset to the co-pilot as he took control again, "but I'm not certified for this particular model. Is there a procedure for all this?"

"Hold steady on oh-nine-four," came the co-pilot's shaky voice.

Cutter did as instructed, but without any power coming from the engines, he was having a difficult time keeping the plane on any kind of straight course. The co-pilot ran his hands over a series of switches too quickly for Cutter to see clearly in his peripheral vision, but the alarms began to shut off one by one.

Then the STALL WARNING light started blinking.

Cutter cleared his throat. "Is this thing even capable of a zero power landing?"

And the co-pilot didn't even shrug or say another word. He seemed to be reviewing his life and all the choices he had made in it.

Another alarm started.

HYDRAULIC FAILURE.

The co-pilot came out of his trance long enough to silence the alarm, then he spoke over the radio in a frantic, high-pitched voice.

"Mayday, Mayday. Golf-Sierra seven-seven-four-four. Request immediate clearance for landing. Both engines out. Hydraulics failing. Mayday, Mayday. Please respond."

*He's gone on autopilot.* Cutter lightened his grip on the controls again and waited for a response on the radio call.

None came.

The co-pilot repeated his plea, this time in Russian.

# ~15~
## *HARD LANDING*

Ahead was a mush of gray, and Cutter was flying blindly into it without instructions from the tower, and without anything other than the seat of his pants for guidance—in a plane he would be lucky to land even in the best of circumstances on a cloudless day.

He worked his grip on the wheel, wondering what in the hell he was going to do.

*Not a damn clue.*

But then the clouds parted, and the sun appeared, bright and bold and yellow in the haze of day. His first instinct was to shield his eyes from the sudden change in relative brightness. Instead, he squinted and continued to hold his death grip on the hard plastic wheel, fighting against the glare while trying to keep the plane level and biting enough air to avoid a stall.

Ahead, the single strip of gray concrete that was the Vuktyl airfield loomed large. Behind it was what appeared to be a small community of homes scattered among the random assortment of green treetops. Behind them was a murky river, tinged red.

"Altitude?" he asked into the mike he was practically chewing on, not wanting to spare a moment to look down and check the display himself.

"Three-zero-one-fiver," the co-pilot said. "Runway is zero-three-fiver-zero. Wind oh-seven-oh, ten knots."

"How about that?" Cutter said, slightly surprised.

"What?" the co-pilot asked, then, "Repeat?"

"Never mind," Cutter breathed back into the static.

He reached for the landing gear control to begin deployment then clicked the flaps an additional notch to account for the increased drag. With both engines out, electrical power was scarce, but to his almost overwhelming joy, he felt the wheels deploying, so he pushed forward ever so slightly on the control yoke to compensate a wee bit more.

*Gentle.*

Having the wheels down though wasn't enough to give him any kind of confidence that the landing would go well overall, but it was enough to provide a tiny flicker of hope. Landing with the gear up was never a good option. No matter what, the approach was going to be steep, and during the last leg of the descent, everything would happen very quickly. He'd only get single, solitary shot at it.

*Make it count.*

He drew a deep breath and said into the mike, "It's just like shooting womp rats in my T-16 back home."

Glancing over, he spared a moment to check in with the co-pilot. The guy didn't seem to get it, which was just too bad.

*Some people—*

Cutter rocked the plane back and forth, bleeding off more altitude. They'd been cleared by the tower, and the runway had been swept clean of planes and vehicles. The landing strip was almost five-thousand feet of reinforced concrete when even ten-thousand feet might not be enough.

"Here goes nothing," he said, hoping God was planning to spare the rod today.

As the G4 neared the ground, the buffeting of the airframe increased to a violent, head-rattling shake. This time, Cutter was firmly strapped to his seat and as sober as he'd been in well over a year.

"One thousand feet altitude," the co-pilot said.

"Five hundred."

"Four."

Math told Cutter that he had just fifty feet left to go, given that the runway was at three-hundred and fifty feet above sea level. As they got closer, the concrete strip seemed to flatten and stretch out to the horizon, but that was only an optical illusion. The town and residences quickly vanished below the treetops and the blackened, tar-filled cracks in the runway all seemed to blur together as they streaked past.

*Twenty feet.*

He pulled back on the yoke, flaring the nose of the plane, feeling the near-to-ground effect giving the G4's wings a needed final boost of lift.

*Ten feet.*

*Leveling.*

*Flaring.*

With barely a squawk from the rubber tires, the plane touched down, and those cracks in the runway shuddered the airframe and shook him hard in his seat.

*Uh, oh.*

With a terrible sinking feeling, he realized he had used up too much runway on approach and had landed halfway down it. From the corner of his eye, he spotted the airport buildings to his right whooshing past, as well as the single taxiway that shot past. He was going hard on the brakes and deceleration kept him punched up against his restraints, but he was also struggling to keep everything going in a straight line over the bumps and cracks in the rough concrete. The plane began to shimmy violently and veer to the right no matter how much control he exerted in the opposite direction.

*Closer.*

*Stop, please…*

With a sudden jolt, the plane shot off the last of the runway. The landing gear bit into the dirt and grass and pointed them on a new heading—directly toward a cluster of short green trees in the near distance.

The plane started to rotate further and skid sideways, bucking wildly. Cutter bit down hard and forced himself to relax his grip again on the steering yoke. There was nothing he could do other than hang on for dear life, hope for the best, and ride it out until it stopped. Still, he tried what he could, instinctively turning the useless wheel in the opposite direction of the skid as if he were driving a car on ice.

*Come on—*

And with a sudden, bone-jarring jolt, the plane came to a halt, flipped up, lingered there for a brief moment, and then reversed course and came crashing down, finally settling with an almost perceivable sigh of relief.

For a very quick dozen heartbeats, there was almost complete and utter silence. The only sound was that of fatigued metal reaching a new equilibrium. Cutter blinked twice and shook his head. He licked his dry lips and worked his jaw.

The co-pilot next to him was alternating between beaming wide smiles and mouthing, "Wow."

Glancing at the man, Cutter said, "So that's how you do it."

The smile vanished from the man's face, replaced by a look of abject fear, as if he'd suddenly realized the obvious—that Cutter truly hadn't known a damned thing about dead-sticking a G4, which was the gods' honest truth.

Cutter unbuckled himself and worked a kink out of his neck as he stood. When he went rearward to check on the others, he found Morgan already cleaning up all manner of things that had shaken loose or had come spilling out of cabinets and had been bouncing about the interior.

Gauge was still in his seat, nodding and grinning in his own way, which always made it seem as if he were laughing at some cosmic joke only he was privy to.

Outside, the sun was getting ready to set, and new flashes of light visible inside the plane started coming from behind them. Cutter glanced out the window and spotted a single emergency vehicle speeding toward the G4.

He could hardly keep from smiling as he slapped a hand on one of the seat backs and began making his way to the forward exit, where he twisted the control handle to manually lower the door and stairway ramp.

"Company's coming," he said as he deplaned and stretched his arms wide and shook the numbness out of his rubbery legs.

# ~16~
## *COLONEL SUVOROV*

Taking long strides in a way that blended well with a forceful, military-like clockwork precision, a man wearing a dark-colored beret cocked to one side and dressed all in black and white camouflaged fatigues marched toward Cutter and the smoking plane with purpose. Two additional men accompanied the guy, taking care to remain to either side so that if the guy were to reach out an arm, neither of his two followers would be struck by it.

Cutter remained firmly in place by the jet's small stairway, scratching his chin, figuring he had about another day's worth of beard growth in the past hour. Or, maybe it had just gone a bit gray.

"Jackson Cutter?" the man in the beret said in acceptable English as he closed the distance. He had a touch of an accent but sounded as though he'd trained hard to eliminate it.

Cutter remained silent and let the man continue his approach. He'd found that it was often better to wait for others to speak first. It was a power thing, and he sort of got off on that, especially now. He was already about as high on adrenaline and joy juice as he had ever been sucking on a bottle.

When the guy was exactly two feet in front of him, the man came to an almost orchestrated halt, as did his men. The two behind the man in the beret thrust out their chests and locked their hands behind their backs and raised their chins. The lead guy in the beret was tall enough that Cutter had to look up a little to stare into the man's smoke-gray eyes. The guy was clean-shaven and well-tanned and had a jawline that made him look as if he'd often used his teeth to break rocks into gravel, but his belly betrayed him as someone who also enjoyed a good meal or two, or three.

"I'm Colonel Suvorov." The man thrust out his hand. "Welcome to my country. I expect you had a pleasant flight?"

Cutter said nothing while he shook the man's well-calloused hand, returning the firm grip received and squeezing even harder.

"You were expected earlier, Mr. Cutter." The colonel released his grip. "Though, shall I say, we did not expect you to arrive in such a fancy and yet disturbing way. It is a real mess that you have caused for us, yes? I am fully expecting this to cost your employer extra if they desire it to remain private. I hope you can understand."

"Expected." Cutter shrugged and scratched his belly. "Bill them. They'll pay it." Frankly, he didn't much care. He'd make sure all the repairs to the rented G4 didn't come out of his cut. Those backing this expedition would end up paying for it in one way or another. They always did.

Colonel Suvorov continued to stare forward, not moving, not blinking, not perturbed in the least. The stare was meant to bore deep into Cutter's own returned gaze as if the guy were attempting to expose a hidden weakness. When Cutter returned that same steely gaze, the colonel snorted, glanced away, and grinned a thin smile. It had been just like their handshake and was that same butt-sniffing, alpha-dog thing that all men in their line of work did when meeting each other for the first time. The colonel was just testing him, and when the man blinked, Cutter knew he'd passed the test. But the dominance and pecking order between them had not yet been properly assigned. It would—given enough time.

"Good." The man nodded almost imperceptibly. "We will get along well, you and I."

The colonel snapped his fingers, and the two men to either side of him double-timed it over to the airplane and helped the others to disembark. Dr. Martinez was the last one to get off the plane, bags in hand.

A few minutes later, Cutter heard the steady whomp, whomp, whomp of a big chopper coming in from the east. Then, from over the treetops came a fat Mi-8—an old Russian helicopter capable of transporting an entire squad of troops.

"Our ride?" Cutter asked the colonel.

The big man nodded once and pointed to a spot just off the runway where all of the G4's cargo was being offloaded by four other men who had just arrived. The colonel's two aides ran to the helicopter and waved their arms to redirect the big bird where to land.

The big chopper beat the air into submission as it hovered over the field, first pivoting to face the plane then turning and landing rear wheels first. Cutter shielded his eyes from the kicked up dust and held his ground. The massive twin blades were kept spooled up, which told him that Suvorov was in a hurry to depart.

A few seconds later, the rear hatch descended on hydraulics, and a group of soldiers dressed in identical camouflage to the colonel's hustled out and ran to the cargo containers taken from the G4 and quickly manhandled everything back inside the helicopter.

Less than five minutes later, Cutter and everyone except the co-pilot of the G4 were airborne and heading northwest over the muddy river to their destination, presumably the mine site.

Cutter glanced out the window as the airport faded into the distance, wondering if they were going to taxi the plane back somewhere and fix it up, or just leave it in the field along with another wreck he'd spotted from the air. The G4 was their primary ticket home, and he hoped it hadn't broken like Humpty-Dumpty.

After the airport had vanished into the haze, he scanned the assembled men sitting on the bench seats around him. They were little more than scared and scrawny. The colonel appeared to be cut from a different cloth entirely, but the men under his command had not been fed well or cared for. He'd heard stories that the true Russian military was made up of many of these types, and except for the elite soldiers, or the ones used in parades on television, most of the men that made up their Army were conscripts too poor to know better, finding military service a way of getting out of the squalor in which they were raised. But what they seemed to find by joining up was only slightly better than what they left behind. Which, as Cutter examined each man in turn, meant that these guys were going to be about as reliable as a politician's promise on election day.

# ~17~
## *HOMEWORK*

Under a dull overcast of gray, twilight began to purple the sky. The big Mi-8 helicopter entered the airspace above the mine site and fell into a lazy circle.

Inside, arrayed on twin benches running the entire length of the craft, the young men sat with their hands folded across their packs, some stoic, some showing fear, which didn't fill Cutter with much confidence. But he had Gauge and Morgan to rely on, so as long as these young guns kept their weapons on safety, there shouldn't be any troubles. In fact, it should be a simple shoot and scoot mission. Get Dr. Martinez in, scoop up the artifact, and get the hell out. Maybe then find a ride back to Texas and figure out what the hell the FBI and Homeland Security had up their collective asses.

He sat forward, near the cockpit. Gauge was directly across from him, slumped low, next to Dr. Martinez. The man was still about a head taller and a foot wider than her. Morgan rested next to him, separating him from Colonel Suvorov.

In a voice loud enough to cut through the whine of the twin turboshaft engines, Cutter leaned across Morgan and asked Colonel Suvorov, "What can you tell me about this place?"

Shaking his head, the colonel grunted his disapproval and said nothing more, so Cutter leaned in close to Morgan's right ear, and asked her the same question.

She turned and said in his ear, "Didn't you do your homework?"

Cutter glanced away then back. "And start doing something new?"

Morgan pulled back a few inches and stared at him. She most likely hadn't heard him, but she'd read his lips and had probably understood his meaning.

"This installation is not supposed to be here," she said in his ear. "It's an illegal mining site."

"Come again?" Cutter said, and she shook her head. He bent closer to her to repeat it in her ear.

She said in return, "This whole adventure is illegal, Jack. The mining operation. What we are doing. Everything. The Komi Forest is a World Heritage Site. Which means that any kind of mining in the area is strictly prohibited."

"Then why hasn't someone put a stop to it?"

She nodded toward Colonel Suvorov. "How much do you think he gets paid?"

Cutter had no idea, so he shrugged.

She frowned, then said into his ear, "The equivalent of about fifty bucks a month by the Russian government. That's all they pay for a colonel like him this far out on the fringes of their former empire. The others make even less. Many far less, and probably gamble it all away first chance they get."

She took a breath before continuing. "How much do you think he makes doing whatever chores Mr. Moray's operation has him performing on the side?"

Again, Cutter didn't know, but he could guess. He shrugged. "More. A lot more. A hell of a lot more."

"Right. A heck of a lot more. Same with the miners. And with most of Russia in the same miserably corrupted state, it is easy to overlook a single mining site that is making money in defiance of the UN's various decrees. Even one this big. Plus, those pompous fools at the UN are too busy hosting dinner parties to notice what is going on anyway. As long as their checks clear."

Grinning wryly, Cutter pulled away and glanced at Gauge, who remained unmoving and poker-faced with his arms crossed over his chest and thumbs pointing upward. Morgan really knew her shit, even though she would never use such a foul and nasty word to describe it.

He let the matter drop as the helicopter continued to circle above the mining site.

Colonel Suvorov shifted positions and slid the forward side door open, creating a loud rush of wind that filled the interior. The air smelled dusty and slightly of pine. The man grabbed the side rail next to the door and hung out over the edge, looking downward.

Cutter moved into a squatting position next to the man and squinted against the onrush of air as he peered through the open doorway and down at the site.

Below him, nothing was stirring.

*This late in the day? Something should be moving. Trucks hauling supplies? Men going to and fro? Some smoke or dust trails at least.* He followed the two narrow roads leading out of the area with his eyes, searching for any vehicular traffic along them.

*Nothing. Nothing at all. Weird.*

Then, catching his eye, he spotted something. There was a figure moving far down below. It was running across a barren stretch of gray, which could only be crushed gravel.

*What the—?*

The hairs on Cutter's arms all stood on end at once, and an icy chill tickled his spine.

It was a guy. He was running for his life.

*What the hell was he running from?*

# ~18~
## *SHARON CUTTER*

Seeing the guy below, running for his life, reminded Cutter of the day he'd lost his wife. It was hard not to be reminded of her. But, sadly, she'd never had the opportunity to run, and he could imagine hearing her anguished cries over the beating of the rotors and the whining of the twin engines of the Mi-8.

Those same screams had cut off so abruptly when she'd died, but those screams had not died out in Cutter's mind. *Never*. He heard them day and night, awake or asleep.

Only the alcohol helped keep them at bay.

On that terrible day, he'd tried to get to her. Hell, he'd tried to with every fiber of his being, but Gauge and Morgan had stopped him and dragged him away before the final explosives had gone off and brought the entire mountain down on top of them. Only later had he realized he'd broken his arm at some point along with two ribs. And, somehow, he'd also cracked open his skull in a futile attempt to save her.

There was blood everywhere—all of it was his.

Sharon had repelled deep inside the mine, down to where the artifact had supposedly landed after they had been attacked by some kind of crazed people. Those people looked human, but they didn't act human.

Cutter had said he would make his descent first, but she argued how he barely knew his elbow from his asshole when it came to this kind of thing, and he would not be able to properly handle the artifact, so he capitulated, and she had gone before him.

That had been his mistake.

When Morgan's call had come over the radio to evacuate immediately, he was ready to make the climb back to the top. He urged Sharon, who was below him, to climb up to him so they could both get out together. But she'd yelled back up to him that she was almost to the artifact. She could even see it a few feet below her in the mineshaft and only needed to descend another few feet to reach it.

Morgan's repeated radio calls then became more and more insistent.

Still, Cutter trusted his wife completely. She knew what she was doing. If she said it would only be another few seconds, he could give her that time. So, against his better judgment, he ignored Morgan's cries of alarm and let Sharon finish her work while he began to climb in anticipation of pulling his wife up when she had the artifact in hand. There was still plenty of time. There always was. He was certain of it. He'd set the charges himself, so he knew just how long they had before they were scheduled to go off.

But he was wrong. The clock in his head had been wrong. And everything from that point forward had gone so terribly wrong.

He'd just started to pull her up when the concussion wave from the first charge knocked him flat on his ass. He lost control of the rope that held her, letting it slip right through his fingers before realizing what had happened. He tried to lunge for the rope and snatch it. But, before he could reach it, the line went taut, and the first anchor cam jerked free. Then another blast wave hit, and he fell again and the second cam broke free. And as that shiny metal anchor disappeared over the edge and into the gloom, so too went his wife, Sharon.

# ~19~
## *CHUDOVISHE*

Cutter's eyes focused on the man running below across the large stretch of gray. The man fell. Got up. Ran faster, arms pumping hard. Tiny puffs of brown dust followed his footsteps as he raced across the open space. It appeared he was heading for the thick line of trees at the edge of the clearing.

*What the hell are you running from?*

Cutter suddenly had a very bad, bad feeling about all this. It was all eerily similar to what had happened in Ecuador when they'd been attacked by those crazed people hopped up on some kind of drugs. Cutter had no idea how many of them had died when the mountain came down on top of them, but they had tried to kill him, so they had gotten what they deserved.

The helicopter continued to circle above the cluster of buildings while Cutter and Suvorov watched the man below. With a jolt, the helicopter nosed over and plunged into a steep descent.

Cutter lost sight of the man as the Mi-8's heading changed to intercept the guy near the tree line. When he glanced over at Suvorov again, the colonel was speaking into the microphone of his headset while balanced on the balls of his feet and peering out the open doorway.

Suvorov was directing the pilot. *Chase that guy,* he was probably saying in Russian. Cutter returned to his seat and pulled his own headset on to listen to the conversation. It did him little good as they were conversing only in Russian. He waved for Morgan to slip hers back on and interpret what was being said.

With another shocking jolt, he felt his stomach float into his throat as the helicopter fell from the sky into an even faster descent, sinking like a stone. His stomach began to settle down right as Morgan managed to get her headset on. He shook his head at her and removed his headset and hung it on a hook above his shoulder.

The engines on the Mi-8 raced, and the pitch of the whine grew higher and higher, almost screeching, and about a second later, a green light winked on near the rear hatch, and the hinged back door released downward before the helicopter had even set down. The men onboard remained seated until touchdown, then all of them stood up and filed out two at a time and spread out, crouching low, guns raised, nervous, but ready.

They looked as if they had practiced the maneuver before, but it was also easy to see that they weren't very good at it, either, because one guy stumbled and the rest piled up behind him causing them all to nearly fall over like toppling dominos.

Cutter glanced at Gauge, who was drawing his polished Desert Eagle and grinning with pleasure as he followed behind.

Morgan rose from her seat next to Cutter and prepared to exit, but he indicated for her to stay behind with Dr. Martinez. *Stay there*, he gestured in his haste, like he was commanding a dog to obey. She looked wounded by the order that he had meant to be a suggestion. *Sorry.* He grinned an apology at her then grabbed his gear. After exiting the helicopter, he ducked low on instinct and jogged to where everyone was assembling outside the rotor wash. The man who had been running across the field stood on a patch of grass, surrounded by Suvorov's men.

The frightened man had his hands on his knees and was bent over panting. He was covered in dirt and muck and filth as if he had come from the mine. There were also wet streaks that were probably blood.

Flailing his arms, the guy came alive and spoke rapidly in highly-animated Russian.

"What's he saying?" Cutter asked as he closed in on Suvorov.

"It is nothing for you to be concerned about," the colonel said from the corner of his mouth.

The man continued to point back at the cluster of blue buildings in the distance, stabbing his finger repeatedly at them and saying, "*Chudovishe. Chudovishe.*"

Colonel Suvorov left Cutter standing with Gauge and grabbed the gibbering man firmly by the shoulders, held him still, and then shook him hard, snapping the guy's neck like a kid shaking a rag doll. The colonel then forced the man to remain still and spoke in slow and reassuring tones. The guy calmed somewhat, coughed, and resumed stabbing his finger in the direction of the buildings making up the mining complex. There was blood under three of the man's fingernails, and two of them were completely missing.

"What's going on?" Cutter asked as he stepped alongside the colonel.

Suvorov did not initially answer. Instead, he made a series of hand gestures that sent four of his men running toward the cluster of distant buildings. The soldier's boots crunched with each double-time step they took, and their heads swiveled left and right, and their guns came up, and their backs were bent as if they expected to encounter trouble at any second even though the way ahead was clear.

That earlier bad feeling Cutter had had was growing worse by the second. "We should get out of here. No amount of—"

The colonel cut him off with a snort and hand wave. He then said something in Russian to his remaining troops. A laugh rippled through the men.

*What?* Cutter could not understand what was being said, but he could discern the meaning. It wasn't good.

"He's calling you a coward," Morgan whispered in his ear. "Specifically, he's calling you a '*trusikha*,' which means a fema—"

Cutter whirled on her. "I thought I said for you to stay behind and keep an eye on Dr. Martinez?"

She smirked. "And when have I started listening to you when you didn't make any sense?"

*Never*, was what came to mind. When it was truly important, she listened. Both she and Gauge did. Still, she should have remained behind in the helicopter. Someone needed to watch Dr. Martinez carefully until they knew if she could take care of herself and not jeopardize the entire mission.

"Okay, then," Cutter said. "Suvorov can think whatever he damn well wants, but I'll tell you this. We need to scoot on out of here, and do it now."

"Should we call you a '*trusikha*' as well?" Morgan said. She waited a beat and added, "Just suck it up, buttercup."

Cutter looked to Gauge for support. He found none there either. And they were right. He was acting far too fearful for the facts that they knew to be true. *Shit.* He'd lost his nerve for a moment. *That was all, yeah. God, I want a drink. A double, maybe. Or triple.*

"I'm fine," he said. "Let's go do this. We'll play along for now. But I won't let it get anywhere close to how it went last time. *No way. No how.* We'll bail first, okay?"

Morgan asked, "And you think you can do that all on your own? You think you can tell us to leave when we haven't even seen a good reason to go yet. You are better than this, Jack."

"Seeing that guy doesn't—" He stopped himself. He was slipping again. *Let it drop.*

The colonel asked the panic-stricken man another question, holding him by the shoulders and glaring into the man's eyes. Then he let him go. The guy fell on his backside and started pointing frantically again at the buildings, mumbling nonsense. About half the soldier's heads turned in that direction, looking somewhat nervous, not liking the way the situation was developing much either.

In the extreme distance, the men who had been sent were already rounding one of the largest of the blue steel buildings.

Then they vanished from sight.

Everyone watched, waited.

Cutter took a few calming breaths, chastising himself for his onset of fear. It had never been this bad for him before. *What the hell has happened to my nerve?* His deep breathing calmed him just enough to begin to put the pieces back together again. *We have a full complement of men. Yes, they are probably not the highest quality, but we've got Gauge, and Morgan, and a mini-arsenal. What trouble could there possibly be that we can't handle?*

A few staccato gunshots rang out. It was enough to cause the soldiers near Cutter to shift into a more defensive posture, fanning out to cover all angles of potential attack—from the trees behind, from the left, from the right, from whatever might come charging at them from the clustered buildings.

Then more shots went off—rapid, erratic shots.

A scream.

Another.

And then silence.

The spooked man sitting on the ground clawed his way back to his feet and began jumping from foot to foot like a madman and pointing and repeating the same word over and over.

*"Chudovishe! Chudovishe!"*

Cutter had to know what that meant. He leaned over and asked Morgan.

"Monster," she said. "It means monster."

# ~20~
## *GUN UP*

Inside the helicopter, Cutter broke open one of their three crates of supplies—the biggest one with all the guns in it. To Morgan and Gauge, he handed an MP5K and six spare magazines. He grabbed the same for himself and stuffed the spare mags in his tactical vest and left behind their fancy assault rifles, helmets, and body armor for now. They'd come back for it later if necessary. He figured with all the soldiers there to escort them into the mine, they probably wouldn't need all that. It would just slow them down.

He nodded to Gauge and Morgan in turn, and his two teammates stepped forward to fetch their favorite sidearms from the crate. Morgan, who always professed to hate guns, grabbed a Glock 19 and strapped it to her hip. Gauge, who was already well armed with his Desert Eagle .50 protruding from its resting place closest to his heart, grabbed an additional Glock, then another, stuffing both guns into hidden pockets in the hulking vest and harness he wore over a long-sleeve T-shirt, black.

Cutter grabbed the Glock that had been brought along for him, racked the slide, and inspected the condition—brand new, just broken in. Then he switched to his familiar M1911 Colt .45 that he'd found in his desk drawer back in Texas. He weighed both in his hands. *Which one should I take?* He only wanted to bring one and wanted the one that had the least chance of jamming. He grimaced and put his old Colt .45 automatic away. It was a great gun, but it had been fired so many times that he just couldn't count on it any longer. It needed a complete rebuild. But he loved that gun, so it was difficult to just leave it there. He did, though, giving it final look as he rested it on the foam inside the packing crate. Instead of bringing along the .45, he snatched up a few extra magazines of 9-millimeter for the Glock and stuffed them in the pockets of his tactical pants.

"What are you doing?" Colonel Suvorov asked, poking his head back inside the helicopter.

"Getting dressed." Cutter racked the slide on his MP5K and checked the chamber, looking for that reassuring sparkle of brass.

"You will not need your own guns. We are in charge of security here. My soldiers will protect you."

Cutter shared an uncertain glance with Gauge and Morgan. He had seen the colonel's nervous men, who were really no more than pimply teenage boys drafted into service and escaping impoverishment. That made them soldiers that could not be counted on, and Cutter would not risk his life on them, or the lives of his two teammates.

"Sorry, but we brought our own."

"You will not need them," the colonel said. "I assure you they will not be necessary."

"We'll see." Cutter, satisfied with his weapon choices, let the slide slam forward on the MP5K.

"I must insist," the colonel said. "Leave them here."

*Like hell, I will.* The colonel's statement also caused another nervous glance from Morgan, who had her back to the man.

"Okay," Cutter said slowly, and he stood to his full height. "You can just come take them away from us then."

Colonel sized Cutter up again. Gauge pulled out Betty and racked the slide, checking the chamber as Cutter had on his MP5K. The big gun remained pointed in the colonel's general direction while Gauge inspected the mighty weapon.

"Very well," Suvorov said, turned, and disappeared.

Gauge whispered to Cutter, "I do not trust them. Young boys make poor soldiers."

Cutter nodded. "Then they'll need someone to show them just how it is done, won't they?"

"And I am supposed to do that?" Gauge said, then growled.

Moving beside him, Morgan added, "They are a bunch of pathetic little monkeys, aren't they?"

Gauge grunted his approval while Cutter considered the implications. Colonel Suvorov was in it for Colonel Suvorov. They would have to watch the man closely.

*Anyone who asked another to disarm was a potential threat—* Cutter understood that lesson very well.

"Dr. Martinez," Cutter said when she appeared from behind Gauge. She'd come back inside the helicopter. "Would you care for a weapon? We brought along extras and—"

She waved him off. "I don't care for guns," she said and adjusted the collar of her shirt. "I find them distasteful."

Gauge flashed a vulpine smile at Morgan, and she shook her head in disapproval. Cutter just stared ahead at Dr. Martinez, wondering what in the hell was wrong with her. Morgan at least realized the dangerous situation they were in and the value of a quality weapon to mitigate it.

*I'll just have to keep an eye on her.*

"Best we get the show on the road," he said before motioning to them to exit the helicopter.

After assembling with the young soldiers outside the Mi-8, as a group, they approached the outskirts of the large blue buildings. The gravel crunched under their boots, and the air was still and calm. Perhaps too calm. Bugs swarmed around Cutter, and he batted them away. He was doubly wary of what they might be walking into. He kept sniffing the air, picturing in his mind that he would be able to detect trouble before it happened. It was a mental game he often played that kept him on his toes. Sometimes it worked.

One of the young soldiers took the point position in their walking formation. He was a tall, thin, blond-haired kid who could not have been more than seventeen years old. He still had acne on his face and neck. The other soldiers followed him, scanning for trouble, but seemed completely unprepared for any trouble that might find them.

Cutter and team followed the soldiers with Colonel Suvorov and his two bodyguards. He held the MP5K loosely in his grip, trigger finger stiff along the trigger guard, ready to bring the weapon up and fire it should the need arise. It was a strange dilemma he faced. Having so many soldiers at the ready should allow them to take down almost anything they might encounter, so he figured the four men who had been sent earlier had to have been taken by surprise, which also meant the colonel was making every effort that any mistakes those men had made would not be repeated. Still, he was not at all reassured. *Not in the least*, and that was feeding his growing unease and tension. And, judging by the pale glances Gauge and Morgan were giving him, he was not alone.

As they approached, the buildings became larger than he had first thought they were when he had flown over them. They seemed broader, yet more squat. It was probably the multi-shaded blue paint and the fading light. The sides had been textured in a way that looked almost like a diffused-edge camouflage that would make them appear far smaller from above, or from any oblique angle. From space, probably even smaller. Red Cyrillic writing adorned the buildings, not English. Even so, it was relatively easy to make out the Roman numerals. And it was not difficult to guess the purpose of each building.

The first of the buildings was long and narrow and two stories high with deeply inset square windows running along at each level. External metal stairs led up to the second story, and it was topped by a grooved metal roof. Just outside the lower landing, a pair of barren trees stood alongside a series of park benches surrounding a concrete fire pit. Stained plastic chairs were arranged haphazardly around the blackened ring, and the ground near it was stubbled with crabgrass and littered with cigarette butts.

Cutter wondered if there were any cigarettes left that he could get a hit or two from. Morgan had taken his last pack and crushed it before they had boarded the plane in Texas. He glanced at her, wishing she hadn't taken away his cigarettes.

"What?" she asked, then shook her head. "These are the dorms," she added as the passed by the building's entrance.

As they swung around to the other side of the building where the four soldiers had disappeared, Colonel Suvorov ordered his men to fan out. Cutter and Morgan both raised their guns and followed. Gauge stood guard next to Dr. Martinez, who had remained silent and observant the whole time. She seemed curious and self-assured—if nothing else.

As they rounded the corner of the building, taking slow steps, preparing, they all drew to a halt behind the colonel's outstretched arm signaling for them to stop.

But there was nothing to see.

No soldiers. No bodies. *Nothing.* Just more mud, dotted bits of grass, and murky brown pools of water with bootprints. There were so many it was hard to tell what was what. Cutter scanned the area and followed the edges of the buildings up to the rooftops.

*Where were all the lights?* It was getting dark already, and not a single light had come on. They were there, mounted under the eaves and on round metal poles, but—

*Nothing.*

Almost in lockstep, they moved forward another fifty feet, and Suvorov again held up a hand to call a silent halt, then motioned for his soldiers to regroup into a new, wider formation next to a concrete wall that was about waist high.

Cutter came up to join the man. There were bootprints in the muddy earth along the wall—multiple sets, some big, some small, some uniform, some not. He squatted on his haunches and examined the prints. It was impossible to sort them out and tell what they meant, but then glints of yellow caught his attention and he rose and made his way closer to the building that was next to the wall. He let his MP5K drop and hang on its strap.

Brass casings had bounced off the sides of the building and landed in the mud there, showing him the direction from which the men had fired and where they had been standing when they did.

But that was it. *Just casings.* The men who had fired those guns were long gone.

One of the soldiers called out for the colonel. Cutter followed along and squatted next to them in the mud. Long streaks led off in a squiggly trail across the muddy ground as if someone had been dragged away. Those tracks led around the side of the building and then disappeared.

"Wouldn't there be blood if they were hit?" Cutter asked no one in particular.

"Not if they were attacked and hit from behind," Morgan answered. She'd snuck up behind him and was looking over his shoulder.

Gauge joined them. "What do you think this is?"

Cutter shrugged. "Not sure yet. Who would attack these guys? The miners? If so, why?"

He rose and repeated the question for Colonel Suvorov's benefit. "Who do you think attacked them?"

"That is something we must find out," the colonel said. He shouted orders in Russian at his troops, and the men regrouped and tracked the drag marks on the ground.

Cutter grabbed Suvorov by the arm, which drew a nasty return look. The colonel then shrugged him off and marched forward. Cutter said to his back, "We should think about going."

"Those were my men," the colonel said. "We are going to get them back from whoever took them."

"And you are going to die too if you go after them," a new voice said.

All heads pivoted toward Dr. Martinez. She was standing about ten feet away, but she quickly closed the gap between them.

"What do you know about this?" Cutter asked.

Just then came an agonizing cry that split the air. Birds took flight and flapped past overhead. Cutter tracked them back to the source. The cry had come from somewhere that was hidden from view by the largest of the buildings in the complex. It was a hulking structure three or more stories tall.

"What the hell was that?" Morgan asked, coming up from a crouching position.

Gauge had Betty out and looked as though he was ready to shoot whatever dared to move next. Cutter motioned for him to calm down.

The terrible cry came again. It was a nightmarish cry of anguish and pain and sent shivers down his backbone, locking him in place. Morgan shifted to stand closer to him while Gauge cocked his head left and right.

Cutter lifted his own weapon on the strap and scanned the area for threats. He saw none. "I think we should get back to the chopper."

"You can go," Suvorov said. "But I'm not leaving without knowing what has happened to my men."

"They are dead," Dr. Martinez said. "And the others will be soon if you do not recall them."

"What the hell haven't you told us?" Cutter asked, eyeing her with budding anger. "How would you know all that?"

She said nothing.

"Okay," he said, "that seals it. We need to get back to the chopper and away from these buildings. We can regroup and reassess there. We're too exposed here."

The anguishing cry came once more. It was an inhuman wail, and this time, it went on for nearly ten seconds before it cut off abruptly with a gurgling choke. Cutter was sickened by the noise, but he was no longer frozen in place by it. His feet were already starting to move him back toward the helicopter.

A new distant shout rang out.

It repeated.

The new shout was something in Russian Cutter could not understand, but the universal tone of terror had been enough to tell him that now was a really, really good time to bug out and get the hell back to the chopper. Then that shout cut off and was replaced by another wailing scream, pitched higher, and made by the same tortured throat as the first shouted cry.

Colonel Suvorov barked fresh new commands. His men reacted this time and responded almost instantly. *Fear does that to men*, Cutter knew. Those with little real experience almost always look to someone else to save them. The colonel was supposed to be that man. But just then, the same guy who had been wanting to go after his men, grabbed Cutter by the shirt and yanked him forward and off balance. "We go now. We must go now, right? Back to the helicopter?"

Cutter nodded in surprise and let out a held breath.

# ~21~
## BAD TIMING

Cutter wasn't the first to reach the Mi-8, but he was the first to climb inside through the open rear hatch, which hadn't been open when they had left. And when he climbed the ramp, his nose told him that something was wrong—*terribly wrong.*

Outside, the sun had almost set completely. Nightfall was upon them, which made it even darker inside the helicopter—too dark for Cutter to see anything until his eyes fully adjusted to the dim light. He felt his way along with his feet and with one arm outstretched and touching the right side of the helicopter. His other he waved directly in front of him to avoid running into anything unexpected.

Then his right palm brushed against a damp patch, and he jerked his hand away and flexed his fingers, rubbing them against his thumb. Whatever his hand had landed in was sticky and warm, and the fluid oozed between the tips of his fingers. He sniffed it. The iron and copper scent was unmistakable. *Blood.* But it was what he saw next when he entered the cockpit that sent his pounding heart into overdrive.

*Oh, God—*

The two pilots that had stayed behind with the craft were still upright in their seats—most of them, anyway. Someone or something had wrenched their heads completely off. *Impossible.* But there it was. Proof that it could be done. And it made a hell of a mess. There was so much blood in the cockpit that the forward windscreens and instrument panels were bathed in spatters of crimson that glittered faintly in the last bit of light. The stink alone was overpowering. Cutter gagged. His stomach roiled, and he had to turn away and collect himself.

He groaned and sucked in a shallow breath as he shoved his forearm against his nose. His eyes were already watering, and he blinked away the tears while swallowing his disgust in one big, fat lump.

Because they had no other readily known means of escape, he had to prepare himself for what he would have to do next. Closing his eyes, he let his stomach settle. *You can do this. Yes, you can.* Reluctantly, he grabbed the pilot by the shoulder straps, pulled him off the seat, and dragged what remained of his body out of the cockpit and set him on the floor.

Morgan, who came up from behind him with a flashlight in hand, touched him on the arm and shook her head. Her eyes were squinted, and her lips had narrowed in disgust. She folded her arm over her nose like he had and ran for the exit, taking the only source of illumination with her. He continued to watch her scramble out of the big Mi-8, wishing he could follow her.

*Got a job to do.*

Gauge's square head emerged from the backside of the helicopter. It appeared ghost-like in the beam of his own flashlight as it shone from below, making him all angles and planes. His head seemed to float up the ramp at the rear as if it had become separated from his body. *No.* Cutter shook his own head and shivered to wipe away the terrible vision of a headless Gauge.

*Just the dark. That's it. That's all.* He sucked a deep breath, realizing his breathing had been too shallow to do much good.

Gauge came forward, crouched low, and pointed his flashlight downward to not blind Cutter. Colonel Suvorov was following directly behind him. Suvorov came to a stop before he reached the cockpit. He glanced at Cutter and the body on the floor.

"Can you fly this?"

Cutter had only flown a helicopter once in his life. The principles, he knew, but the specifics of flying such a big Russian bird, with Russian instruments, through Russian airspace, at night? Everything was so unfamiliar and far, far beyond his abilities.

"Yes, I can," he said reassuringly.

"Good," Suvorov said and backed himself all the way out of the helicopter.

With Gauge there to help him, Cutter grabbed the co-pilot's body from the seat and tried to drag it out of the cockpit to join the pilot.

"What happened to their heads?" the big man asked.

That was the obvious question Cutter did not have an answer for yet, nor had he the time to figure it out, nor could he even imagine how those heads had been removed in the first place. With so much blood everywhere, it was impossible to tell for sure just what had happened.

He located a terrycloth towel the pilot had stashed in the pocket next to his seat, presumably to dry his hands. It had remained relatively free of the twin fountains of blood that had erupted and coated almost everything else in gore. He used the rag to wipe clean a spot on the windshield, but the action did little more than smear and streak the blood around, and soon the cloth became too saturated in wet stickiness to clear much of anything. But he had exposed a tiny section that he could peer through if he kept his head low and tilted to one side.

"*Morgan!*" he yelled over his shoulder and almost into Gauge's face.

No response.

He yelled her name again.

Grimacing as if she were going to be sick at any moment, she joined him, avoiding all the spattered blood as best she could.

"Do you know how I start this thing?" he asked as he checked the controls. He wasn't about to start randomly flipping switches until he was reasonably sure what he was doing.

She scanned the forward instrument panel, running her fingers over the various buttons and mouthing the translations as she thought them through.

"No, these," Cutter said, pointing with Gauge's flashlight at the switches about his head. She leaned past him, narrowed her eyes, and touched one of the toggle switches. A single drop of blood was transferred to her fingertips, and she drew back with her eyes going even wider.

"Come on," he said, "we've been through this kind of shit before."

She grunted a nervous laugh. "Not like this," she said, head shaking. "Never ever like this. This is…terrible."

"Yeah, it is," he admitted. "Here goes." He flipped the switch she had indicated.

There was a mechanical clunk. The entire craft shuddered.

"Try that one," she said.

"He flipped another switch and the instrument lights all clicked on and started blinking red."

He flipped the first switch she had indicated again, holding it against its stop. He figured it was an engine start.

But nothing happened. Red lights on the instrument panel continued to flash.

"You sure that was the right switch?"

She checked again. "Yes, it has to be. *Engine Start*, right?"

Cutter sighed and waved a hand in the air. "Then something else is wrong. Short in the system from all this—maybe?"

"Maybe," she agreed, seeming not so sure.

Suvorov joined them. "You fly? No?"

"I can, yeah, but this Russian shit-pile won't fire up," Cutter said. "There's a fault somewhere and it's not allowing the engines to start."

Cutter and Morgan both looked to Suvorov for reaction. He remained blank-faced. Finally, he said, "Outside, maybe? We think they may have gotten to the engines."

"What the hell? *Who got to them?*" Cutter rose and hurriedly pushed past the others, heading for the back of the craft.

He exited and rounded the helicopter and came to a halt near the front. He aimed Gauge's flashlight at the outside hull. Dark bloodstains led up to the twin engine intakes above the cockpit, and it appeared that someone had jumped onto the helicopter and somehow had climbed up the side of the airframe.

*Impossible.* But, it hadn't been.

He eyed the path and streaks of blood for a beat. He turned to Gauge. "Give me a boost."

With locked fingers, Gauge lifted him up the side of the craft until he could twist his foot sideways and use a seam in the aluminum skin to boost himself even higher. He felt wetness seeping into his shirt as he clung to the side. *More blood.* He pushed his fear aside and centered himself again.

The old rituals of quickly regaining self-control were beginning to return to him—and they had picked a damn fine time to start doing so. Still, he would have traded it all for a bottle of tequila, a carton of smokes, and a beautiful, well-tanned, big-breasted island girl. Preferably one he didn't have to pay for.

By hanging onto the side of the Mi-8 by his fingertips, he was able to work up enough grip to pull himself just high enough to see into the port side engine intake. There was an obstruction. He strained to get closer, scooting up on his belly and toes and practically shoving his entire head into the oblong intake.

What he saw made him flinch and nearly lose his grip on the helicopter. A single lifeless eyeball stared back at him from a head that was covered in blood and had been partially crushed by the engine's compressor blades.

"I think I found our pilot," Cutter cried. His voice echoed inside the tube.

"What?" Morgan said from below.

He backed out a bit so he could talk to her. "I found some of him. His head is up here. The colonel was right. It's the engine. It's not going to start. The intake's all jammed up."

He grabbed the head by the hair and tried to pull it away from the turbine blades, but could not get a good grip while holding himself steady with his other hand. The short, blood-soaked hair kept slipping through his fingers. *Damn. Can't get it.* He left the disembodied head in place and made his way back down the side of the helicopter. He landed in the soft dirt and stopped to wipe his hands dry on his black cargo pants. He smelled of lifeblood, which was an odor that once experience was never forgotten.

"No idea how anyone could do that to a man," he said, "let alone two. But the colonel is right." He drew a breath. "We might just be stuck here for a while, so you'd better start unpacking and setting up a solid perimeter. *Got that?*"

Morgan and Gauge both professionally nodded an affirmative. Wheeling, Cutter grabbed the colonel by the shirt and directed him to the cockpit. When they got there, Cutter grabbed a headset from a hook behind the pilot's seat, shook off the blood, and held it out for the man.

"Call in reinforcements," he said. "*Now.* Call in another helicopter. Another hundred soldiers. *Any damn thing!* Whatever it takes to get us the hell out of here before anyone else dies."

But Colonel Suvorov did nothing, so Cutter thrust the headset at the man's chest. "I don't give a good goddamn about this mission any longer. So you call them, and you call them...*now!*"

Suvorov pursed his lips and shook his head, refusing to accept the headset.

"*Seriously?*" Cutter sucked in a long, deep breath, and then in a lower tone said as he nodded his understanding, "There are no reinforcements to call in, are there? These are all the men you have available to you?"

The colonel said nothing.

"*Goddamn it,* what about those taking care of the G4 back at the airfield?"

"We have enough men here with us," the colonel said. "Plenty. We will find out who killed my pilots and then we will—"

"And your other four that just died screaming somewhere," Cutter added. "I don't give two squirts about getting any kind of revenge for this, or even finding out how in the hell it was even possible to rip a man's head clean off. What we need to do is get the hell out of here before anyone else gets killed. So get on the damn radio—*and call someone!*"

"We have enough men to handle any problem."

"*That's total bullshit.* You don't have nearly enough. Whoever it was that attacked us was able to do so on their terms. Not ours. Don't you see that? They're going to pick us off one by one if we don't get out of here."

"We Russians are not cowards, Mr. Cutter. We are not afraid. We stick together. Not like you Americans, who always turn tail and run."

"What the hell kind of comment is that?" Cutter asked. "You think this is about *fear?* I'll be the first to admit that I sure the hell am afraid. But a little fear and retreat are better than being stupid and dead. Now call someone in, and do it *now!*"

Cutter thrust the headset at the colonel again.

The man refused to take it and turned his back on Cutter and made his way down the aisle and out of the helicopter, leaving Cutter holding the former pilot's blood-stained headset. He was practically shaking with rage. He gripped the headset and ripped it free from its tether and chucked it as hard as he could toward the back of the helicopter.

The headset bounced off the cargo netting above the bench seats, then caught an edge and started to tumble through the air. And at that precise moment, Gauge had the misfortune of coming up the ramp at the rear of the helicopter at the same time—and got hit square in the face.

# ~22~
## GODDAMNED ZOMBIES

The impact of the helmet had busted Gauge's nose. This wasn't the first time Cutter had broken that same nose, but the last time there'd been a valid reason for doing so.

"Shit," he said as he held out a gauze pad he'd pulled from their medical kit to stop the blood flow.

Gauge grabbed the pad and held it against his nose without comment as he sat on the bench. The large man's eyes were watering, and he was blinking rapidly, but he wasn't complaining.

Cutter sucked in a deep breath. "Let me see if one of those guys out there is a medic." He left the helicopter shaking his head, disgusted with himself for having harmed the guy, who was probably one of the only two friends he had left in the world. *And I left him sitting next to a pair of headless corpses? Great, Jack. Just great.*

Outside, it was well past sunset. The purples were already darkening the sky and painting the clouds in shades of black. The first stars were already visible in between the small gaps in the cover, but the moon was nowhere to be seen.

"What happened?" Morgan asked Cutter as she huddled with him.

"I smashed up Gauge good, real good," he admitted.

"Did he deserve it?" she asked.

Cutter drew a breath. "Of course not. Any of these guys strike you as a competent medic?"

"These guys," she said, drawing it out, "strike me as the types who are looking for any excuse to pull either us women folk aside for some alone time."

"Keep a close watch on her, okay?" Cutter nodded toward Dr. Martinez. He knew that Morgan was sharp enough to take care of herself in pretty much any situation, but he didn't know enough about Dr. Martinez yet. *Too many horny teenagers nearby. Never a good thing.*

Cutter left her to her various tasks and went to find Suvorov, who was scanning the distant compound through binoculars.

"See anything?"

"Plenty," the man said, not taking his eyes away from his binoculars. "But not my men."

"You have a medic in your outfit?"

"Why?"

"My guy has gone and got his nose all busted up."

The colonel lowered the binoculars for a moment, returned a puzzled look, then nodded toward one of his men, a short guy with clipped blond hair and a bag slung over his shoulder.

Cutter picked out the guy Suvorov had indicated, and talking to him with hand gestures, got the man to understand what was needed.

"Still think you should have ducked," Cutter said to Gauge while the medic worked on him.

The big man pushed the scrawny medic to one side with a sweep of his hand. "I didn't think you could throw so hard."

Cutter stifled a chuckle, and Gauge leaned back and let the medic work on him again. There were no hard feelings on Gauge's side. There never were. It was just a stupid accident. They'd share more jokes about it later. Maybe some retorts about payback. But all was good between them. And it was hard to take it either way with a headless corpse just feet away under a blanket.

Morgan soon joined them and examined the work the medic had done as he was finishing up. "I think it will look even better this time around when it heals. Can you breathe okay?"

Gauge grunted once and scratched at the dressing.

Dr. Martinez also reentered the craft, bent forward, and began digging through a satchel she had stowed under the bench seat. Since that put her backside about three feet from both Cutter and Gauge, they both watched her in admiration from behind while Morgan shook her head, scolding them. Cutter ignored her while Gauge just forced a grin and rubbed his jaw and stroked his cheeks around the bandage on his nose.

"There's no getting out of here tonight," Cutter said loudly enough to cause Dr. Martinez to turn. When she noticed the angle he had been watching her from, she frowned.

Cutter smiled. "So we need to figure out what is going on here, and do it quickly."

"You don't think we should stay here in any case, do you?" Morgan asked.

Cutter shifted so he could look out one of the porthole windows. "We may have to, though. I don't see many five-star hotels nearby."

"We certainly can't stay inside here tonight," Morgan said. "One of those buildings has to have an area we can secure."

"Maybe." Cutter chewed on a thought. "But we would have to get there first. Ideas?"

"Might I make a suggestion?" Dr. Martinez injected into the conversation as she backed herself against the bench across from them.

Cutter nodded. "By all means." The plan he was hatching in his head was coming out all wings and elbows.

"I know what is going on here," she said. "I've been briefed beforehand, so I know what it was that killed those men."

"Well, then," Cutter asked in a slightly irritated tone. "Enlighten us, Doctor. I heard a 'what' in that and not a 'who,' so how about first telling us *what* the hell is going on? Those two guys up front probably would have appreciated knowing a bit more about the situation they had just flown into before having their damn heads torn off. And, even knowing this as a possibility of what could happen, I'm not sure I would have agreed to come here in the first place. Not after—"

Morgan bumped him. He got her meaning. "Okay, okay. Who? *Who* is doing this to us? It has to be a 'who,' not a 'what.'"

Dr. Martinez said nothing.

Cutter stared at her for a long, hard second. *What the hell?* This was supposed to be a simple retrieval mission. Go in, fetch what they'd been sent for, and scoot the hell out. The guns they'd brought along were only a formality after what had happened in Ecuador. For show, mostly, or so he had first thought. *Now they're a damned necessity.*

A shout came from outside. He tilted his head and held up a hand for silence.

*Gunfire.*

"Zombies," Dr. Martinez said.

"What?" Cutter's head snapped back to stare at her. "Zombies? What the hell is that supposed to mean?"

More gunshots.

Dr. Martinez leaned forward. "What killed those pilots—they were zombies."

"Like TV? Walkers? Biters? Roamers?" Cutter asked.

"No, of course not. Not any of those. That's a fictional TV show filled with misinformation and certainly n—"

She was cut off when another rapid burst of gunfire came from just outside the helicopter. Cutter pushed himself up and weaved through them all and made for the back ramp in a hurry while raising his weapon. *She had to be crazy. Zombies? That made as much sense as—*

As soon as he exited, he spotted a distant shadow flitter past on one of the buildings, a shape in the night. It moved shark-swift against the backdrop and was about a hundred and fifty yards away.

Two of the colonel's men were kneeling in front of the man. Their automatic rifles were balanced on their knees, their arms bent, rifle straps wound around their arms to stabilize their weapons, just like they had probably been trained to do. But they were doing it wrong. They'd been firing at the fast-moving shapes. Bullet casings littered the ground and reflected what scant light was left.

Now the two men were holding fire. Cutter crabbed sideways to stand beside the colonel and put his fingers in his ears. The men resumed their fusillade of lead, and the gun muzzles flashed in the night—quick bursts followed by assessments of damage.

The salvo had been completely ineffective. The shapes vanished behind another building and out of sight. Even at a hundred and fifty yards, these kids couldn't hit diddly squat, which made Cutter wonder if these guys had been trained at Stormtrooper School.

When their target had completely disappeared into the night, the colonel struck one of the young soldiers in the back of the head, nearly knocking him over. He said something to the kid in Russian, but it was not hard to grasp the disgust in his voice.

"What was that?" Cutter asked the man.

"*Chudovishe*," Colonel Suvorov said.

"Monsters?" Cutter asked. "What the hell is going on here?"

"Maybe you should tell me, Mr. Cutter. Do you believe in monsters?"

"No," Cutter said. "Our 'guest' thinks they are zombies. The undead. Like in the movies. You have movies here, right?" He stopped and changed his tone. Now was not the time for jokes. "Those things tore the heads off two of your pilots, so they seem a little more than zombies to me. Whatever the hell those things are, I'd rather we not stick around tonight and find out more about them. Have you reconsidered? Is there another way out of here other than by helicopter? Some other vehicles, maybe? It's a mining site, right? Where are all the trucks?"

"No," the colonel said. "We are not leaving tonight. Not yet. Not until I find out what has happened to my men."

Morgan and Gauge arrived, with Dr. Martinez between them. Cutter jerked his thumb at Dr. Martinez. "She's the one who claims these things are zombies. I saw something similar to these things once before, but I never got this close to them. We heard them more than we saw them, and that was close enough for me. Natives said they were hopped up on something."

"Hopped up?" the colonel asked.

"Drugs. Something that turned them into psychopaths. But I'm thinking that was bullshit now."

The colonel eyed Dr. Martinez carefully while he considered. Then he nodded. "There is a secure space inside the building just past the large one over there." He indicated the dormitory building. "We should be safe inside for the night."

"We just have to get there first," Cutter added. Then he remembered something. The thought that had started in the back of his mind earlier dinged that it had finished baking. He'd been so damn stupid. He'd been relying too much on others to do his thinking, which was always a bad idea.

"Morgan, where's the sat phone?"

With her help, they rushed to the stacked supply crates and dug the phone out. Cutter pressed the green button to turn the phone on. Then he stared at the dial pad. *Who do I call? And what do I say? Help, I'm stuck in a Russian mining complex in the middle of nowhere. Please come rescue me from zombies who have already ripped the heads of two men clean off? Yeah. That was not going to fly.*

"Ideas?" he asked.

Morgan grabbed the phone and began to dial a number. Cutter stopped her because the colonel and his men were already heading across the expanse of dirt and scattered tufts of grass toward the dormitory building.

"We can get to that later," he said to her. "Grab what you can and we'll follow them. They may be a bunch of chimps with guns, but there's safety in numbers—if we watch them closely. I don't want to stick around here waiting for whatever ripped those heads off to come back."

Grabbing various packs, Gauge and Morgan swung them over their shoulders and handed one to Cutter. The bag weighed about sixty pounds.

"What the hell did you put in these things?" he asked.

"Just a bit of this, and a bit of that," she said, smiling.

"You coming, Doc?" Cutter asked Dr. Martinez.

"Yes, may I have the phone?"

"Why?"

"I was given an emergency contact in case of troubles."

He took the phone back from Morgan and slapped it into Dr. Martinez palm. "Call them and tell them to send the cavalry. Horses and all."

Then he turned away from her and shook his head. A whole lotta things changed in his mind. Their whole mission to Ecuador just took on an entirely new perspective.

"Zombies," he said to no one in particular. He shrugged to adjust the straps on his heavy pack. "We are going after a bunch of goddamned zombies."

# ~23~
## *REBELS*

"*Run*," Cutter barked, and as Morgan began to move, he swung in behind her. Just ahead, Colonel Suvorov and his men spread out, guns sweeping left and right. The colonel shifted to the middle of the group, well protected by those surrounding him.

Gauge came up from behind Cutter. Dr. Martinez was with him. "Thaw thomething," Gauge whispered, nose plugged. "Think they are trying to get at us from behind."

"I know," Cutter said, pushing forward. He'd picked up the same movements, more of a sense of movement as it was too dark to tell for certain.

"Not much we can do about it now," he said. "Keep going, and for God sakes, keep her safe."

"I can take care of myself, Mr. Cutter," Dr. Martinez said.

"I'm sure you can." He snorted and jogged ahead to check with the colonel. "Where exactly are we going?"

Colonel Suvorov said nothing and kept marching forward. *Asshole.* Cutter checked his various guns just to be sure he could get to them in a pinch and fell into the same rapid step as the colonel.

As the group moved deeper into the compound, the purple twilight twisted into darkness. They broke out flashlights and slipped from one building exterior to the next, clearing each and reacting to shadows while staying low and seeking out signs of pursuit. There were no sounds except the crunching of gravel under boots and the whispering wind, which had begun to pick up, bringing scents of pine and pollen.

With his back pressed against the corner of a building, Suvorov called a halt to their advance, raising a hand to keep everyone held in place. Next, he waved rapidly and sent two men accelerating across a clearing between the buildings.

Cutter pulled alongside and whispered, "You are sending them in like you expect them to get shot at. I've seen no signs of return fire."

"There are others out there," the colonel said.

"Others?" Cutter asked.

"Rebels."

"*Rebels?*" Cutter asked, letting the odd answer sink in.

The colonel remained silent.

Cutter shook his head. *What is the man thinking?* Had it been one of these rebels that had snuck up from behind and had ripped the heads off two men while they remained in their seats? Whatever had done that to the men had to have been immensely strong. Dr. Martinez's zombie idea had a tiny bit of truth to it. *But rebels? No, it can't be rebels.*

"Okay, Colonel, time to level with us. What's really going on here?"

"It is none of your business, *svoloch.*"

"Of course it's my goddamned business. I—"

Before Cutter could finish, more gunshots crackled in the night. He could still see the two young soldiers who had separated from the group, but he wasn't sure if it had been their shots he'd heard. Muzzle flashes then came from the two soldiers' guns as they fired and retreated from something. Finally, they held up, turned tail, and ran all the way back to where the main group was assembled.

"*Chudovishe,*" said one of the wild-eyed kid soldiers.

# ~24~
## *SEPARATED*

"Where to now?" Cutter asked.

Colonel Suvorov led the way still, but it was unclear as to where he was headed. Away from whatever his men had encountered, at the very least. Cutter was about to fall back and check with Morgan when a scream split the air.

Everyone froze.

Cutter scanned for targets. In the beams of all the crisscrossing flashlights, he spotted movement coming from the building directly across from them. There was a man. He was dressed in a white shirt with a narrow tie. The shirt was stained red and brown. *Mud and blood.*

The flashlights converged on the guy.

There was something wrong with the man's face. His lips had pulled back, and his teeth were grotesquely exposed. They gleamed eerily yellow in the beams of light. The muscles of his face had pulled taut, and his eyeballs had bulged from his head. There was blood, lots of blood. He didn't even hold his hands up to shield the light. He just stood there like a spotlighted animal.

Cutter realized it wasn't a man he was seeing. *Not anymore.* It was something else entirely. He hadn't seen those that had chased him a year ago so up close and personal. They had been natives on drugs that had driven them psychotic—*or had they been something else?*

Whatever this thing standing in front of him was, it started shambling in his direction. Much as he hated to admit that what he was seeing was a 'zombie,' it did become the predominate term in his mind. *But zombies only existed in television and movies, right? These look so real. What they hell are they?*

One of the soldiers raised his gun and prepared to fire. Then another. They glanced over their shoulders to check with the colonel, who shook his head no, so they held off.

The thing came closer, shuffling on its feet like a drunk, dragging one leg behind it as if that leg were broken. To Cutter, it was more of a curiosity than a danger. They had plenty of firepower to kill whatever the hell it was. Perhaps the colonel was thinking like him and wanted the thing to get closer so they could identify what had happened to the guy. But that curiosity was short-lived. Cutter was pretty sure now that whatever had happened to this man and had turned it into whatever the hell that thing was, it was the same shit he'd faced in Ecuador. And that made his skin crawl.

The thing drew closer.

The men shifted. Two more dropped to their knees and prepared to fire.

Still, the colonel refused to give the order.

Then the thing moved just a little faster, closing the distance quickly. Cutter could feel the fear growing in the men around him. They wanted to kill it. He raised his own gun to fire and chanced a look at Gauge and Morgan. Gauge had Betty out and was also ready to shoot whatever the hell that creature was. Morgan stood next to Dr. Martinez, quietly whispering to her. And then the thing took another step closer.

"Colonel?" Cutter asked.

Suvorov twisted toward Cutter, but also kept watch on the approaching creature.

"Aren't you going to neutralize that threat?"

"He is one of my countrymen. I will not have him killed. We can—"

One of the soldiers ignored the order to hold fire and opened up on the thing, causing it to fall into a spastic dance. But it somehow kept coming at them, snarling, lips curling back to reveal a fierce row of stained teeth as the bullets slapped into its body, sending off an almost constant spray of red. To it, though, it moved like it was only encountering a strong headwind.

Cutter raised his own gun to fire, but before he could, he heard the bark of Gauge's Desert Eagle, and the head of the thing exploded like a ripe melon.

"*Stoyte!*" the colonel yelled.

And then from the side, the real attack came.

Rapid movement.

A scream. A soldier's scream.

Chaos. Red. Loud.

A dark mass of movement collided with the assembled soldiers, pushing them back and hitting them from behind where they were not prepared.

Cutter skipped backward on his heels but spun and quickly recovered and began pulling himself through the scrambling bodies of the bunching soldiers, trying to get to Gauge and Morgan.

More screams.

As flashlights turned, he saw faces coming at them. Terrible faces. *Teeth.* Those teeth began sinking into the flesh of the young soldiers.

Flashlight beams crisscrossed and strobed. Blood flowed. Sprayed. Hot wetness rained down on Cutter and stuck to his exposed skin. The soldiers on the edge of the group tried to get out of the way of the attack, but were being pushed to the ground, and the creatures were pouncing on them like wolves and viciously tearing into flesh.

Many tried to scatter in panic, taking their flashlights with them. Others backed away, looking for clear lanes of fire, finding none. One soldier raised his gun and pointed it in the direction were Gauge and Morgan were holding off the attack. Cutter bumped the guy off line, and the kid's gunfire spilled into the air.

Gauge had a grip on Morgan when he came out of the melee. Betty's slide was locked open. He needed to reload. Cutter covered for him, firing at one of the approaching zombies, dropping it with a burst of lead to the face.

"Where is she?" Cutter shouted over the din. He scanned those remaining, trying to sort out where Dr. Martinez had disappeared to in the mayhem, but he could not see her anywhere.

Morgan turned her back to the battle. "We have to find her, Jack."

"I know. We can't do that if we're dead." He pulled Morgan behind him a split second before a leaping zombie landed on her. Gauge finished reloading, spun and fired, blasting the rapidly moving thing in the head. It stopped moving and collapsed.

"Where is the colonel?" Morgan asked.

"He was just here a second ago." Cutter scanned the area, but the colonel had apparently abandoned them too, along with about half of his men.

"We have to go. *Now!*" Cutter yelled.

Gauge swung his flashlight, and the fat beam lit another one of the creatures. He fired Betty once more at the approaching zombie. What remained of its head snapped back, and it fell to the ground, arms flailing. It then twitched and jerked in a wild shudder of rupturing flesh, spraying blood everywhere.

But it was only one of many. More were coming. Many more.

# ~25~
## *IN A FLASH*

"We'll keep going," Morgan said. "It's close, I think."

"Think or know?" Cutter asked as he stayed beside her, lightly touching her on the arm so he could tell where she was going. He could hear Gauge mouth-breathing on the other side of her but could barely see the man. The clouds had thickened, and the sky had gone pitch black. Not even a hint of the deep purple existed any longer, and a certain expression about being stuck up an indelicate part of a miner's anatomy came to Cutter's mind.

After they had become separated from the colonel and his men, they'd followed Morgan's lead. She was the only one wearing night vision goggles, which made her the only one who could see what the hell was going on around them. So, all Cutter could do was rely on her to lead them all to safety. Though, he wished he could have relied on her to have packed another set of NVGs for him as well, but, this time, his *go in light, get out fast* mantra had worked against him. She had instead chosen to load his pack down with bullets and explosives. But he figured that if he couldn't see anything, whatever the hell was out there couldn't see him either. Still, he also wanted to be a little wary about stumbling into another ambush with whatever those things were, doubly so in the inky darkness.

And those zombies were not exactly like most of the zombies he'd seen in the movies. These seemed to be able to think and reason on their feet better than those slow-moving shambling types. They had coordinated the last attack. And the implications of that—? He didn't want to go there. *Not yet.*

Since the power was off throughout the compound, they had agreed to make for the primary generators for the complex. Morgan claimed she knew where they were located. Maybe they could at least get the lights back on and see what the hell they were up against. *Or maybe it's better if we don't see them,* Cutter had suggested earlier.

"Think or know, Morgan?" he repeated.

"Heck, Jack, I only just memorized the map. You want me to chance looking again?"

*Shit no, that's not what I want.* She'd have to pull out her tablet to check, which would light up their current position and ring the dinner bell for all zombies in the immediate area. No, they'd separated from the colonel and his men because those guys were shining flashlights everywhere and getting themselves killed faster than red-shirts on a Star Trek episode. But, regrettably, they had also lost Dr. Martinez in the ensuing chaos. He hoped she was still with Suvorov's men, and he could find her again once they got the lights turned back on, and the situation was under control.

"No, I trust you. Just lead the way. Get us to safety."

She started forward again. He used his ears, trying to pick out any stray sounds that might alert him to danger.

*Nothing.*

In the darkness, though, he felt he could see purple-edged shapes moving at the far edges of his vision, which caused his already palpable fear to keep growing to a level bordering on insanity. *Hold it together. It is only—*

Morgan stopped suddenly.

"Hear that?" she whispered.

He had. "Can you see them? Anything?"

"No," she whispered back. "Just a little farther ahead. Fifty feet, I'd guess."

And she was right. They stopped again in about fifty feet. Cutter sensed something in front of him, something hulking and giving off warmth. He held his hand out in front of his face and probed for it. He touched metal and could feel the textures of a painted surface. Morgan shrugged his other hand off her arm, and he heard a new sound—a metallic ticking. Then, right as he identified the noise as a doorknob turning but not opening, he heard something else that pushed him close to all out panic.

*Footsteps. Lots of them. From behind. No flashlights. Bad.*

"Morgan?" he whisper-barked as he drew the Glock.

"Two secs, Jack."

Cutter figured they actually had maybe three seconds and no more—because the sound of footsteps growing closer was all he could focus on, and he realized he was doing so to the point of obsession but couldn't stop himself. He couldn't tell the exact direction from which they came. They were echoing off walls and multiplying somewhere out in the black beyond. He turned his head left and right, seeking the primary source for the confusing noises, but quickly realized the many footfalls could be coming from almost any direction.

He sucked a breath and held it for a beat while forcing calm on himself. New noises reached his ears. Slipping, crunching gravel. Groans. Moans. Wet sucking sounds. Icy fear trickled down his spine, which raised his anxiety to even more epic levels.

"*Morgan,*" he said with a bit more insistence in his tone, perhaps bordering on desperation.

She did not answer. He sensed her turning away from the door and shifting to get behind him. But there was nothing he could do to protect her.

*Can't see shit.*

"Get the door unlocked or tell me what the hell you are seeing." He raised the Glock he'd been gripping tightly and risked flicking on the tiny flashlight he'd affixed to it earlier. When the beam ignited, he almost wished he hadn't turned on the light at all.

There were more targets than he had bullets for, and even with Gauge's assistance, there was no way their combined marksmanship skills could stop the horde arrayed in front of them before it overran them completely. He and Gauge still had their MP5Ks, but to raise them would mean putting his only source of illumination down. He wouldn't be able to see what he was shooting at.

Escape to the left and right were also being cut off by more of the zombies. Cutter sucked air through his teeth. There would be no running. The only way to any semblance of safety was to shoot their way out or get through the door behind him—*the door that was still locked.*

He felt a tug at his back. "What?" He shifted and prepared to turn around and see if he could help get the door open any faster.

"Hold still, Jack."

Morgan was pulling items from his pack.

"Here." She dropped something weighty into his left hand. His fingers instinctively clenched around it.

The creatures continued to approach at a run. He could start shooting and take a few out, but it would do little good.

*How many—?*

Gauge jumped one step ahead of him. The big man leveled his miniature howitzer and opened up all kinds of downrange fifty-caliber hellfire. Betty spat hot lead and zombie heads exploded, one after another. It was sheer conditioned reflex that caused Cutter to join in and send his own head busters downrange to slap wetly into skulls.

A creature dropped with each round fired, but they weren't dropping fast enough.

They kept coming.

And, just then as the realization hit him that they were going to be overwhelmed, his gun clicked on empty. He was about to shift the Glock to his left hand and raise the MP5K when he again took notice of what Morgan had placed there—an M84, flash bang grenade. He lifted the grenade and pulled the pin with his right-hand pinky and lobbed the canister in front of him so it would roll in front of the advancing zombies. Morgan had already spun toward the building and was working on the door again. Gauge continued to drop bodies with each shot.

"*FB out!*" Cutter barked and clamped his eyes closed. The grenade went off with a loud bang that he felt deep inside his chest. He saw a mass of red spidery veins through his closed eyelids. When his vision darkened again, he half-opened his eyes and scanned the scene.

The creatures had all stopped as if they'd hit a wall of fire. Some had fallen to their knees. But those that had were already reeling and getting back up, one by one, while the rest continued their forward stagger.

In the spill of light from his Glock-mounted flashlight, Cutter noticed that both Gauge and Morgan were observing the aftereffects of the grenade as well. The bright flash and thundering explosion had slowed the things, but it had not stopped them for more than a second or two.

"I can't get the lock open, Jack. It's going to take too long on the door," Morgan said. "I don't know how many tumblers it has in it yet. I thought I had most of them bounced, but—"

"But what, Morgan?" he asked quickly. "Work fast. I mean faster than you have ever done this before. Those things aren't going to stop and wait for you."

"I know," she snapped as she turned again.

*Wait? Oh, yeah.* Cutter realized then what he could do. He should have done it the moment Morgan had hesitated.

*Back away, shoot the lock—*

*No…wait…that would—*

The big steel door behind him suddenly swung open.

"Hurry," a voice inside the building said.

# ~26~
## *CULLING*

"About time you showed up," Dr. Martinez said as she closed the door behind them all and shined her flashlight on the floor in front of them.

Cutter breathed a sigh of relief. "How in the hell?" he asked her as he backed away, head cocked sideways.

"You were hired to protect me, Mr. Cutter. And yet you abandoned me with those stupid Russian children."

A loud boom sounded behind them. The zombies had reached the door. Gauge was already working with Morgan to roll a large spool of coiled wire up against the doorframe. She had lit a small hand-held lantern that gave off just enough light to see by, which she had strapped to her arm.

Cutter stared at the nearby door with a single thought on his mind. Those things had ripped the heads off two men. They had to be immensely strong to have done that. A simple steel door wouldn't stop them for long.

*Not much I can do about it now.* Shaking his head to clear it, he turned. Dr. Martinez was staring at him. In the light spill of her flashlight, he saw that her brows were scrunched behind her glasses and her lips were drawn up tight. She was pissed—*probably for abandoning her. Couldn't be helped.* He ignored her silent protest and turned a bit further toward the sprawling interior that unfolded behind her.

Huge machines filled most of the empty space, along with man-sized ceramic insulators and metal conduits and connector junctions tucked neatly inside of steel cages. The room smelled of ozone and old grease. All the signs hanging on chain-link dividers were written in big bold Cyrillic lettering, which he couldn't read. But also present on the signs were the familiar lightning bolt symbols, which themselves were a fairly universal marking for "touch this when you don't know what the hell you are doing, and you will die."

Dr. Martinez blocked his path. "Have you been listening to me, Mr. Cutter? Do you understand your responsibility here?"

"Yeah," he said absently.

"Then you should know—"

"Shhh," he warned, finger on lips.

"What?"

He stood there for a moment listening to the booming echoes from the door Morgan and Gauge had barricaded. *Can those things get through? If they—? Could they even—?* He was drawing a blank.

*Do what's important first.*

"Morgan, do you think you can get the power back on? Find a way to fire up these—generators. That's what they are, right?"

She nodded an affirmative and grabbed Gauge by the sleeve and led him away.

"I do not appreciate you shushing me, Mr. Cutter," Dr. Martinez said.

"Call me Jack."

"Mr. Cutter," she said with emphasis, "I do not appreciate the very fact that you abandoned me so easily. That was very unprofessional. You were hired to—"

He held a hand up to interrupt her. "Yeah, I know about that. Neither do I. Not happy about it either. I'm sorry."

His answer seemed to stop her in her tracks before she could build up any kind of steam. She gave him a puzzled look of reappraisal and folded her arms across her chest. "You still shouldn't have left me with them."

"No, I shouldn't have," he said with conviction. "How did you get in here?"

"Long story," she said. "We have to do what's important first."

He nodded. His appraisal of her clicked a notch into the positive direction.

She continued, "We need to find the artifact, and we don't have much time to do it."

*One click negative.* He stared at her for a long moment. At first, he wanted to ask her why it was so damn important when compared to the flesh-eating monsters pounding away right outside the door.

Then he changed his mind.

Then he changed it again. "Are you shitting me? What we need to do right this very minute is find a goddamned way to get the hell out of here and away from those…those zombie things."

She backed away a step. "I am indeed not 'shitting' you, Mr. Cutter. You were hired to help me retrieve the device—the artifact. And I plan to locate it, with or without your help. But you were paid to help me get to it, so I expect you to do everything in your powers to assist me short of dying."

*Short of dying?* He said nothing more. She had also said, "device," letting something slip by that. *What the hell did she mean?* He opened his mouth to ask, but she continued to talk.

"You do realize just how important it is that we find it, don't you?"

"No, I don't understand. Why don't you enlighten me."

She puffed air out through her tight lips. "You wouldn't be able to understand it if I did tell you the truth."

"Try me."

"We just need to find it." She nodded her head up and down.

Cutter said nothing again in return. He folded his arms over his chest.

"Your wife, Mr. Cutter, would have understood why it is so important that we locate it quickly. She comprehended the importance of such a discovery and what it could mean for the world."

He growled a little. "With a hundred of those goddamned zombie things just outside the door knocking to come in and eat us?" He sucked a whistling breath through his teeth. "No, my *dead wife* would have been smart enough to have recognized the reality of our situation and been recommending already that we should be working together to get the hell out of here. And that's what I intend to do, Doc."

"So you would just abandon me again?" Her hands raised in the air and she shook them and backed away.

*She's faking it.* He knew it. He'd seen it before. But he didn't care. He didn't have the time right now to argue. He stepped past her.

"*Morgan!*" he bellowed over the pounding coming from the door behind him.

He found her next to a control panel filled with colored buttons that made little sense to him when he examined it. She was running her hands up and down the buttons and switches as if she were searching for something specific. Gauge stood behind her, holding his penlight steady and moving his lips as he tried to sound out the Cyrillic writing on the panel. He wasn't having much luck.

"Have you met your match, Jack?" Morgan asked, not looking back at him.

He shook his head. "How long?"

"I only need to find—"

"You walked away from me, Mr. Cutter." It was Dr. Martinez. She had followed him. "Don't do that again. You will lead me to the artifact, or your team will forfeit all payment for this assignment. That's four million dollars, might I remind you."

"Is that so?" he asked.

She held out the satellite phone he'd given her earlier. "Yeah. Go ahead, call home and find out."

Cutter took the phone and clipped it to his belt. "We didn't sign up to fight zombies."

"You are being paid extremely well, Mr. Cutter. We are going after it, and that's the final word on the matter." She turned and walked away.

He watched her go, then let go of a held breath. *Damn woman.* She had almost made the short list of women he just could not get along with.

"That went well," Morgan quipped. Gauge grunted a laugh.

Cutter fondled the phone he'd clipped to his hip. "Just get the damn power on, Morgan. We'll figure something out from there."

"We bugging out then, boss?"

"Yeah," Cutter said. *No amount of money is worth this much bullshit.* He couldn't lose Morgan or Gauge—not after losing Sharon in an all-too-similar situation. His own life didn't matter so much, but their lives did. He'd gotten them into this by agreeing to take the gig, but he'd also find a way to somehow get them out. He only had to persuade Dr. Martinez to see things his way as well.

*For her own damn good.*

"Dr. Martinez?" Cutter had just about returned to where he thought she had disappeared to. He heard a noise just behind him and started to turn and—

A heavy weight slammed into him from behind, driving him to the ground and knocking the wind from his lungs. Something had landed on top of him, snarling in his ear like a rabid dog. He felt hot saliva trickle down his neck. He tried to turn.

*Can't—*

Then fear took over, and his right hand came free. His shoulders bunched and rolled forward an inch, two inches. Somehow, he broke loose and rolled onto his back. Both hands shot up and grabbed at the blurry shape that had jumped him.

As the shape came into focus, red, satanic eyes filled with bloodlust stared down at him. Fetid breath expelled in his face and washed over him. He cringed and tried not to inhale. Slavering, pulled-back teeth clacked together and came for his throat, meaning to tear out a meaty chunk. The zombie on top of him was immensely powerful, much stronger than he was.

Twisting, rolling, he grappled with it, back and forth. It may have had more brute strength than he had, but it lacked the dexterity to use its strength. The thing shifted and went for his throat again, and he was suddenly free and able to get his left arm up and under the zombie's chin before the slashing, carnivorous teeth could bite into his flesh.

Shrieking, the zombie redoubled its efforts, ripping at him with flailing arms and snapping at him as it struggled to get closer. The creature's thrashing legs came up, knees first, narrowly missing his groin. He pushed with everything the sudden onset of fear had given him and gripped it by the throat and raised the thing's head and—

The top of its head exploded like a rotten pumpkin.

The report of Gauge's gunshot echoed from the distant walls in the cavernous building. Panting with relief, Cutter continued to hold the thing by the neck as he rolled out from underneath the dripping gore. He shoved what little he was still holding onto to his right side. He stared back at the thing as he lay next to it on the cold concrete floor, breathing hard, recovering.

In the sharp-angled shadows of the penlight Gauge held on the scene, Cutter saw that the thing next to him had once been human, but it was no longer human. It wore the gray overalls of a worker, but they were little more than shredded rags, and the flesh underneath was ravaged and torn as if it had been clawed and bitten many times. And after Gauge's timely shot, it was nearly headless as well.

"Thanks," Cutter breathed up at the man, his friend. Probably his best friend at the moment.

Gauge lowered Betty and the flashlight and nodded once.

"Where the hell did that thing come from?" Cutter asked, sucking in a final breath of recovery and expelling it languidly. Sitting up, he shook his arms to fling away some of the blood and gore that now covered him from head to toe and had added to his already damp shirt and tactical pants. *Am I ever going to be clean again?*

Gauge smiled a thin smile and held out his left hand. Just as the big man was pulling him up, a new scream split the air, echoing from the far end of the expansive interior space.

The post-fight-or-flight shakes that had just started to effect Cutter fled in an instant, and he again came to total and complete alertness.

# ~27~
## *FINDING MORE*

Only a fraction of a second passed before Cutter had finished reloading and was moving toward the new sound, the new danger. Gauge was with him, elbow to elbow, making just enough room to operate their weapons without jamming each other up. They spread out as they raced past Morgan, who had just come to help them with the creature that had attacked Cutter.

"Eyes open," Cutter said as they passed by her. "Protect her."

She nodded an okay.

He raised his Glock with the mounted flashlight and swept the space in front of them with the fat beam. There were three paths they could take, left, right, and up the middle—the old Monty Hall problem. *Which door has the prize?* He didn't know, and there was no game show host to open the door with the goat behind it and alter the odds.

"Where did that thing come from, do you think?" Cutter asked. Gauge indicated to the left. Cutter sighed and went with his gut. It was all he really had to go on. They approached the massive generators and split up when they reached them. He took the middle path between them while Gauge went to the right.

Cutter figured that there was still a good chance he'd guessed wrong, but he didn't have much of a choice, either. He had to be correct, he thought as he glanced over his shoulder, worrying a bit about the two women he'd left behind, virtually unprotected. Morgan was sharp, though. She'd sort it out. Dr. Martinez, he was still unsure of how she would react to any true threats, but she'd survived well enough so far.

Half-a-second later, he heard Betty's powerful bark, but no second, follow-up shot. One target dispatched, certainly. Gauge required only a single round to neutralize anything smaller than an elephant.

No sooner than he had processed the gunshot and what it meant when his own light was falling on a moving shape in front of him. He zeroed in with the Glock, instantly spotlighting the new target and identifying it as a threat, closing quickly. He fired twice, a double-tap. He was a crack shot, but given the relatively small size of a 9-millimeter Parabellum, he needed to be certain that what he wanted to shoot dead, stayed dead.

Both his bullets slammed home less than an inch apart, causing the creature to fall sideways and drop into a convulsive fit as it bounced off the series of leg-sized pipes running alongside the massive generator to his right. As the thing died, it sprayed blood like a busted fountainhead then slumped into death.

He dropped a step, almost tripping over his own feet. *Why do they bleed?* It didn't make any sense at the moment. All the zombies he'd seen on TV were just dead bodies filled with brownish goo, which was supposed to be some kind of putrid, rotting bodily fluids. These still sprayed oxygen-rich lifeblood, which meant they still had a heartbeat.

*And that means—*

He didn't even want to consider the implications now as he prepared for more that might attack, but nothing else came at him.

Working his jaw back and forth to clear the lingering effects of the loud report, he skipped to make up his missing step and quickened his pace past the crumpled form of the dead zombie. He arrived at the end of the row the same time that Gauge did. They converged to cover each other and worked their way to the back of the building. Offices were to either side of them and were separated by painted walls and hip-high glass windows. Running down the center of them was a darkened hallway.

The terrible scream sounded again.

"You first." Cutter gestured with his Glock.

Gauge nodded once professionally and led the way with Cutter holding his Glock up as well, scanning the way ahead over the large man's shoulder and covering where Gauge was not. The floor changed to thin, industrial carpeting. At the far end of the office row was another sturdy door with a push bar on it. It was shut tight. There was a body resting against it—a soldier's body. The guy was slumped in a heap on the floor, not moving.

As they approached, the guy resolved into one of Suvorov young conscripts. The kid was missing a large section of his upper arm, and his shoulder had almost been torn completely off by something. The limb was dangling uselessly at his side, held there by overly stretched tendons and skin and fabric. Blood trickled from the wounds and was congealing like paste.

Suddenly, the motionless body stirred and the kid raised his eyes to the heavens and screamed a hideous throat warbling cry that sent shivers racing up and down Cutter's spine. Both he and Gauge raised their guns and approached the soldier with caution, holding their fire.

The kid tried to stand. He did so jerkily, bouncing his head against the closed door and clambering to his feet like a marionette whose strings were being pulled from above. He made it to his feet and stumbled forward a shuffling step, dangling arm flopping uselessly against his body. Ribbons of fresh blood ran freely down his side and leaked onto the carpet.

"What the hell?" Cutter said as he watched the suffering thing in horror. If it had been alive, there was no way it could have moved like that. The pain would have been excruciating.

The young soldier began to move faster, as if he were learning how to walk. He bumped into the walls to either side of him, which caused him to spin and shift sideways, but he kept coming.

*Is this how it happens—? Is this how they turn into zombies?* Cutter's revulsion turned to fear. More than anything, he did not want to turn into one of those things.

He watched the thing learning to walk. *That's what it had to be doing, right? Learning?* Even so, he had a hard time seeing the zombie as anything other than a sick pimply-faced teenager. He did not see him as a monster. Not yet. But as the young soldier drew closer, *it* became the prominent identifier in his mind. Whatever the kid had become, *it* was no longer a peaceful human being, and tragically, *it* had to die.

The new-born zombie bared its teeth and snapped at Cutter. It shrieked and fell into a slow, clumsy run, making it an imminent threat that needed to be neutralized.

"I got this," he said. A strange, sinking feeling overcame him— like he wasn't supposed to shoot and kill the kid. He would have much rather restrained the thing until figuring out what the hell had gone wrong. Maybe whatever was afflicting it could be cured. He knew if he shot it there was no turning back. He'd be ending a life with his next trigger pull. *Is there even a chance the kid can be saved? A remote one? What if I trapped it—didn't kill it?*

In his moment of indecision, the thing crossed much of the distance between them and was preparing to attack. There was no denying it. His lizard brain reacted, and his deepest animal instinct took over. He had to kill it before it killed him.

He raised his gun to fire. "Sorry." Turning away slightly, he pulled the trigger, already instinctively correcting for the recoil so the next shot would complete the familiar double-tap.

Nothing happened.

He squeezed the trigger again.

*Nothing?*

He reached up to draw the slide back. His gun had jammed. A well-maintained Glock almost never jams.

*Almost never.*

The thing was upon him in a flash. Cutter's arms shot up protectively, but they were bent, and he was off-balance. The zombie had the advantage. It came for his face, and he drew back in horror, not wanting the thing to take a bite from the exposed flesh of his cheek.

Then Gauge was there, kicking the thing away with a booted foot, driving the thing back against the opposite wall. The big man kicked it again, knocking the zombie to the ground. Gauge hovered over his fallen adversary for a beat and then fired a single shot from Betty downward into the thing's skull. The zombie's head cratered and the skull pan emptied onto the carpeted floor beneath it as the booming echo from Gauge's hand cannon died away into nothingness.

Cutter stuck a finger in his ear and shook it to clear the ringing pain. As his hearing returned somewhat, he heard another short series of gunshots. *Small caliber.* They had come from where Morgan and Dr. Martinez were working to restore power—*at the opposite end of the building.* Morgan was shooting at something. She was trained in basic marksmanship, but she hated guns.

*Shit!*

"Go!" he urged Gauge, hoping the man could reach the women in time.

Gauge did not hesitate. He took off at a run. Cutter shook his head as he sprinted down the narrow hallway looking for any other entrances to the building, then checked to make sure the sturdy outside door was secure. He found it was slightly ajar. Anyone could have come through it if they had wanted to. A cold fear ran through him, and his heart rattled in his ribcage. *Is Gauge about to walk into a whole group of those things? Were Morgan and Dr. Martinez already dead? Did I just send them all to their deaths? Can I shoot them if they turn into one of those things—?*

He pulled the door closed and felt it catch. He tested it to make sure it was locked. It didn't seem sturdy enough. Nothing seemed sturdy enough right now. He'd just have to hope that it would hold. Spinning on his heel, he raced back through the narrow hallway and out into the expanse of the generator room. He took the middle path and ran as fast as his legs would take him.

And then on the other side came to a skidding halt and doubled over, panting, wheezing. All three were there—Gauge, Morgan, and Dr. Martinez.

*Alive.* They were all alive and well. He wanted to throw his arms around them all—*but that would be weird.*

Dr. Martinez had a small pistol cradled loosely in her hand. It was a Walther PPK, the kind James Bond might use. The gun had very little firepower, but it had been enough to get the job done. *Where did she get it?* It was nothing they had brought along with them. *One of the soldiers, maybe?* Something that small would definitely not be Gauge-approved.

And what worried him even more was that it hadn't been Morgan who'd fired the shot. He spared her a quick glance. She'd remained completely defenseless. She didn't even have her sidearm out. It was still strapped in its holster on her hip. He'd have to speak with her about that. *Guns are tools that keep you alive,* he would tell her for the umpteenth time. While she'd so often been so damn stubborn about that particular fact, she wasn't a complete moron.

On the floor at her feet was another one of those things. A shot had entered the creature's head through the left eye socket. Another had bored its way through the nasal cavity. Two shots, well placed. That was a surprise. *I've underestimated you.* She *could* take care of herself when pressed. She'd also saved a defenseless Morgan, which made him doubly mad. He should have been there, or Morgan should have done something. But mostly he was pissed off at himself. He'd guessed wrong earlier, and one of those goddamned things had gotten past him. His hand clenched on his gun, and he worked to clear the jam in his Glock, yanking perhaps a bit too hard on the slide.

He turned to Morgan. "I thought I told you to get the goddamn power back on. *So do it!*"

She flashed him a grim look, as if to say, "Back off!"

Cutter cleared the jam and holstered his weapon. He tossed the chewed-up round from his gun and bent over the corpse of the zombie on the concrete floor. He shivered a little as he went to touch the thing and then pulled his hand back with a jerk. A slick pool of blood was forming around its head and had matted its short, curly hair. The thing's teeth were exposed, and the torn lips were stretched as if someone had grabbed it by the hair and pulled all the loose skin taut from behind. Cutter ran his light up and down the body. There were bite marks and chunks of missing skin and shredded clothing. It was basically just a big, bloody mess.

"How the hell is this happening?" he asked, looking up at Dr. Martinez. "You need to tell me right here and right now. We just witnessed one of these things turning. One minute it was a human—the next? I don't know what the hell it became. Can we save them from this?"

She nodded slowly, and as she did, emergency lights clicked on, bathing the room in shades of red.

"Almost got it," Morgan said from a short distance away. She gave Cutter a quick nod and disappeared behind a wall next to the control panel. Mechanical noises started—deep rumbling vibrations that shook Cutter to his core. One of the massive engines behind him came to life like a demon rising from hell. The noise level grew as the generator came fully online and finished with a whine that sounded like a thousand electric motors all spinning up at once.

The lights all about him began to flicker and strike.

Morgan returned. "One of these generators should be enough to get the lights on throughout the complex," she said with a hint of pride in her voice. "Probably down inside the mine too. Pumps, air circulation. We can go down there now—if we are still going."

"Don't know if we are," Cutter said. "But fire everything up anyway."

"It's all computer controlled, Jack. I'm sure of that. I suspect there are terminals around here somewhere to operate everything."

"Maybe the offices in the back?" he offered.

"Perfect," she said. She gave Gauge a look. He fell in beside her, and they made their way to the path between generators, leaving Cutter alone with Dr. Martinez.

"We should join them," he said. "Then I want to hear the whole story about what is really going on here. Everything—okay?"

Dr. Martinez gave him a nervous look and then nodded.

# ~28~
## *ZOMBIES?*

Back in one of the offices, Cutter rested on the edge of a desk. Dr. Martinez sat in a chair off to one side. She had the satellite phone in her hands and was turning it over and over. He'd given it back to her so she could call her bosses back home and have them send reinforcements, or even the Russian Military. At this point, it didn't matter much to him that he and his team were in the country illegally. There were a few more pressing issues—the flesh-eating zombies being the primary concern.

Gauge was leaning against one wall, keeping an ear in the room while keeping his eyes on Morgan, who was working in the office across the hallway from them.

"So what the hell are these things?" Cutter asked. "The whole idea of undead zombies seems a little farfetched, maybe even a little juvenile."

"Obviously," she said. "They require too much effort to suspend disbelief. But, it is an appropriate term, nonetheless. Undead, maybe not. Zombies—yes. Do you know the etymology of the word 'zombie'?"

He partially understood what she had meant, something about Haiti and Voodoo curses and such. "Entomology? Isn't that the study of bugs?"

She let out an exasperated sigh. "No, not bugs, Mr. Cutter. *Ety-*mology. It is the study of words and their historical origins. I was asking if you knew where the word 'zombie' first originated."

"No, afraid I don't. We didn't study that sort of thing in military school." For half a second, he wanted to take that back. Didn't seem appropriate.

She shook her head side to side and adjusted her glasses. "'Zombi,' spelled without the 'E,' was originally a West African deity. It later came to mean—" She cleared her throat. "It means the vegetative state when the life force that makes us human escapes the body and leaves only a hollow shell behind. Some call it the fleeing of the spirit or soul, but the basis for the actual condition is much more definable, scientifically speaking. So, essentially, the term refers to any being that more or less lacks any self-awareness or individual intelligence."

"But," she continued, "unlike all those fictionalized stories about them, zombies are indeed real. Ask any Haitian. The difference here is that their version of zombies start out dead and are brought back to life fully under the control of the priest or priestess who resurrected them. Some say the reference even goes back as far as biblical times. You've read the Bible, yes?"

He nodded. It had mostly been when he was eight or nine or ten, so it mostly consisted of picture books and stories about animals marching two-by-two. But he knew what she was referring to. Sharon, who was far more intelligent than he had ever been, had first offered a theory related to the many references to zombie-like creatures in the Bible. She had just never actually stooped to calling them that and had often scoffed at all the odd names the many television shows, books, and movies used to refer to them. She'd simply called them 'The Resurrected.'

"Yes," Dr. Martinez said as she watched him closely. "I can tell you understand me now. Your wife did know a lot more than you currently do about these matters. Maybe you should have paid more attention to her."

Cutter tightened his jaw and considered walking away. By sheer will, he held himself in place.

She smirked at him. "You see, one notable Biblical verse that applies here is Revelation 9:6, 'And in those days people will seek death and not find it. They will long to die, but death will flee from them.' Do you understand the implications of that, Mr. Cutter? There are many such referrals throughout ancient history to these so-called 'resurrections' where those who are supposedly dead walk the earth."

"And how does that apply here, specifically?" he asked.

Gauge was listening with interest. Morgan was also at the door, looking from Cutter to Dr. Martinez in puzzlement. Noticing them, Cutter held up a hand to interrupt Dr. Martinez for a moment while he dealt with the more immediate issue.

"Are the lights on?" he asked Morgan.

"They will be soon. It'll take ten or fifteen minutes for them all to come back online, but I think the entire site should soon be blanketed in bright, white light soon enough. Pumps should come online soon after, as will the ventilation systems."

"Good," Cutter said. "How about cameras? Are there any cameras in the mines or anywhere on the property?"

She snapped her fingers as if she had forgotten something so trivial. "No," she said. "No cameras at all. Might have to do with this being an illegal mining operation."

"Uh, yes," Dr. Martinez said. She swiveled back to address Cutter directly. "These 'zombies' that we have encountered so far are sensitive to bright light. They will shy away from it, but it will not stop them completely. Nothing will short of—"

"Severing their brain stems?" Gauge added. He scratched at the bandage still on his nose.

She nodded, but said nothing.

Gauge grunted.

Cutter bobbed his head in agreement. "So, what else can you tell us about these things? Can they be stopped another way? One that doesn't mean we kill them? Can they be—helped?"

"They can be killed, yes. Helped? I do not know. But to kill them you will need to shoot them in the head to destroy their hypothalamus—their primitive mind. That will stop them immediately. But—"

"But, what?" Cutter asked.

"You should know that the person whose body has been resurrected—probably remains a part of the entity."

Cutter made a fist and leaned closer to her. "What—? What does that mean?"

"They, Mr. Cutter, are—in my best estimation—still sentient and fully aware of everything they are doing, but remain unable to consciously control their actions."

He leaned back and sucked his lips together. "You mean who they were is still a part of them? Thinking and feeling everything they do?"

"Crudely, put, yes. It's who they are—their essence. Or it is what they once were—their original mind. It is what we call our waking state of consciousness, which is present and very active and alive when we are not sleeping. And this leaves these entities able to feel everything that's being done to them, but they have no way of controlling it or acting to change their behavior."

"That's horrible," Morgan said. "I get it." She faced Cutter. "Think of it like being a passenger in your own body, Jack. Wow—heck, if that ever happens to me, just shoot me in the head and put me out of my misery, will you?"

He nodded slowly as he further absorbed the implications.

Morgan rubbed her cheek nervously. "Is what they have infectious? How is it happening to so many, so quickly? And are you sure it is not some kind of disease these things are spreading? Like getting bit by one of those things? With the way their teeth are—"

"No, assuredly not," Dr. Martinez stated. "The original infection behaves much like chorea, but it is not that."

"St. Vitus's Dance?" Cutter asked, recalling something his wife had once said.

Dr. Martinez turned to him and gave him a look of reappraisal. "That's one term for it. But no, it's not that. We don't know for sure what causes it, or what the foreign entity is that controls those it infects. It is either a hive mind or a central control scheme. Right now, it is beyond our understanding. That is why I'm here to determine what is happening to these people and how to control it."

Cutter asked, "Whatever the hell it is, can it be stopped?"

"Maybe," she said. "If we find the source of the control."

He stated the obvious, "The artifact, right?"

"Yes, the artifact," she said. "If you destroy it then the influence over all those who have come in contact with it should end as well."

"Should?" he asked. "Are you sure?"

"Yes, I'm fairly certain," she stated.

It was the typical answer from the scientific types—always one-hundred percent certain of something right up until the moment they are inconclusively proven wrong.

He'd also detected something in the way she had answered, some hidden deception lurking just below the surface. He sat back on the desk and folded his arms across his chest. He had a lot of thinking to do and not much time to do it. On a corner bookshelf, he spotted an old copy of a magazine that looked like a Russian version of Sports Illustrated. Next to it was another magazine featuring a well-endowed topless woman on the cover. He had a simple decision to make and then a much larger one. To make that decision, he needed to go somewhere he could make it alone.

He selected the sports magazine and picked it up and thumbed through it briefly. The other magazine would have proven too distracting for what he had planned and would have not allowed him to think through the next few steps under consideration.

"Is there a restroom nearby?" he asked.

Morgan indicated there was one outside the door and just down the hall. Cutter grunted, tucked the sports magazine under his right arm, and left the small office to go do some serious thinking.

# ~29~
## *THRONE OF THOUGHT*

Cutter sat on his temporary throne, flipping through the sports magazine, looking at the strange pictures inside of Russian athletes and letting his mind wander. The restroom was remarkably clean and the plumbing was much the same as any he'd encountered in the States. It was an odd quirk of his, but he always did his best thinking while his body worked its daily cycle.

Something important wasn't adding up. If these zombies were all infected by a single artifact, that meant they all had to touch it or somehow come in contact with it directly. He and his team had not been infected, and they'd been here a while. It also was true that the young Russian soldier had been bitten—there were marks everywhere on him—so what Dr. Martinez had said couldn't be entirely correct. There had to be another form of transmission—through saliva, or blood, or something else. *Why would she want to mislead us about that?*

Sharon had mentioned that the artifact they were going after in Ecuador was dangerous, but she had also said it could be handled safely with the proper precautions. So, that meant proximity was not what could lead to becoming one of those things. Sharon had also said that if anyone tried to touch the artifact, they had to be wearing gloves.

*Was it as simple as that?*

If so—*then how did the infection spread so quickly and so broadly? And if it spread as far as it had here, what would stop it from spreading further? Maybe it could spread beyond the mine? How far? Worldwide epidemic?*

The thought of it spreading gave him the chills. It seemed the isolation of the operation here was the only thing keeping the infection from spreading to the much larger general population. There had to be towns nearby. *Had it already spread there?*

Which all meant that this infection had to be transmittable in a way other than by touching the artifact—*or as she had called it, 'the device.'* It had to be transferable through multiple bites, or some other trauma because he'd come in contact with enough blood and slobber from those things that he should have been infected by now.

The dilemma now, too, was if he could keep shooting those that had been infected. If they could somehow be cured, maybe turned back into normal people—*then wouldn't the right thing to do would be to go after the source of infection and destroy it? Locate the artifact? Was it some sort of control device itself? Maybe some kind of central mind?*

*Or should they all just get the hell out of there and wait for re-enforcements to arrive?* It was down to only the four of them now going up against all of those monsters. Hundreds, perhaps. *How many will I have to kill to get to the artifact? All of them? Will they try to protect it if it were being attacked—?*

He sighed. All his thinking was only raising more questions, not reducing them. Maybe he was the only real leader that was left, but his primary thought at the moment was getting the hell out of there and letting someone else solve the problem. He didn't owe anyone an explanation for that—*not one bit.*

*Screw the money.*

But, on the other hand, it wasn't just him that was in danger. Morgan and Gauge were hip deep in it now too. They might be thinking differently about all this. They might think that they could save all those people by going after the artifact and would try to convince him likewise.

He drew a deep breath—let it out. *Screw them. It is for their own good.* He had his answer. It was the right answer.

Finishing, he got up and washed himself in the sink to get the dried blood off his skin. His clothes were another matter. He'd have to discard them at his earliest opportunity.

He checked himself in the mirror and nodded at his own reflection. He was right. It didn't matter what they said. He'd collect everyone still alive and get them the hell out of there. Then he would go—*alone.* It would be just as he had planned in the beginning.

It was just too damn dangerous to risk the lives of his team, his friends. No—*his only remaining family.* No amount of money was worth watching any of them become infected. He'd been with Sharon when she'd died. That had been enough for one lifetime.

He returned to the office and found Morgan working behind a computer monitor, typing away and staring at the screen as lines of gibberish scrolled by. Gauge was resting in a chair behind her, half-dozing like he was wont to do, but with a hair-trigger readiness lurking just beneath the surface.

"So?" Morgan said, turning to him and lifting her fingers from the keyboard.

"We are bugging out," he said then squared his shoulders, expecting her to fight back.

"You sure about this, Jack? I think we should stay and go after that thing. Destroy it so this doesn't keep happening."

Gauge grunted and sat up. "I'm with her."

"I'm sure," Cutter said. "This is not worth it. Not for any amount of money. There are just too many unknowns."

"Okay, Jack," Morgan said. "I agree with you."

"Thank you," he said.

"For what?"

"For not challenging me on this one. We need to get the hell out of Dodge, and we need to do it without killing anyone else."

"That's not going to be easy," she said.

"I know," he replied, nodding and scanning the room. "Where's Dr. Martinez?"

# ~30~
## *ALTERED PLANS*

When Dr. Martinez did not return after five minutes, Jackson Cutter began to worry, and two minutes after that when she still hadn't returned and he had finished checking all the offices and the restroom, he went beyond worrying.

He stopped at the office where Gauge and Morgan still were and poked his head inside. "Stay here. I'm got to go look for her."

"Wait," Morgan said.

He turned toward her. "What?"

She held up her tablet computer. "Already found her. Watch this."

And as he did, he saw four green dots on the screen. Three were in close proximity. The fourth one was moving away. It stopped, then started moving again.

"Is that her?"

"Yes, I slipped a tracker chip into the pocket of her cargo pants. You each have one too. That way I can keep track of you."

"Sly. What about the—?" Cutter reached to his waistband for the satellite phone. *What the hell?* It wasn't there. "Where do you think that dumbass woman is going?"

"*Hey!*" Morgan said. "Sitting here."

"Didn't mean it that way. I meant that particular woman."

"I know, but still—"

"But still…what?"

"You can be a jerk sometimes, Jack. You know that?"

"Yeah, I know that. And we are talking about this now—why?"

She said nothing while he chewed on his bottom lip. He couldn't win for losing, or lose for winning. But, hell, he knew what she meant when she'd said it. He hadn't been himself for some time. *Too much anger.* He used to be a hell of a lot better when he wasn't so pissed off with the world. *Now?* He really didn't know who he was. But he planned to find out. And that started with finding Dr. Martinez, wherever the hell she went.

"Give me that." He didn't wait for her to respond. He grabbed the tablet from Morgan's hands and yanked it away. "You stay the hell in here. I'm going the hell after her."

"No," she said. "No, you are not."

"Like—" He wanted to say, "hell," but he realized he had been overusing that word to the point of absurdity. "You two are staying put. Right there." He used his pointer finger to emphasize the seriousness of his statement.

Frowning like only Gauge could do, the big man rose from his chair. He crept into Cutter personal space, nearly going chest to chest. Cutter looked up into Gauge's eyes, which were inches away and stood stock still. He held the man's unblinking stare. Gauge breathed calmly through his mouth. His cheeks had puffed up, and purple bruises had formed under his eyes, but the man did not move out of the way.

Cutter blinked first. *Shit. I've been a real asshole, haven't I?* He swallowed thickly. "Okay. Okay." He backed off a step. "We are going after her. All of us. That okay? Like old times?"

Morgan nodded, as did Gauge.

Cutter checked the tablet one final time before handing it back to Morgan. The green dot representing Dr. Martinez was still moving away from them. They were going after her, for her own damn good. Then they were going to find the damn artifact and destroy the damn thing, and *then* they were going to get the *hell* out of there.

"Okay," he finally said. "Let's go put some lead in some heads."

# ~31~
## *WHICH WIRE?*

Cutter could smell death in the very air around him, cold and foul and sour. Sodium vapor lights burned incessantly, casting the entire scene in a yellowish orange.

He and Gauge and Morgan were crossing the compound between the various buildings, stepping gently, weapons up and at the ready. Bodies littered the ground. Some were soldiers, some were dressed as civilian miners. All were damaged beyond repair. Those that had not been shot in the head or had other catastrophic injuries, writhed on the ground, or moved like inchworms on missing limbs. All seemed to be traveling in the same direction—back toward the entrance of the mine.

Which, according to her tracker chip, also happened to be the same direction Dr. Martinez was headed.

Cutter did not want to shoot any of those poor wretches who still survived, even if it might put them out of their misery. There still might be a chance to save some, at least. He planned to go after Dr. Martinez in the mine instead—maybe find her or that damned artifact and destroy it. But, before he could do anything else, he had to get to the crates near the helicopter and retrieve as much death-dealing firepower as they possibly could carry between them.

As they passed by the writhing dead, all Cutter could feel was sympathy for the poor men. If they were being controlled by some unknown entity and were still conscious enough to understand what the hell was happening to them—*and cannot do anything about it?* That was a horror beyond imagining.

They rounded the large dormitory building, lit brightly by floodlights mounted on the side of the blue building. Nothing stirred outside the structure, but a few of Suvorov's young soldiers lay dead nearby. Cutter checked them for movement before squatting to pick up one of their AK-47s. He had to lift the guy with his foot to get the strap over the guy's shoulder, doing so cautiously. He kept picturing the guy's single remaining eye opening and displaying that red, satanic look he'd seen in the others. But the guy was nothing more than a rag doll—a very heavy one.

Once he pried the AK free, he worked the bolt and checked the magazine—*empty*. Gauge checked another of the young soldiers with the same results. Both had large chunks of flesh missing from their upper arms, and both had been shot through the head, leaving their jellied brains exposed and the air above them smelling like ivory soap and copper.

Cutter said over his shoulder, "Don't let those things touch you if they get near, I guess. I don't care if there are still people inside those bodies, or what the doctor said. If they bite you, that might just be it for you. I'm pretty sure of that. And it would be a hell of a shame if I had to shoot either of you."

Morgan and Gauge said nothing, and Cutter grunted at his own bad attempt to lighten their collective mood.

Gauge had Betty out and was frequently turning and making sure their rear was covered as if he'd been hearing things. But nothing was coming at them—nothing from the shadows, and nothing from the light.

The entity that had taken overall control here seemed to have no desire to infect Cutter and his team, or to neutralize them as a threat. To which he was extremely glad, but puzzled. He also reconsidered whether they should just leave when they reached the helicopter. If he could get it going again, he could fly them out and to safety. It had been a while since he'd flown a helicopter, but he knew he could do it. There hadn't been an aircraft made yet he couldn't fly—fixed wing or not.

They soon reached the stacked crates near the helicopter. Nothing had tried to stop them. Cutter took it as a sign that perhaps they should get the hell out of there and come back with re-enforcements.

The lights on the buildings in the distance created just enough illumination to see the outlines of the crates and cause them to cast long shadows. Cutter holstered his Glock and set his nearly empty MP5K against the stack of crates and flipped the first latch on the topmost one.

"*Wait!*" Morgan said, running to his side.

He froze as she circled to stand beside him. "Hold still, Jack. Hold very, very still."

He moved only his eyes, watching her drop down to one knee and pulling out a penlight. Next she ran the light up and down and around the latch.

"What is it?" he whispered, not wanting to draw enough breath to speak any louder.

"Just keep holding still." She reached into a pouch on her belt and drew out a pair of diagonal cutters. "There's something not right here, Jack. I sealed these crates myself. They've been opened by someone."

"Suvorov?" he whispered.

"Maybe," she said. "Stay there. Stay still." She got up and circled the entire crate, examining it closely in the cone of light from her penlight.

"Jack, we can't open this."

"Why?"

"I think it's been booby trapped."

"What makes you say that?"

"I can just tell. Just trust me. Okay?"

"But we need those weapons."

"And chance having the whole thing blow up on us?"

"Who the hell would booby trap our supplies? It doesn't make sense, unless—"

*Yes...yes, it had to be Dr. Martinez. She is not who she appears to be. She had time to do it. But why the hell—?*

"It has to be the doctor," he said. "Or Suvorov."

"Right, Jack. Whatever the case, don't open that crate."

"Is there any way you can check if you're right?"

"I know I'm right, Jack."

"No, I mean check. We need what's inside. Or we need to scoot on out of here."

"I thought you weren't planning on leaving."

"What do you think?"

"You are asking me what I think? *Really?* That's a big step for you."

"Morgan. Just let me know if I can move—and how we can get these damn crates open."

She thought about it for a moment and nodded. She set her pack down, and he watched her bring out the NVGs she'd stashed inside and slip them over her head. She drew a knife from a sheath on her belt and slammed it into the side of the supply crate. She twisted and worked the knife blade to make a hole, and then crouched lower.

"Can I move now?"

"No, not yet. Don't even breathe if you can, okay?"

*How?* Not breathing when there was the potential for a bomb going off right next to you was a seriously difficult thing to do.

She finished making the hole in the side of the crate a little bigger and flipped the goggles down and shut off her pen light.

"What do you see?"

"I was right. There is something in here. Looks like maybe a contact trigger tied to a detonator. And that detonator is stuck to a brick of our own C4. *Huh?* It was a hasty job and would have been effective if I wasn't here stop you."

"Yes, that's why I love you, Morgan."

She snorted. "Yeah, right, Jack. I love you too."

He didn't even have to ask her if she could disarm it. He was relatively certain that she could, so he remained silent.

"*Hey!* This is not so good."

"What?"

She tapped the NVGs. "All the wires attached to the trigger are the same color through these things—all green."

Cutter almost laughed, but doing so could have cost him his life, and that of Morgan as well. Gauge had the good sense to stand off at a distance once he realized what was going on. Cutter also knew that only movies and television shows made a big deal about which color wire should be cut. It always added to the tension that someone might just cut the wrong damn one. *Cut the red or blue—?* That would be the question. The hero would then wipe sweat from his brow, clamp his eyes shut, and then cut the opposite color wire. Or if the hero was a *she*, she'd cut whatever damn wire she thought wouldn't blow them to hell—and be right about it.

But he knew that was all just bullshit. You cut one wire, you break the entire circuit. Without a secondary ground, or a path that allows the current to flow, there could be no detonation, no explosion—*no boom.*

"Gotta make another hole here, Jack. Spread your legs just a little bit wider."

"What?"

"Trust me." Morgan got behind him, and he felt the knife blade scrape the inner seam of his tactical pants as it slammed into the side of the crate. Half an inch higher and she would have stabbed him right in the—

"Cutting it kinda close there."

"I said to hold still."

He held as still as he possibly could, but he could feel his toes wanting to lift him from the ground while she turned the knife blade back and forth to make another hole in the crate. He could not easily see what she was doing, and that was probably for the best.

Then he felt something else scrape against his legs then heard a sharp click.

"Okay," she said, "you can open it now."

*Here goes.* Wincing, he lifted the lid slowly and shut his eyes.

Nothing happened, so he opened his eyes and lifted the lid all the way. She had been right. There was an entire circuit that had been hastily assembled from their own supplies.

"Thanks," he breathed.

"Don't mention it. That's the closest in a while that I've been so near to a man's—never mind."

Cutter let out a burbling chuckle of relief as Gauge joined them. "So, how much of this stuff can we actually carry? Looks like you two brought enough shit to blow up the entire mine."

"Close," she answered. "If I put the charges in the right places, I could probably bring down the entire mountain. Just like—"

She cut herself off, but he knew what she had meant. *Just like the mine in Ecuador.* But she hadn't been the one who'd set the timers on the explosives—he had.

"Fine," he said. "Let's take whatever we can and get going before—"

Jaw going slack, he stopped talking when he realized that the large ramp at the rear the helicopter had been raised and sealed.

He'd somehow missed it when they had returned for the crates. The hatch had not been fully closed when they'd left the Mi-8 behind earlier.

## ~32~
### *COLONEL SUVOROV REDUX*

Cutter jogged to the helicopter. He lifted himself up by the footholds and peered inside the front windscreen. It was too dark to see anything, so he raised his flashlight and shined it inside. Other than the forms of the two dead pilots under blankets, there appeared to be additional bodies in the back of the helicopter. They were all gathered against the rear hatch. He raced around to the backside of the helicopter and joined Morgan. She had the panel to lower the ramp already open.

He stopped alongside her. "Didn't see anything to lead me to believe it's trapped. But there are bodies in there, so be prepared."

She glanced at him and nodded, then toggled a switch, and the large hatch opened like the mouth of a giant guppy.

The stench immediately hit him. The reek of unwashed bodies, the soured sweat of fear, blood, and grime. It was all one big soup of stomach turning funk. But he also detected an acrid odor that he could not quite identify. When the ramp descended halfway, he spotted six men all crumpled together inside the craft, huddled up near the rear hatch.

*What the hell?* None of them appeared injured. He shined his light on them and stopped on one man in particular. It was Colonel Suvorov. Drool and mucous streaked the man's face, but his mouth was still open, and his chest was moving up and down rhythmically.

"What the hell?" he said, this time out loud.

"Gassed," Morgan replied. "Still alive, though—it seems."

"This is just getting weirder and weirder. You think it's safe to go in? I'm not going to pass out, will I?"

She shrugged and backed away. "Maybe. I don't know for sure."

Cutter ignored her and went to check on Suvorov, bending over and feeling for a pulse—it was strong. He tapped the man on the cheek, trying to wake him. *Nothing?* He hit the guy harder. *Nothing.* Finally, Cutter slapped the man with the back of his hand, hard enough that he had to suck his hand back and shake away the pain.

The colonel stirred and began to wake. Then he came alert with a start, squirmed, and reached for the gun on his hip.

"Whoa," Cutter said. "It's okay. Hold still."

The man blinked in confusion, and Cutter could see what was about to happen the instant before it did, but could do nothing to stop it. *Oh, shit.* He scrambled, pushing himself back and away as the colonel bent forward—and expelled the contents of his stomach onto the grooved metal floor of the helicopter.

Cutter waited for more, but the colonel coughed once and wiped his mouth on his wrist. The guy tried to stand. He said something in Russian and then shook his head, jaw all rubbery. Long streamers of drool dribbled from his mouth and nose and reached almost to the floor. He wiped them away with his fingers and flung them aside.

"What…what happened?" Suvorov asked, this time in English.

Cutter moved closer to the man and checked him over. "You tell me, you were knocked out by something. Some kind of gas, probably."

The colonel eyed him suspiciously.

"And, we just found out that one of our crates was rigged with explosives. Did your team do that?"

Cutter didn't expect the colonel to answer, or for the answer to be entirely truthful, but the man shook his head no.

*Then who the hell did?* he wanted to say but held his tongue. He quickly ran down a list of other possibilities. If the colonel's team hadn't done it, that left only Dr. Martinez as the only remaining suspect who could have set the trap on the ammo crate. *If she is willing to kill us over this, and knock out Suvorov and crew, what else is she capable of doing? And, if she planted that bomb, why didn't she kill the soldiers? Were they her ticket out of here?*

In an instant, his desire to save her switched to a desire to figure out what she was up to. Much more was going on here than he first thought. He didn't know exactly what that was, but he damn well intended to find the hell out.

# ~33~
## *INTO THE DEPTHS*

Cutter added to his pile, taking as much as he thought he could carry from the crates. He'd slipped spare clips into the pockets on his vest and adjusted to the different weight of the .30-caliber ammo for the ARs.

As he grabbed a few extra clips for his Glock, he debated again if he should bring the MP5K instead. It was lighter and the ammo could be swapped with his Glock, but Gauge kept insisting they'd need the extra punch the Badger AA6s provided. Ultimately, he deferred to the man's better judgment on the subject—*would be silly not to.* He also grabbed his ACH and slapped the helmet on his head but did not strap it.

He was still bothered by the question of why only one crate had been booby trapped. *Why not all of them? She must have figured she needed to wire up only one.* It had almost worked. If it hadn't been for Morgan's quick thinking, they'd all be dead now, and he felt that in his bones. *I owe her big time.* But, again, he couldn't figure out why Dr. Martinez had just left them outside to die with those zombie things earlier. *Why did she let us in—?* It was all very puzzling.

Morgan was rifling through one of the now unstacked crates and stuffing things into her pack. Cutter joined her, getting down on one knee. "What else you got for me?"

She kept drawing various items out and inspecting them. "We can leave most of the explosives near the exit. If I set the charges there, we can collapse the entrance and leave whatever those things are trapped inside without necessarily killing them. At least until we can get re-enforcements."

"That's supposed to be the colonel's job. Where the hell is he?"

"Search me, Jack."

He regained his feet and found Suvorov working behind the helicopter with his remaining men. They had one soldier who they were not able to wake. The man had apparently suffocated when he'd been smothered by another after they had all been knocked unconscious.

That left five soldiers still alive and the three total in his crew. *Not the greatest odds going up against all those zombies.* But he implicitly trusted his people. Suvorov and his men had already proven untrustworthy, perhaps even dangerous. There was little choice, though. He had to work with what he had.

Standing alone now and staring at the compound, he ran through his final mental checklist. First, they had to wire up the mine with the explosives. Then locate Dr. Martinez. She'd probably lead them to the artifact directly. After they figured out where the artifact was, they could perhaps destroy it, which should save all those people instead of having to kill them all. Each one was essentially still a human being on the inside, with dreams and desires and value—*or so I hope.*

"Here," Morgan said as she joined him, "put these in." She gave him a set of small earplug devices. He put them in his ears and followed her back to the assembling men.

She gave a pair of the earplugs to Colonel Suvorov. He looked at her suspiciously as he lowered his short-barrel submachine gun and let it rest on the strap.

To head off his question, Cutter said, "They'll keep your eardrums from bursting if we get into a firefight in an enclosed space, especially with all those unsuppressed AKs of yours."

"They are far better than those," the colonel said, nodding toward Cutter's AR and shaking his head side to side. "Too fancy. Too complicated. *Too American.*"

Cutter grinned back at the man as he yawned to adjust the fit of his own earplugs. He quickly figured out that the tiny devices were also amplifying faint sounds. He could hear the buzzing of insects and the breathing wheezes of those around him, and maybe even faint heartbeats. *Hmmm. Interesting.*

"What about NVGs?" he asked.

"I think I got all the lights down there turned on now. We should be able to see just fine. NVGs will just hinder your movement and mess with your head."

Cutter nodded. *And these earplugs won't—?*

"You'll need these, too." She passed out small black boxes to Cutter and Gauge that looked like old cellphones or pagers. "Our radio comms don't work so well underground, but these will if we get separated. These work on VLF. They'll take a bit longer to send messages, but they'll travel through nearly a mile of rock."

Cutter examined the device. "We didn't have these last time."

"I know. New tech. Problem is you have to type the message. Like texting. It will take about 30 seconds for a three-word message to transmit, so don't get chatty."

Cutter figured he wouldn't need the thing and put it in his back pocket just in case. He wasn't going to let them get separated. He planned to keep everyone together.

# ~34~
## *LATE ARRIVAL*

John Wayland peered through the porthole-size side window of the helicopter, looking down on the field below. It was just as his advance team had described it, but the expected outcome had not occurred according to the established plan. He was very disappointed in the performance of his team, and that was why it was time for him to step in and clean up the mess.

He stepped off the helicopter, instinctively ducking the rotor wash as he cleared the landing field.

"What happened?" were the first words out of his mouth, directed at the soldier standing in front of him, NVGs still lowered and glowing green.

The man he had hired, dressed completely in black and armed to the teeth, nodded once and cleared his throat. "We did not expect them to find it so easily."

"Any additional hostiles in the area?"

"No," the soldier reported.

Wayland stood there for a minute, thinking. The man with him waited patiently, wordless. Every part of his carefully laid-out plan was falling to pieces. After his team had staged the brutal killings of the two helicopter pilots, Dr. Martinez was supposed to have returned and stuck around and rendezvoused with him here at the landing zone. But the tracker chip he had put inside the outfit he'd purchased with her indicated that she had indeed abandoned him and was going after the device directly. Which was a big mistake—*that selfish bitch*. She must have learned something about the device he wasn't aware of yet. He intended to find out post haste. And then he intended to finish the job he had started well over a year ago.

He would kill Jackson Cutter and his team for what they had failed to do for him in Ecuador. Everything had been their fault.

Wayland sighed. "You've failed me here, Mr. Briggs," he said in a tone of complete disappointment. "I've compensated you very well." And he had. He'd spent everything on this. Every last dime he'd stolen from that asshole Moray. This would be his swan song.

He would sell the device to the highest bidder and live the rest of his life as a king among men.

"Sir, we did not expect them to find it."

"But they did."

The man said nothing.

Wayland swatted at an insect that had tried to crawl into his mouth. He spat air, trying to shoo it away. "Well, I guess we are just going to have to kill them ourselves now, aren't we?"

# ~35~
## SURPRISE PARTY

"Did she go this way?" Cutter asked.

"Not sure," Morgan replied. "Too much interference. The signal in here is almost non-existent. But there is one way to find out. We go find her."

Cutter held up a hand to keep Colonel Suvorov and his men arrayed behind him as he knelt and examined the dust on the mineshaft floor immediately outside the lift they'd taken to get deep inside the mine. The elevator ride had taken almost ten minutes from start to finish, and by Morgan's calculations, they were at least half a mile down inside the earth. Probably deeper underground than he had ever gone before, and he just hoped he hadn't descended into deep shit.

The ride down had been uneventful. Morgan had maps of the mine stored on her tablet, and she'd shared them with him on the way down. There were other ways to get to where they planned to, but it would take far more time to do so. In fact, it would have meant miles of walking down crisscrossing access tunnels. At best, though, that would keep those things up top from getting to them for some time to come. Unless, of course, those zombies could somehow work the lifts—*or are down here already.*

He swept his fingers across the dust at his feet and used the mini-flashlight strapped to his tactical vest to highlight the various ridges of the individual tracks. There were many prints—almost too many to count—but one set of bootprints stuck out from the rest. They were fresh and sharp and somewhat smaller than the rest. He figured they had been made by the newly purchased hiking boots that Dr. Martinez was wearing. And those prints led off into the brightly lit shaft to his left.

"She went that way." He stood and headed down the tunnel he had indicated. He heard hesitant shuffling coming from behind him. Words were being exchanged in Russian, but he chose to ignore them. The men would follow Suvorov no matter what Cutter said to them, or what they each thought of him personally. They had no choice but to follow the man. All he wanted to ensure was not being anywhere near them if they decided to panic and started rattling off those noisy Russian AKs indiscriminately.

Gauge raised his Badger AA6 and stepped alongside Cutter. The beams of their green lasers crisscrossed each other and stabbed into the distance, reflecting off dust particles hanging in the air. With as much tunnel-clearing firepower as they were carrying, nothing coming from the front stood much of a chance of lasting much longer than a half-a-second post target acquisition.

Cutter held his AR one-handed at the hip with the lanyard supporting most of the weight on his shoulder. It was slightly heavier than he would have liked, but now he fully understood Gauge's reluctance to bring along the smaller MP5Ks. In the end, Gauge's decision had been the wisest approach. Those tiny 9-millimeter sewing machines could throw out a lot of lead quickly, but they just didn't have the same kind of punch that the .30-caliber assault rifles had. And Gauge had also chosen the more powerful supersonic loads for their kits, which, given the mining helmets some of the zombies had strapped to their heads, meant a clean, penetrating shot right straight into the brain pan each time with only a small chance of deflection.

"*There!*" Morgan whisper-shouted. The blip representing their target had reappeared on her tablet. She pointed in the direction Dr. Martinez was taking. Cutter signed to Suvorov to follow closely. His men remained behind with him, huddled together like a little a brood of rabbits seeking safety in numbers. But it was a bad formation for them to take. Being that close together, they would all get in each other's way if the shit actually did hit the fan. And they were making far too much noise.

He was about to warn them to be a little more quiet when—

From out of a side shaft came a whole host of zombies. Gauge sprang into action first, pushing Morgan ahead of him. Cutter joined them, and they formed a line from which to pour hot lead into the group of approaching zombies.

Colonel Suvorov and his men tried to separate as well, but one of his soldiers collapsed when a creature put on a burst of speed and landed firmly on the young soldier's back, knocking him sideways into the others.

The thing's teeth sank into the soft flesh of the kid's throat, and he fumbled and got tangled up while trying to raise his strapped weapon. He quickly went down under a pile of the swarming things. Their teeth bit deeply into the soft flesh of the poor kid's quivering throat. He pushed one by the head, trying to shove it away, but as he did, his fingers slipped inside the thing's mouth, and its exposed teeth bit down hard. The kid yanked his hand back and screamed as blood spurted from the remaining stumps of his missing fingers. His wail soon turned to a gurgle as more of the zombies bit into the flesh of his face and tore away skin and muscle from bone.

The two remaining soldiers with Suvorov fumbled for their weapons and turned to fire at the creatures that had flanked them while Suvorov backed away from the mess and raised his submachine gun and fired into a new group of zombies coming from their right. He was yelling at his men in Russian, but they had frozen in place and were spraying bullets into the horde like a pair of out of control firehoses.

It worked for a little while. Then their guns ran out of ammunition.

Cutter did not have the proper angle to open fire, not unless he wanted to chance hitting Suvorov's men.

Desperately and heroically, Suvorov tried to save his men. He grabbed one by the collar and tugged him backward, away from the flailing arms of the zombies. But it didn't have the desired effect. The man tripped and fell. Suvorov then tried to help the man regain his feet, but by that time, the creatures were already pulling themselves on top the guy.

"Come on!" Cutter yelled. "*Clear a path!*" He chanced it and fired once, killing the first zombie already digging into the shrieking kid. "*You can't help them! They're dead already. We have to go!*"

But Suvorov still tried to help, crouching low and tugging on the guy, locked in a tug-a-war game with three zombies each wanting the kid as its own, while another one gnawed on the kid's ear and tore it off. It raised its head, and its exposed teeth ground back and forth on the stolen flesh.

Cutter and Gauge joined Suvorov, stepping to each side of the man and adding their combined firepower to the mix. The green laser beams from their weapons flicked between targets, and bright muzzle flashes accompanied the virtual wall of streaming death as they switched to the approaching mass of zombies. Lead slammed into the creatures, dropping them like bolted cows. Gooey splatters and chunks of gore flew off and slapped wetly against the rock walls behind them while their guns clacked efficiently and effectively, barely audible above the horrible cries of the dying creatures.

Cutter backed away like a fireman retreating from a hot blaze and kept shooting at the approaching zombies, watching his bullets destroy heads, popping them open like rotten pumpkins. Each man he was forced to kill, though, hurt him a little inside. He wanted to save them if he could, but he also wanted to remain alive.

*Kill or be killed*—the apex law of nature.

He raised his AR and moved between three targets, firing single rounds in rapid succession as soon as the laser marked them for death. Three zombies dropped to the dust, but another five immediately took their places. Howling, the newly arriving creatures charged, stumbling over the bodies of their fallen brethren.

Cutter spotted the deception and could hardly believe it. *What the—?* He blinked. More creatures were circling in behind them and arriving even faster and in greater numbers. They would soon flank them completely.

*Get out. Go. Go. Go.*

Reacting instantly, he raised his weapon and fired again and again one-handed while signaling Gauge to clear a path through the horde.

Gauge hot-swapped another clip before going into full fury mode, shredding bodies and sending brass bullet casings pouring out of the side of the gun. The brass shells bounced about the shaft chaotically, making high-pitched sounds that Cutter's earbuds selected for after filtering out the supersonic cracks of the bullets in flight. Gauge kept his attack going until his clip ran dry. He hot-swapped another and went searching for fresh targets. But he did not fire at first and seemed momentarily satisfied with the damage he had wrought. He then reset the stock against his shoulder and pressed the trigger and more flames and fire and lead streamed from his gun. Now he was being more surgical about his kills, and Cutter just held fire and watched. All the lead going downstream was having the desired effect. The flow ahead of them had slowed to a trickle as the bodies piled up and created their own stream-damming effects.

Cutter then knew what he had to do. He couldn't wait around to explain it, nor could he save anyone else. He grabbed Morgan by the arm and shoved her next to Gauge.

"Go! That way!" he yelled, pointing in the direction they had come with his barrel. "We'll be right behind you. Hustle!"

Cutter spun and fired at the remaining zombies that were attempting to flank them. He kept short bursts of fire going. Each new shot crashed into the head of an approaching creature, dropping it before it could come near.

"*We can't leave you, Jack!*" Morgan yelled, or that is what he thought she said. He ignored her and nodded a *get-the-hell-out-of-here* to Gauge. The big man let up on his trigger, nodded back his understanding, and grabbed Morgan by the upper arm and pulled her alongside him. He opened up again with his AR, parting the zombies in the tunnel ahead of him like Moses parting the Red Sea.

Cutter chanced a peek. The temporary gap that Gauge had created would only remain open for a few more seconds and would quickly collapse when they got through it. The big man was already moving, pulling Morgan along behind him. Zombies reached out to grab them both as they went past, but each one that managed to lay a hand on Gauge got its head exploded in return. With a final burst of rounds, they made it through the last of them to the end and into the cleared spaced behind them.

Morgan stopped to signal Cutter, but he ignored her and turned again to refocus his effort on the creatures that had gotten behind him and Suvorov.

Cutter swapped clips just as Suvorov's gun clicked empty, and the colonel went for a spare clip, but ended up only patting himself and not finding one. Cutter selected three more targets for neutralization and fired his AR to drop them then let his gun go slack and hang from the strap temporarily as he drew his Glock left-handed. He tossed the handgun to Suvorov who raised it and used it to shoot the next few zombies that were almost upon them. In the enclosed space, the report from the Glock was many times louder than the AR's, but the earbuds were doing a damn fine job filtering all the noise.

*"We gotta go through that way!"* Cutter shouted. "Go the opposite way from them." And as he said it, he headed in the direction with the least number of the creatures, weapon raised, but not firing to conserve ammunition.

Many pairs of mottled arms in shredded clothing grasped at him, attempting to drag him aside to attack him. He hit back at them with the AR's stock and tried to drive them backward and on to their heels, but the creatures grew more frantic and began snapping at him with their yellowed, slavering teeth. He dodged and weaved their attacks like a boxer while keeping watch on the colonel. The man was right beside him, being attacked by the same creatures, and striking back at them with his own weapon, sending blood and bits of flesh flying off in all directions with each impact.

A zombie lunged at Cutter, and he smashed it in the face with the butt of his gun. The telescoping stock then collapsed sideways and sheared off, leaving him with a stunted weapon that he wasn't sure how he was going to be able to fire. Chancing it, he yanked the AR up and fired off another two rounds, dropping the next two zombies in their tracks. Then he leaned forward and dug in his heels and pushed his way forward, weapon turned sideways to clear a pathway to freedom.

A few seconds later, he and the colonel stumbled through the last of the mob and broke free of the pawing grips and found themselves on the far side with nothing trying to attack them.

His hasty plan had worked. He just hoped separating them into multiple groups and trading distance for time was going to work out in the long run.

Spinning on his heel, he fired his crippled weapon again into the group. More creatures died, but it was not going to be enough to stop them completely. And he could feel by the weight of the gun that he was nearly out of ammunition. He had only a few rounds left, and he did not have any spare clips readily available. He'd have to open his pack to get to them.

*Make 'em count.*

He fired at the forward-most zombies, wanting to clog the rest up and get them all tripping over each other. He backpedaled again as Suvorov shot a stray zombie that had snuck up from behind them.

He turned and scanned the tunnel behind them as he backpedaled. The way to safety appeared clear.

"Watch my back," Cutter said as he committed to a quick reconnaissance and sped past a sloping ramp leading to a downward tunnel to his right. He peeked inside. *No thanks.* It was dark inside, too dark to see. The lights that were strung along the upper right continued at the same level. They bypassed the downward offshoot and continued far into the distance before disappearing around a bend. He didn't give the side route a second glance. He was not about to go descending into the darkness of an unknown passageway.

*No way. No how.*

He rounded the next corner and skidded to a stop in the dirt. He could hear the colonel still firing single shots from the Glock just behind him, so he ran back to where he had left the man. The colonel turned and bumped into him, knocking them both off balance. Together, they held each other up and stilled. Cutter tilted his head to one side and listened. The earpiece Morgan had given him was amplifying the sounds of approaching footsteps, but he couldn't tell from which direction they were coming.

He twisted his head left and right. The colonel did the same. Then he sorted it out. *Ah, Crap.* Neither direction inside the tunnel was going to lead to any kind of safety.

"Blocked," Cutter said, spitting the word out with a mouthful of disgust. "Both ways."

"Where then?" Suvorov asked.

He grabbed the man by the shirt and dragged him back to the ramp that led down the dark path that he swore he would never take, realizing now that he had no other choice but to take it.

"I'll be right on your tail," he said to the man as he unhooked two flash-bangs grenades from his vest, pulled the pins with opposing fingers.

He tossed the M84s in opposite directions inside the tunnel. Then he pushed the colonel down into the darkness and slid in after him.

# ~36~
## *FIRST OBSTACLE*

John Wayland and his team made it to the bottom of the elevator shaft. As his hired man opened the lift gate for him, he held up the small tablet in his hand and found the odd signal the artifact was giving off. But it was impossible to pinpoint. There was too much interference to get a solid lock on it. Still, he knew generally where it was. He pointed to the largest shaft to the left.

"That way," he ordered.

A few minutes later, they arrived at a scene of utter chaos. Blood was everywhere. Bodies were everywhere. Inanimate creatures lay scattered across the mineshaft floor like so many discarded dolls. Most were missing large chunks of their skulls. Many had literally been cut to shreds by some seriously heavy firepower. He had to give Cutter that. The man traveled with a team that could become a virtual meat-grinder. The big man, Gauge, was most likely going to be difficult to bring down. *But not too difficult.* A single shot from a small-caliber gun would be enough—if fired into the back of his head.

As Wayland scanned the area, he saw no indication the zombies had inflicted any damage at all to Cutter and his team. The dead were just men dressed in Russian uniforms.

"They must have gotten away." He started making a clucking noise with his tongue.

The man next to him, Briggs, turned to him. "This is too much bad shit. We didn't sign up for any of this, sir."

"Don't lose your nerve now," Wayland said calmly. "You are being paid very well. Extremely well."

"I cannot guarantee your safety any longer, sir. Or that of my men. I recommend we abort and return to the surface and wait for them to come to us."

"Are you kidding me?" Wayland said, irritated. "No, of course we are not returning to the surface. Not until Mr. Cutter and his team are dead, and I have that bitch's throat firmly between my fingers. I will—"

He stopped cold. He'd heard something.

# ~37~
## *MORE COMING TO THE PARTY*

A third helicopter landed behind the other two already in the clearing. Dawn was just about to break, and the sky was turning a slightly lighter shade of blue. This third Mi-8 had come in heavy because it was carrying a full complement of highly trained and specialized Russian troops. Most were former Spetsnaz and had turned mercenary after their unit had been disbanded by an uncaring bureaucratic government. While not quite as deadly and well-equipped as US Special Forces, these were the very best troops that money could buy on the open market.

Anton Moray always paid top dollar for the best people. That was how he had clawed his way to the top of his industry. He could spot value, and he could spot frauds. And he'd pegged John Wayland for the fraud that he was the minute he had laid eyes on the guy. But he was a useful idiot. He knew the man would betray him on this project, which was why he had set his plan in motion two days before Wayland brought in Jackson Cutter and team to retrieve the device. That was why he was here now, and the last one to the party—*last, but soon to be the first.*

Everyone else were just pawns. One of them was bound to get lucky and retrieve the device. Anton Moray didn't need luck. He made his own. There was only one way out, and he simply had to wait long enough for them to return to the surface. Then he could just...take it from them.

"Establish a perimeter," he told the battle-hardened major to his right. "I want to know the second one of them returns."

Orders were given, and supply crates were unloaded, and guns were readied while he watched—and waited. A chair was brought for him and a bottle of some expensive sparkling water. He twisted the top off and chucked it into the weeds. Then he raised the bottle in toast toward the mine.

"Let's wait and see who wins," he said to no one in particular.

# ~38~
## *SACRIFICE*

Cutter spat damp earth from his mouth. It tasted foul. He coughed once, then said, "You okay?" He said it half to reassure himself and half to discover the status of the man he was certain had tumbled down the shaft beside him.

Colonel Suvorov groaned, proving that he was still alive. Cutter fell into a hacking fit while feeling around for his flashlight. Each cough hurt. It also hurt to move and to think, but as he moved, he ran through a mental checklist of his various bones and limbs and discovered that nothing had apparently broken. Maybe just a rib or two, which made it difficult to breathe, but not impossible to do so. Still, that did not stop the pain that afflicted his entire body. It felt like the very hand of God had attempted to smite him down in a series of blows—and had almost succeeded.

Suvorov hadn't answered with anything other than moans of pain by the time Cutter found the switch on his flashlight and clicked it on. He shined it around the cramped space and found the colonel lying nearby. The guy didn't look so good. A splinter of white bone was protruding from where the man's kneecap should have been, and his leg was twisted at an unnatural angle with the foot significantly out of alignment with the knee. The colonel winced at the pain and blinked as the beam of light fell on his face. He raised a hand feebly and batted away at the glare, causing dust to swirl in the air in front of him.

Cutter crawled over to where the colonel was resting in the dirt. He tried to help the man sit up, and it became quickly apparent that a broken leg was the least of the man's worries. The fall had been much harder on the guy than it had been on Cutter, which had been bad enough.

Colonel Suvorov raised his left arm and patted his chest pocket. Cutter shined the light there and nodded. He unbuttoned the pocket and removed a pack of cigarettes and grinned at the odd lettering on the cellophane-wrapped pack, then back down at the colonel.

"Lighter?" Cutter asked. "Don't have one of my own."

The colonel nodded to his pants, and Cutter found a metal lighter there, though he felt a little weird digging around inside another man's pockets. Leaning back, he tapped out two smokes, lit them both, and set one on the colonel's lips. The man inhaled and coughed spasmodically. His eyes closed and then opened slowly.

Cutter backed away and rested his battered body against a rock and tried to get comfortable. It didn't work out so well. With a twist, he clicked his flashlight to the widest beam setting possible and propped it against the wall, which gave them just enough light to smoke by.

He looked around for the small pack filled with grenades that Gauge had affixed to his vest, but it was not immediately visible. It had probably been torn off in the fall and not made it to the bottom of the shaft yet. Or maybe those zombies had it. Maybe they would find a use for it. Maybe even blow themselves up. *If I could be so lucky.* His only wish was that he could have grabbed another clip or two before taking the plunge. He also searched the ground for his helmet, but no dice. It was gone as well. The angry swelling lump he felt growing on the back of his head reminded him that one should buckle one's helmet first if one should decide to go tumbling down a mineshaft into the darkness.

He figured he'd just have to forget about all that and focus on his immediate problems. His AR was nearby and had made it to the bottom of the sloped shaft. He dragged it over to him with the heel of his boot. Then he remembered the comm device Morgan had given him. It was in his side pocket, so he reached for it only to find it broken. He tossed the useless thing and glanced back at the colonel.

The glowing tip of the man's cigarette was dim, and growing ever dimmer. Then, suddenly, Suvorov startled and took a big puff, causing the tip to glow cherry red. Cutter sucked on his own cigarette and sampled the foulness of the Russian cigarette.

"These things taste like shit," he said, holding his out at arm's length and then coughing against his forearm. When he finished his fit, he took another drag and contemplated the real meaning of life once given to him by a one-eyed guy dressed like Jimi Hendrix.

*Life happens until you die, man.*

He didn't have much more time than that few seconds of contemplation because he was already beginning to hear the small avalanches of rocks coming from the shaft they'd both tumbled down. It was only a matter of time before one of those zombies dared to make the descent. Perhaps one had even started down it already. Maybe it got stuck. *Wouldn't that be something?* Or, maybe they were proving smarter than he was by not taking the heedless plunge. He drew another breath and chuckled to himself grimly. He figured he was well enough to get the hell out of there on his own, but it was going to be doubly hard doing so while also supporting Colonel Suvorov.

*Suck it up, buttercup,* he remembered Morgan telling him. She was right. He would just have to find a way out and stop worrying about it. Worrying got him nowhere fast.

As he turned back Suvorov, he recognized the grim look on the man's face. The man was dying. It was only a matter of time. Maybe a minute, maybe two. Maybe ten. But he was going to slip the mortal coil.

*Soon.*

Cutter stabbed out his cigarette. "Time we get the hell out of here, you old Russian bastard. I'll race you to the top."

The colonel started to laugh, but it turned into a coughing and choking fit, and during it, he lost the cigarette dangling from his lips. It rolled away, and the tip sparked and broke off and then went black.

"You go," Colonel Suvorov said. "I'll stay here and keep them company."

"No, we are both getting out of here. No one gets left behind, right?"

"*Bah!* You Americans and your slogans. Go on. Get going. I will catch up with you."

Cutter watched as the colonel struggled to draw his sidearm and set it in his lap. He went over to the man and picked up the gun and checked it. "Now, come on. Put that thing away and let's get going."

Suvorov stifled a laugh and grimaced. Nodding, Cutter continued to inspect the man's weapon. There was only a single round remaining. He made sure that round was loaded and handed the gun back to Suvorov.

"I will save it," the old soldier said. "I will not become one of those things."

Cutter took the man's cigarettes and tapped out another. It was the last one in the pack. He crumpled the pack and tossed it aside. More rocks came tumbling down the sloped shaft.

"Take this," Suvorov said. He held out Cutter's Glock, which he must have fallen on. "I have what I need. I want a Russian bullet and die on Russian soil."

Cutter then heard the sound of something else falling. Acting on instinct, he bent forward and yanked Colonel Suvorov out of the way. One of the zombies came tumbling down the sloped tunnel and fell into the room.

Letting go of Suvorov, Cutter fumbled for the Glock, but the colonel acted faster. The man raised his own weapon and fired. The zombie's head exploded, and it went limp.

As the sound cleared, Cutter spotted something the zombie had knocked loose—his small pack. He snatched it up over his shoulder and backed away as he shared a grim look with Suvorov.

More zombies were coming. The noise of falling stones was getting louder. Cutter swapped a fresh clip into his Glock and tried again to pick up the colonel.

"Go," the man said, shaking his head. "I do not need the bullet. Those boys became men today. They were too young to die for this. I am old. It is my time. I will be gone long before they get here."

Cutter dragged the colonel away from the bottom of the shaft. The man was bulky and every inch he dragged him was excruciatingly painful. But he got him far enough away that he wouldn't have one of those creatures land on top of him if it came tumbling down the shaft.

Nodding as Suvorov settled against a rock, Cutter adjusted his flashlight and clipped it to his vest so it would light the entire space in front of him. Then he checked the M203 bolted to his AR and felt the weight of a single remaining HEDP round still in the chamber. If he fired it close enough to the support beam at the bottom of the shaft they had tumbled down, he could bring that section of the tunnel down on top of them both. And if he didn't fire it, the zombies would certainly overrun them.

It mattered little. God was in no mood to spare the rod this time. Cutter was ready to go if fate had it in for him. Gauge and Morgan were probably dead already too, and it was all his fault. There was no way they could have gotten through such a large horde of those things. And where could they have run to? They'd been cut off, most likely. And he had been the one that had gotten them killed— just as he'd gone and gotten his wife killed a year earlier.

*If I go right now, it won't be so bad.*

He heard another noise, and a split second later, a group of zombies made it to the bottom of the shaft, slipping and sliding. They had tumbled into one another but were already regaining their feet. It wouldn't take them long to mount an assault.

Cutter gave one last look of respect to the colonel. The man took a puff on his cigarette and raised an arm in salute, touching fingers to forehead. Cutter nodded and backed away as far as he could then squeezed the trigger on the M203. The business end of the tube whooshed as the modified forty-millimeter HEDP round left the barrel.

# ~39~
## FOUND HER

Somehow, Cutter found himself hovering high above the ocean and watching the waves moving lazily across the water. It was just giant gray ocean as far as the eye could see. The occasional cloud passed him by, obscuring his view, but it was unmistakably the ocean.

*Flying? Am I dead?*

Then he blinked and realized the flashlight on his vest was illuminating the ceiling of the cave, and the water was simply the facets on the rocks, and the dust hanging thick in the air were the clouds floating above him.

Groaning, he pushed himself over and stumbled to his feet. The dust lay heavy in the mineshaft. He coughed again and fell against the wall for support. As lucidity returned, he checked the way he thought he wanted to go, and could barely see squat in the tunnel ahead, but the way behind him was covered by an unmistakable cave in, so there wasn't much choice. None of the zombies had made it through, which was good, but Colonel Suvorov had not made it either, which was bad. It would have been a miracle if the man had made it.

Cutter brushed himself off, and stumbled forward, flashlight illuminating the way ahead, cutting a beam through the settling dust. He had no idea where he was going, but he was going somewhere, and that's what counted. As he walked, he dug through the small pack and found another full drum magazine for the AR and a couple of flash bangs. *Damn. Not much. Have to do. Travel light, my ass.*

He paused to swap in a fresh clip and trudged forward, seeing a light in the distance. How long he followed the mineshaft, he did not know, but soon he came to a T-junction with a much larger shaft. Inside were electrical cables and pipes as big around as his waist. He could hear a whispering from the pipes as if something was flowing through them. *Air? Water?* He couldn't be sure. Connected to the pipes was a long string of lights, so he clicked off his flashlight and rechecked his supplies. He found an energy bar and half-consumed bottle of water.

He snacked on the energy bar while working out which direction he was going to take. One direction led up, while the other seemed to descend further into the earth's crust. Normally, his inclination would be to go left, but in this case, he overrode his first thought and decided to go to the right. But first he paused to listen, and the earbuds still in his ears picked up distant echoes, but no signs of immediate threats.

He swallowed the last of his energy bar and chugged his water and tossed the bottle and wrapper. After brushing his hands on his torn and filthy shirt sleeves, he set off.

Eventually, he reached an opening in the expanse that led to another junction. This one led three directions. There were vehicles parked against one wall along with various mining equipment. He stopped to examine the ground at the junction, searching for what he hoped was the path most traveled. He found it, and that path seemed to be leading to the new tunnel to his right. But he saw something else he didn't expect. In the mix of prints, he recognized the relatively small bootprints left by Dr. Martinez. They went into the tunnel immediately in front of him. There were other prints following them that obscured all but a few, and most of those prints were scuffed and from a dragging gait, which told him the zombies had been chasing Dr. Martinez. Perhaps they had even caught her. He gave the potential way out one last glance, shook his head, and followed the bootprints of Dr. Martinez.

It didn't take long to locate her.

As he rounded a corner, he heard the zombies. They were still a long way off, but what he heard was the unmistakable sound of them moaning and sighing with whatever attempted vocalizations they could use.

*Certainly aren't a quiet bunch.*

And when he found them, they were facing away from him and pawing at a metal door on what looked to be a large cargo container, only beefier. When he got close, one of the creatures turned its neck in his direction. Cutter put a finger to his lips and made a shushing noise, as if that would help.

Then another turned.

And another.

One broke free and charged, which caused them all to take notice of him and move away from the container while jostling their neighbors in order to be the first to reach him.

Instinctively, Cutter raised his AR and clicked on the laser. *Nothing.* He slapped the side of the gun and the green beam still did not come on. *Shit. Old fashion way, I guess.* He braced and fired, aiming instinctively and loosing a burst of lead at the oncoming zombies with his damaged assault rifle. He settled into the barrage and let the gun do its work while handling the mild recoil and letting the small blowback walk the assault rifle onto the next target, all while moving sideways to avoid hitting the metal container from which they came. He had no idea how thick or thin it was and if the bullets would penetrate it. Some of the zombies still wore their mining helmets, and the armor-piercing bullets went through those metal helmets like they were no more than baseball caps.

Tragically, every one of the zombies he killed was not a victory, but a defeat. They were once men. Many of them were probably good men, and he was already growing tired of killing them, but he had to keep killing them, or they would kill him. And in a matter of a few brief seconds, he had lured them all away from the large container, corralled them with their own dead, and cleared a space in front of the metal door, which was good because he had just begun to feel the weight of his gun growing a bit too light as it was running near to the end of the large capacity magazine. He took a quick glance down just to be sure. He was right.

*No more buwwets,* he thought in the voice of Elmer Fudd. Somehow, the humor struck him as funny, and he started laughing at his own stupid joke as he drew his Glock and kept up the firefight.

Stilled zombies continued to pile up on the mineshaft floor, raising puffs of chalky dust as they toppled over. He watched them fall, wondering if they were actually dead. *Were they undead before and dead now? What the hell does it mean either way?* Killing them was becoming too easy. His shots had not been precise. They'd been completely indiscriminate in the death they'd dealt out, and he'd cut some of those dead or undead to pieces more than simply going for head shots on each.

"You're slipping, Jack," he said.

Shaking his head to clear it, he stopped when he spotted a brief break in the slaughter. The creatures still active were tangled up in the bodies of the unmoving, so he used the brief window of time to rush the metal door and pound on it.

*"Hey! Open up!"*

Stopping, he rested his ear against the steel door to listen for a response.

Nothing.

*"Hey!"* he shouted and pounded once more, then backed away and checked over his shoulder to see how close the creatures were getting.

Two of the stuck zombies had freed themselves and were coming right at him. His earbuds also picked up a new noise. *Footsteps. Lots of footsteps.* Like a whole holy herd of stomping feet far off in the distance. *Running.* He glanced at the door, searching for a way to open it from the outside. There was a wheel. He grabbed it and twisted, but it didn't budge.

The sounds were growing louder by the second. He raised his Glock and fired off two more quick rounds, this time dropping the two approaching zombies with brain busters placed precisely where he had wanted them to go.

That would buy him a couple of seconds.

But with the sounds of all those approaching footsteps, he quickly realized that it was time to get the hell out of there. But, unfortunately, the container appeared to have been placed at the end of the shaft, so the only path left to him would take him back through the horde of zombies he could hear coming. There was no way he had enough ammunition left in his Glock to make a dent, much less clear a pathway to freedom. And the idea of going for his knife and stabbing them just seemed suicidal.

"Fine mess you got yourself into this time," he said.

Then the door behind him squeaked open.

For a second time, Dr. Martinez was behind the door at his back, but this time around, she said nothing. Still, Jackson Cutter got the message loud and clear. *You owe me big time.*

Letting out a sigh, he jogged back to the door and ducked through it. Dr. Martinez shut the door behind him and spun a small wheel that was set where the doorknob would normally be.

The place was well lit on the inside, with lights running the length of the space along the ceiling. It was an isolation chamber of some kind that reminded him of a deep sea depressurization chamber. There were no exits other than the door he'd just come through. The walls were thick as the place had to serve as a survival chamber in case of a mine collapse.

A few seconds later, the pounding on the door resumed. The zombies were knocking, and he was not about to answer their solicitations.

"Some rescue," Dr. Martinez said coldly. Oddly, Cutter got the reference. He flashed her a wry grin, and his respect for her grew two-fold.

"Here we go again," he said as he rested his AR against the wall and massaged his injured shoulder and tried to rub away the pain coming from the growing bump on his head.

# ~40~
## *PRIVATE MOMENT*

"Fancy meeting you here," Cutter said as he examined the white-painted steel walls of the structure, figuring if it could hold off the weight of the mountain, it could prevent a few zombies from breaking in, even as strong as they were.

Dr. Martinez said nothing. She returned to a pack she had rested on a bench seat and rummaged through it.

As Cutter examined the far end of the space, he found various controls and dials and knobs that looked as if they controlled oxygen and nitrogen mixes. The writing was all different, but he recognized the usage. That meant there had to be a self-contained supply of oxygen available somewhere, and as he thought back on it, he recalled the various tanks bolted to the sides of the structure. *Probably enough for days? Must be. That meant—*

He turned to Dr. Martinez and asked, "How did you find this place?"

She was still rummaging through the pack she had set by the wall. She pulled out a tablet computer and switched it on and showed him a picture of the same chamber from the outside taken by a camera. The image was washed out with noise and overexposed, but it appeared to be the same chamber.

"The artifact was placed in here?" Cutter guessed.

She nodded.

"That's why you came here directly, isn't it?"

She said nothing.

"Where is it?"

"It wasn't here."

"What?"

She glanced away. "I think I know where it is, though."

"Where?"

"Not here."

Cutter stroked his jaw. "Why didn't you wait for us? Why did you try this alone?"

She did not reply, but went to her pack and sat down next to it and rested her back against the wall. She adjusted her glasses.

He sighed, disappointed. *She wants it for herself.* He recognized the greed, all green and slimy. "Were you just going to leave us behind once you had it?"

"You could have gotten out anytime if you had wanted to. You had weapons. You could have left. I thought that was what you planned to do after I left you behind. But getting out of here didn't coincide with my plans."

"True enough," he admitted. He had been ready to run for the hills.

"Why did you come after me? Why didn't you leave behind when you could have? I don't matter. Only the money matters to you."

"Why wouldn't I come after you?"

She appeared stunned. Then she shook her head. "No one would. No one ever has before."

Cutter watched her for a moment. He sucked air through his teeth. She seemed sincere, but she kept turning her head away from him, so he couldn't be sure. She reached up to wipe under one of her eyes.

"I guess we are stuck here now." She turned to face him, confirming that she had been on the verge of tears.

"We don't have much choice. We wait to be rescued. They are bound to send someone after us. I trust my people." Though, he was not entirely sure of his statement. All he had was hope. But even if Gauge and Morgan did not make it out alive, someone would obviously be sent. And he figured if he searched hard enough, there had to be emergency rations to survive on. Perhaps even enough for a full crew to last a week or two. That would give them a few months' worth of supplies if it came down to it.

She lifted her legs onto the bench and folded her face into her knees. She was a strikingly beautiful woman, he thought as he admired the sheen of her mahogany-brown hair. Even the bits of dust and debris that had landed there did not damage her beauty. He'd always been a man who loved the imperfections in the people he kept close. Sharon had had those tiny freckles around her eyes and nose. She tried to hide them, but he appreciated them, just as he appreciated everything about her.

*Damn, I miss her.*

Something about the new vulnerability that she was displaying was getting to him and hitting him with feelings he'd been missing for so long. All he wanted to do was comfort her and forgive her for what she had done. *Where is this coming from?* Suddenly, he wanted to make her feel better. It was an odd sensation. He hadn't felt that way since his wife had died. He wanted the feeling to stop. It was wrong.

But the feeling wouldn't stop.

Even though he ached all over, he sucked it all up and came and sat down next to Dr. Martinez and rested his hands on his knees. She leaned closer to him. The pounding on the door continued, which was amplified by the earbuds still in his ears. He pulled them out and buttoned them in his pocket. When he settled back against the wall, she snuggled up closer to him, and he wrapped his arm around her.

He was a mess, busted ribs—maybe—covered in dirt and dust and stink—definitely—but all he could smell was the sweet scent of her hair, which smelled good to him despite the day and a half of fear and zombies and all the other bad shit he had been through.

And then, somehow they were kissing, and all pain was quickly forgotten. Soon her fingers were running up and down his chest, probing and unbuttoning his vest, then his crusty shirt. He let it happen and kissed her back, harder, and also worked to unbutton her shirt and slide his hand inside and caress her there. Her breasts were firm, but they yielded to his touch, and he could sense her arousal.

Before he could stop himself, he was leaning back and working to remove her shirt while she worked on his. The pounding on the outside door continued unabated, but he hardly took any notice of it.

# ~41~
## *FLOODED*

Right then Cutter wanted another cigarette. Even if it was one of those crappy Russian cigarettes he'd smoked with Suvorov before he'd pulled the trigger and launched the grenade that had killed the man.

He would just have to make do with the relaxed afterglow of one of the wildest rides he'd had in his entire life. It was E-ticket territory. All through their lovemaking, the door continued to pound, and he and the very warm, very welcoming Dr. Martinez had sought to match the rhythm.

She was up now and finishing the buttoning of her shirt. She had said nothing the entire time they had been entangled other than the occasional escaped moan. For someone he had once thought so cold, she was one of the warmest and most passionate women he had ever been with. She really didn't need to say a word. Her body spoke for her. *What other surprises does she have to offer?*

Perhaps it was wrong. Perhaps the fact that death was right outside the door. Maybe that had changed them both. Maybe that had brought about a level of life and desire that had gone beyond the ethereal. Whatever the case—*it was pretty damn awesome.* Or, maybe it was just him wishing he'd had the same opportunity with his wife before she had fallen away to her death.

*Just once more.*

And for the past few hours, he had been racking up even more souls and putting too many deep notches in his own spirit. *They'll be hell to pay one day. A reckoning. But not today.*

He swung away from her and stared at the door. The muted pounding continued, making him wonder if those things would ever give up.

No sooner than he had thought that it happened. The zombies outside seemed to have given up and left Cutter and Dr. Martinez in complete silence.

Then that silence was broken by a new sound.

A faint beeping sound.

He heard it again and rose from where he'd been sitting. He flashed a questioning glance at Dr. Martinez. He caught her eyes moving to a small pack sitting on a bench at the far end of the room. He went to the pack and picked it up. It was heavy. He began to open it.

"Wait," she said.

He returned a questioning look and then unzipped the pack. Inside were various pieces of electronic equipment including a small round device that looked like a remote trigger, three flash-bang grenades, and two bricks of C4 along with detonators. He heard the beep again and dug deeper.

At the bottom of the pack, he found one of the small VLF communications devices Morgan had given him and that he had subsequently broken in the fall down the shaft with Suvorov. *What the hell? How did she get her hands on this?* He pulled the device out and glanced at her. She shook her head and looked away. He then read the message displayed in orange block letters on the screen.

HELP. TRAPPED.

The timestamped identifier preceding the message said it had come from Morgan about ten minutes earlier. He slid open the keyboard and typed a message of his own. Since he was not using the VLF device he'd been given, he made sure to add his initials so she would know who had sent the message.

WHERE? SAFE NOW. JC

He hit send, and the device beeped ten-seconds later letting him know the message had been sent.

"Where did you get this?" he asked.

She shook her head again.

"You take it from us? It was you who set the bomb on the crate?"

"Bomb?"

He stared at her for a few seconds, trying to discern the truth. Part of his mind was telling him that she was lying, but his gut was telling him that she was not. *Why would she try to kill us?* He hadn't stopped to think it through fully. She had saved him twice. If she had wanted to kill him, there were easier ways than setting a bomb in that crate. *But if it wasn't her, then, who—?*

The device beeped again.

WTH? J? WITH L. NO AM. FND ARTFCT.

Dr. Martinez had come over and was reading the tiny display over his shoulder.

Cutter grumbled, "How the hell am I supposed to know where that is?"

"I think I know," Dr. Martinez said. "I mean I can find out."

Cutter turned to her. "How?"

She returned to the pack she'd left on the bench and pulled out her tablet computer and switched it on. Returning, she showed him a map. There were a series of flashing gray markers in the upper right corner.

He put his finger under the markers. "What are we looking at here?"

"One of those marks where it is. But I don't have an exact fix on it. There is too much interference."

"How can you tell for sure?"

"Complicated," she said.

He left it at that and chewed on his bottom lip, thinking.

"So where are we?"

She pointed to one of the junctions, and he traced his finger over the map of the mine. "Is there some way I can I make this bigger?"

She set two fingers on the tablet and expanded the map and showed him how to scroll it left and right, up and down. He studied the screen for a moment and all the connecting tunnels. The small shaft he'd fallen down with Suvorov was not even part of the map that he could make out, but he could tell that if he had gone the opposite direction, they would have returned to the correct junction that would have taken them back to the lifts and to the surface. But it also might have driven them straight into the zombie horde.

He returned his focus to the dots representing the possible locations for the artifact. None were far away. They were clustered together. He would only need to take a few short side tunnels and then make a right at the next junction to get to the primary location, and—

"We can get to them," he stated. "We just need to get the hell out of here first. Are you okay to run? It won't be easy."

She sighed, and nodded.

"Okay," he said as he fished in his pocket for the protective earbuds. He memorized the turns he would need to take. Then he sent one final message to Morgan.

CALVARY COMING.

He gave one last check of his remaining ammo in his Glock. Four shots remained in the magazine. When he clicked the magazine off the AR, he found only two rounds remained in it.

"You still have that PPK?"

Dr. Martinez nodded and drew it from a holster strapped to her back. He checked it. She had a few rounds remaining as well.

"Spares?"

She shook her head no as he handed the weapon back to her. *Great.* He grabbed all three of the flash-bang grenades from the small pack and the explosives. He clipped one grenade to his vest and prepared the first of the remaining two by pulling the pin out and holding the handle down tight.

They both stepped to the door.

"Ready?" he asked.

She nodded.

"Open it a crack and turn away."

She did as he asked, and he tossed one of the flash bangs through the gap and clamped his eyes shut. The door pushed closed under the weight of the sudden surge coming from creatures outside. He heard the dull thud of the grenade and immediately shoved the door open with his injured shoulder, which barked with pain. Blinking away tears, he scanned the area ahead of him with his flashlight. An entire host of the creatures was there to greet him. Many were the former miners still dressed in their overalls and covered in muck and dust. Those same satanic eyes stared back at him in horror. But the grenade had had its desired effect. The horde was momentarily stunned. But it was recovering quickly.

*Hurry.*

He rolled the second grenade as he raised his gun to fire. Clamping his eyes shut again, he waited for the next thud then pushed his way through the crowd, shooting twice to drop the zombies immediately in front of him. Then he covered his face and raised the empty AR and slammed it into any of the creatures that did not clear out of his path. He took a brief moment to check for Dr. Martinez. She was tied to his hip directly behind him with her gun out and raised above his shoulder, ready to shoot anything he couldn't handle. With a final bash to the slavering teeth, he knocked the last of the zombies backward and ran for the junction that was just ahead, bringing his flashlight up and shining it down the long tube he'd chosen to his left.

*Clear.*

He sprinted as fast as his legs would take him. He could hear the doctor running just behind him, but he also heard the sounds of dozens of more feet pounding dirt echoing from the walls.

"*Faster!*" he yelled as he coaxed her to move ahead of him.

She sprinted, pulling past, and he kept his flashlight up so they could see the way ahead.

Then she suddenly came to a halt.

*Crap.*

The way ahead dipped lower, and as he flashed the beam of his light across their path, he realized with a stomach-sinking feeling that the tunnel descended just ahead. And it descended into a glassy pool of stilled water.

The footsteps coming from behind them continued and were steadily growing louder.

*Faster, faster.*

He hadn't expected the way he'd planned to take be blocked by water. But, if he remembered correctly, the tunnel dipped and then returned to the same level probably a hundred feet ahead. *Maybe a bit more?* He could swim that far underwater. *Can she?*

There was no choice. *She had to.*

His mind spun. He'd made underwater swims of even longer distances many times before. But he'd never done it deep inside a mine and in the dark. And Dr. Martinez? *Had she? Would she panic? Would the flashlight even help underwater? Is the water going to seep in and it short out and leave me in the goddamned dark halfway through?*

He sighed. *Suck it up.*

"We have to go under," he said, and to his surprise, she nodded and ran straight for the water as she holstered her weapon and withdrew a flashlight of her own and clicked it on. She shined it on the water and waded in, took a deep breath, and disappeared under the surface. He had expected a little resistance from her. Seeing her moving this quickly without any coaxing left him standing there blinking in stunned amazement. He watched as the glow from her beam vanished into the darkness.

And, yet again, his hesitation had allowed the creatures to gain an extra step. When he heard the sounds of them almost crashing on top of him, he spun and stumbled toward the water. The first few zombies were already shambling directly for him. They were feet away. He raised his Glock and fired the final two rounds he had saved just in case and dropped them cold.

With regret, he secured his weapon and raked his hand across his vest to grab the last flash-bang grenade. He tossed it in front of him, spun, and high-stepped into the water at nearly a full run. Deep enough, he gulped air, shut his eyes, and dove underwater.

The dull thud from the grenade was barely audible, but the water lit up and burned the image of the mineshaft ahead deep into his mind. It looked as if he were swimming down the throat of some giant beast. The water was cloudy, but he could see far enough ahead to spot the glow coming from Dr. Martinez's flashlight. He swam for it and continued to pull himself along with a one-armed stroke while keeping his other hand on the ceiling for guidance and fixating on the question of swimming zombies. He'd seen them learning to walk, so he was sure they could also learn to swim. But how long would it take them and could they do it well enough and did that also mean they could possibly drown as well?

He blew a few bubbles and kept pushing and pulling himself along underwater. His question was partially answered when he hit the first of the bloated bodies floating up against the ceiling where small air pockets still existed. He almost exhaled in surprise when his forearm touched what appeared to be a severed leg floating just above him. Whether it was a piece of a zombie or just a dead miner the zombies had killed, he didn't know. He re-gulped the air that he'd almost exhaled, steeled himself, and kept going.

The light ahead grew suddenly dim and distant, as if it were getting farther and farther away from him. He pushed even harder, feeling the tingles of oxygen starvation creep into his muscles and fatigue him and slow his strokes. Frantically, he searched with his hand for air pockets above him and found none.

Everything was closing in around him, and the urge to breathe was overpowering.

*Hold it, hold it, hold it.*

But he couldn't. He breathed out what was in his lungs, knowing that would buy him just a little more time before he blacked out.

Don't brea—

With a final kick, the hand that had been following the ceiling shot upward, and he realized he was through to the other side. He surfaced and gasped for air, gulping it down as water streamed from his hair.

Dr. Martinez was there, dripping wet and doubled over and also gasping for breath. There were bodies everywhere, or at least pieces of bodies. It was as if a huge explosion had gone off and torn everything to shreds. Charred leg, arms, torsos, and guts, all were splattered against the walls. The stench was somewhere between an overturned outhouse and rotten, roasted pork. It instantly made him sick to his stomach, and right after he exited the water, he fell to his knees, doubled over, and heaved. Bits of the energy bar he'd eaten earlier came out but nothing more. The heaves ended quickly even though the stench did not. He wrinkled his nose in disgust and wiped the drool from his lips and stayed on his knees.

The mine ahead of him opened up into a large cavernous space. At the far end, he could see movement around a shelter that was similar to the one he and Dr. Martinez had been trapped inside. The grim concept of leaving one behind only to get trapped inside another was not lost on him. As he wiped his mouth again, he chuckled to himself. His luck had been running right along the border between bad and good. It could tilt either way in the next few minutes. He just held out hope that it would tilt the right way.

"You okay?" he whispered to Dr. Martinez as he stood.

She remained seated and continued to regain her breath as she opened her backpack and withdrew her tablet computer. Amazingly, it still worked. Cutter's voice had sounded odd, so he pulled one of the earbuds out, shook it and put it back in. It let out a loud squeal, so he yanked them both out and tossed them. The water had ruined them, which was a bit of bad luck to go with all the good.

"What now?" she asked.

"They are trapped in there, right? And we have no weapons, no way to—"

He stopped himself. He was now breathing harder than he should have to, as if he couldn't catch his breath. For a brief half second, he thought it was all the smoking he'd done over the past year and the recent extended stay underwater, but he realized what it really was that was causing him to be so out of breath and light headed.

*Or hoped so.*

He could be wrong. It could be that what he'd noticed was the blackdamp, and the crazy thing he planned to do next was not going to work at all.

# ~42~
## *THROUGH FIRE AND FLAMES*

Cutter almost smiled as he thought through his plan. Almost, because his luck might not hold out much longer. He could end up blowing himself straight to hell if he was wrong.

*But at least it will be spectacular.*

With the flashlight he'd pulled from his Glock, he searched for a shelf that was high enough on which to set the lighter he'd taken from Colonel Suvorov. He was certain that the colonel would be pleased with the use he planned to put it to. He found an outcropping of rock about shoulder height, which he guessed should be perfect for what he had in mind.

"What are you doing?" Dr. Martinez asked.

"Go back to the water," he said. "Get ready to get back in and underwater quickly because things are about to get a little hot in here."

"You can't possibly be serious," she said, taking notice of what he was doing. "You'll blow us up."

"I'm hoping not to," he replied, "but I see little choice. We are stuck here otherwise."

Shaking her head, she turned and went to the water. She did not appear convinced, but she waded out until she was chest deep in the water, and then turned to face him and waited.

Cutter had learned a little of the dangers of methane gas and what firedamp actually was. It was quite a bit different from the oxygen-starved blackdamp. He could sense the lighter than air methane floating near the ceiling, but he wasn't certain it was there since methane in its pure form was colorless and odorless and not at all like what natural gas piped into homes smelled like. But, he wasn't at all sure the concentration was high enough to cause an explosion. That occurred only when a certain saturation level was achieved—*or when pure oxygen is added to boost the reaction in a hell of a hurry.*

When he saw that Dr. Martinez was far enough away, he flicked the lighter open and shut his eyes, half-expecting things to go boom when he spun the wheel to spark the flint.

All he heard was the scrape.

When he opened his eyes, he saw the flame had caught and was burning dimly. The mixture wasn't right yet. But it would be soon.

He stretched and reached up to set the lighter closer to the top of the mineshaft's relatively low ceiling where he was. His shoulder shook from the pain, but he ignored it and reached even higher before setting the lighter on a rock outcropping and leaving it burning.

Then he pulled out his Glock. He raised the gun and took aim at the tanks strapped to the side of the refuge shelter. It was a long shot, bordering on 100-yards or so, the length of a football field. At that distance, his aim had to be perfect. The tanks were bound together, so he had a nice wide target and could miss one and perhaps hit the one next to it and his plan would still work. He only had to account for the bullet drop, which at 100-yards was about a foot. *Easy peasy.* He would aim just a little high to make sure and then let the bullet drop onto the target. That left him plenty of room for error.

*Plenty.*

He checked once more on Dr. Martinez, took aim, and squeezed the trigger. As the near eardrum-busting report died away, the first shot rang true. He saw the tank begin to spew out a mist of pure gas. It looked like steam as the pressure difference froze the gas in the air.

One big problem with his plan, though, was knowing which of the tanks held oxygen and which held nitrogen, and also not knowing the precise moment when the air mixture would reach the correct ratio of methane and oxygen, and then how long it would take to reach the already burning lighter.

*Complications. But a little luck and—*

There was something else he hadn't accounted for, either—the emergency light fixtures burning above the refuge shelter. Could they set off an explosion? Were they sealed correctly? It was a damn mine, so they should be.

*But, what if they aren't?*

As he realized his potentially fatal mistake, he also saw the first flash of ignition, glowing blue in the distance. He spun and raced for the water, his strides covering more ground in less time than he'd ever covered in his entire life. When he reached the water, he dove in head first and ducked under the surface.

The blast compressed the water around him and drove him tumbling through the cave underwater like he'd caught a bad wave under the surf. He hit something, hard, and felt the breath rush out of him, but he somehow kept his mouth closed and did not inhale as he tumbled in the darkness.

As the violence stilled, he opened his eyes and couldn't tell which way was up or down or to which direction he should swim to safety. He chanced it and swam where he thought he saw a light bobbing in the distance. His air-starved lungs burned, and he was already seeing yellow and purple spots. All he wanted to do was let go and breathe. But with every bit of will he had left in him, he found the courage not to. A second later, he saw more of the flashing yellow lights and purple-tinged shapes.

This time, he knew he wasn't going to make it. He was going to die just as his wife had died, stuck inside a hole in the earth. A big part of him didn't mind so much. Death was easy. He'd welcome it. He just wished he would have gone out with the bang and not drown like a rat.

He opened his mouth to breathe and—

Something bumped into him, startling him. In the faint glow from a mysterious light source—he saw a face. It was a ghostly face. The eyes were goggled and glazed, and the skin was torn like ragged cloth with deep furrows carved from it.

His first thought was that he'd blown Dr. Martinez up in the explosion. But he quickly realized it was only the burnt face of one of the zombie creatures. Most of the flesh on its skull hadn't yet been torn or cooked away, and it left the thing looking like it was wearing some kind of evil mask with the lips pulled back and the teeth exposed.

Then those eyes shot fully open and turned redly satanic, and the thing then tried to bite him. He jolted away from it, and his head was suddenly free of the water as he touched the bottom and jerked upward. He gulped air in huge panicked breaths as he continued to kick away from the thing. He got a few feet away from it and found he could stand and walk instead of swim.

All around him the bodies of the former miners burned. Smoke was already filling the air. Sizzling fat and charred flesh kept the fires burning. The smoke hung thick in the air and made it difficult to see much more than a few feet in front of him. He lowered himself closer to the surface of the water and began to make his way through the ash and char to the shoreline.

His hand landed in something hot and wet and squishy. He yanked his arm back as if he'd been burned. What his fingers had landed in had been the body of one of the zombies. He raised his arm and flung away the sticky gore.

"Dr. Martinez!" he called out. His throat was raw from the gathering smoke. He coughed and choked and raised his arm to breathe through the shirt fabric.

He heard no response from her.

He called out again.

No one answered.

If he was going to find her, he was going to have a hell of a time doing it. The smoke was becoming so thick he could barely see in any direction more than a few feet.

He called out again.

Still nothing.

He saved his breath and crouched low, clicked on his flashlight, and moved in the direction he remembered seeing the shelter. It seemed to take forever, but he finally found it when he bumped headfirst into it and could see the side, so he felt his way around it to where he thought the door should be. Reaching up, he banged his fist against the metal three quick times, then three long, followed by three short—Morse code for SOS. He knew that Morgan would recognize the message, Gauge too.

But, nothing.

*Where are you?*

He slumped against the side of the door. They weren't here. They had to have escaped. He shut his eyes.

A second later, he startled when he heard the sound of metal scraping. The door behind him began to unlatch. It creaked open a few inches.

"Jack?" came Morgan's voice through the crack.

He grunted an affirmative, and the door opened wider, and he was sucked inside.

Laying there on the floor, he took shallow gasps and slowly began to regain his breath. He looked up and saw Gauge lying on one of the benches. The man's entire side was covered in white gauze that was spotted with blood. He watched his friend and teammate's chest rise and fall. Coughing, he choked and sputtered and spat until he could speak.

"How is he?" he asked in a hoarse voice.

Morgan shook her head solemnly as he watched her and pushed himself to his feet. He stumbled his way over to Gauge and grabbed him by the hand.

"What happened to him?"

"One of those stupid grenades of his came bouncing back and exploded a little too near. He's got shrapnel stuck in his abdomen. I think he's cut up pretty bad on the inside. He needs a doctor."

Cutter nodded hesitantly, calculating how in the hell he was going to find a doctor in time to save the man if it came to that.

"She was with me," he said.

"Who?" Morgan asked. "Who was with you? Dr. Martinez?"

"Yes, I found her and brought her along with me, but after that little BBQ, I lost her again. She could still be alive. I've got to go look."

"We can't go back out there. Those things—"

"Those things are all dead and crispy." A big part of him resented having to do that to all those poor miners, but it was law of the jungle time, and he'd had to make a snap decision. He just hoped it had been the right one.

"Jack, I found it." Morgan went to one side of the structure and pulled out a metal case. "It's the artifact we were sent for."

She opened it for him and showed him the thing he'd come so far to find. It was nothing special, really, just a long metal bar that seemed to shimmer a little as it caught the light. He reached out to touch it.

Morgan snatched it back and shut the lid. "Don't touch it."

"Yeah," he said, coughing. "Almost forgot."

He paced the inside of the chamber, looking for anything he could use to help him get back out there and find Dr. Martinez—an oxygen mask, or something.

"There's nothing in here, Jack," Morgan said. "We dropped everything and ran for it. We were lucky this place was here. Once I got Lumpy to calm down long enough to sit still, I found some supplies in that compartment—mostly medical supplies and food rations. But that was about it. A whole bunch of nothing otherwise. So what should we do? We've got to get him out of here."

"Yeah. First, though, I gotta see if I can find out if the doctor is still alive," he said while standing over Gauge. The big man grimaced and tried to sit up.

"He shouldn't be doing that," Morgan said.

Gauge winced, but managed to set his feet on the ground and attempt to stand. Cutter helped the man to his feet. Gauge made it, but had to lean heavily on Cutter.

"We don't have a choice, Morgan. He either comes with us and we find her, or—"

"Or what?"

"We just got to find her, okay? And I can't have him die either. So let's get out of here go look."

"Yes," she finally said. "Let's get the heck out of here."

"No, Morgan, let's get the *hell* out of here."

# ~43~
## *BIGGEST LOSS*

Cutter was still soaking wet when he opened the door and surveyed the damage he'd wrought. Only one of the lights on top of the shelter remained lit, and it was covered in soot, so the entire area took on a sickly, yellowish cast. There were smoldering bodies as far as he could see into the darkness, and they probably stretched all the way out to the furthest walls.

He'd killed so many. *Too damn many.*

And, perhaps, he'd also killed the one woman who had given him what he had needed most, when he had needed it most—renewed hope. But that woman was dead. She had to be. So that hope was now lost. Still, he had to check. Just to be sure. Maybe she hadn't been blown to bits. *And if she had—?*

"Wait here," he said to Gauge and Morgan.

He raised his arm to breathe again through his damp sleeve to mask the godawful stink that filled the air. It didn't do much good. He could still smell all those charred bodies. It was like he was trying to walk through the fires of a crematorium.

He'd left the doctor near the water, so he decided to look for her there first. He made it to the water's edge and stood looking at a score of floating bodies and body parts that bobbed and guttered in the inky stillness. Small flames reflected on the water's surface as they continued to consume the skin and fat of the zombies and send greasy tendrils of smoke spiraling to the ceiling of the mineshaft, and then creeping along the bumpy surface.

Flashlight held in front of him, he spotlighted the various bits of debris, searching for signs that reminded him of the doctor—a bit of clothing maybe, hair, something.

He saw no signs of her. *Nothing.* She was just—gone. *What have I done?* But what was one more soul on his troubled conscious? It didn't matter in the grand scheme of the universe. She didn't matter. He didn't matter. *Nothing mattered. Life was a joke with a really bad punchline.* If he somehow got out of this mess, he would go back to his boat, get wasted, find a hot young island girl willing to sleep with him for money, and just get the hell back to the life he had chosen for himself.

*It wasn't all that bad of a life.*

Then when he stilled he heard something. He saw a ripple in the water and watched it with curiosity. The ripple became a shape. The shape took form. And soon that form broke the dark surface of the water and gasped for air.

It was her. *She survived? How the hell?* Shocked, he watched for a brief moment while the water streamed off her head, plastering her hair down against her scalp. Her eyes were wide and filled with surprise at seeing him as well. He almost dropped the flashlight, but quickly reoriented himself and waded into the water and grabbed her under the arm and helped her from the water. She fell on the shoreline on all fours and gasped for breath.

Squatting on his haunches, he waited for her, watching every breath she took and checking her over for any other injuries she might have suffered, but she appeared to have been virtually unscathed by the blast.

"You made it," he said.

"Thanks, Captain Obvious," she said, still recovering. But she turned her head and smiled as best she could after she had said it.

He waited with her for a minute or so while she recovered further, then helped her to regain her feet.

"Glad you are still alive," he said.

"No thanks to you."

# ~44~
## *SPLIT DECISION*

With Gauge hanging on and limping between him and Morgan, Cutter made his way back to the lifts that would return them to the surface. Dr. Martinez followed, carrying her small .38 in one hand, which as it had happened to have turned out, still had a few rounds left in it. But those few precious rounds along with a few precious more in Cutter's Glock and Gauge's Betty were all they had left between them for whatever zombie horde lay ahead. In her other hand, she carried the metal case containing the artifact.

The lights were burning dimly inside the main branch of the tunnel, which provided enough light to see by, but cast everything in a yellowish glow. There were scores of bodies strewn about on the floor. They weaved their way around them as they ascended the ramped path that would take them to the lifts. Many of the corpses were missing limbs or were so badly damaged that they had not risen like the others had, which made Cutter reconsider if those things could actually die from the catastrophic failures of their bodies, or if shooting them in the head was the only way to kill them. What he did know for certain was that shooting them in the head definitely would kill them, so given the chance—and from this point forward—he figured he would do his very best to incapacitate them instead of killing them. Maybe they could all be saved later if he did. He'd killed enough for one lifetime, maybe a hundred lifetimes.

As a young skull-full-of-mush teenager, he'd been trained to kill, but he'd also been told that too much killing led to a very dangerous and nasty place, one which few could ever fully recover from. And if someone grew too accustomed to killing, there was no real coming back from it. It wasn't like the movies or a video game where the good guy would blow the hell out of all the bad guys and then smile and crack wise later. Life was too precious for the human spirit to not be affected by all the lives that were taken.

With Dr. Martinez leading the way, they continued up the mineshaft and surprisingly faced no opposition, a fact that made Cutter nervous but was also a blessing. When they finally made it to the lift, he supported Gauge's weight while Morgan operated the controls. He glanced at Dr. Martinez and tried to smile, but he was certain he looked like some kind of crazy man on leave from the asylum. She did not smile back and glanced away quickly. Whatever they had shared down inside the shelter he was sure would not last once they surfaced and got the hell out of there.

*It was a damn shame.*

The lift came to a screeching halt, and Morgan threw the latch to open the steel cage in which they had ridden up to the surface.

Still, nothing came at them.

At the topmost level, there were even more bodies covering the floor. These had all been shot in the head, but Cutter was certain it hadn't been anyone in his team that had done the damage. That meant someone else was inside the mine. Perhaps another team of soldiers. *Good. Reinforcements.* But then his stomach sank, and he felt a nasty tingle as his mind began to put the pieces together. He indicated toward the ceiling. It was covered with the explosives they had brought along with them. It looked to be all of them and was enough to bring the entire mountain down right on top of them.

Morgan glanced up. "Who did this?" was all she asked.

"Get back," Cutter said.

Morgan had sensed it too, apparently. Together, they began to back away toward the lift.

Bright white lights clicked on in the distance. Cutter saw them and realized that his luck had just run out, and things were about to go from bad to worse.

"Mr. Cutter," a voice said as a familiar man stepped into the light and was haloed by it.

# ~45~
## *DEALS*

"John Wayland," Cutter breathed at the man standing beside three others. The three men beside Wayland fanned out, keeping their weapons raised and locked on target, which happened to be Cutter at the moment.

"So good to see you all again," Wayland said. "I trust that you have not had too difficult a time retrieving my prize for me?"

Cutter said nothing and resisted glancing at Dr. Martinez.

Wayland continued, "Seeing that you are all still alive surprises me, I must say. But the colonel and his men? Tsk, tsk, so sad." He waved a pistol around in a lazy circle, and one of the men went to Dr. Martinez and held out a hand.

"Give him the case," Wayland said.

She did not. Instead, she raised her gun and pointed it at Wayland.

"Oh, come now, Doctor," Wayland said. He smiled in the dim light.

Cutter thought about his own Glock and how quickly he could get to it, but he had to keep Gauge propped up too, and the man weighed a ton. Then he stupidly remembered that Gauge still had Betty strapped across his chest. It would be faster to go for it, but he wasn't exactly sure how many bullets Gauge had left in the gun. Nor was he entirely certain how many remained in his gun. *Two? Three?* He hadn't paid close enough attention when he'd swapped the magazine with what he'd found on the guy. *Big mistake. Probably not enough.* He'd have to talk his way out of this one, or delay until a better opportunity presented itself.

"Give it to him," Cutter said to Dr. Martinez. "Damn thing is not worth dying over."

"Listen to the man," Wayland said. "Drop your weapons and give me the case and no one has to get hurt. You have my word on that."

Cutter knew the man's word was worth about as much as the dirt under his own fingernails. As soon as Wayland removed the threat of her just chucking the case down the elevator shaft, they were all dead.

"This doesn't have to end like it did last time," Wayland said. "Remember, we lost everything thanks in no part to you."

Cutter processed what Wayland had said for a second then turned to Dr. Martinez. "What does he mean by that?"

"Nothing," she said.

"Really?" Wayland waved his gun around, letting it flop in his hand. "He doesn't know?" The man chuckled and stepped closer.

"What?" Cutter wasn't stupid. He had an idea of what they meant, but he wasn't sure about the truth of it.

*But if it were true—? Had she just been toying with him?*

"Dr. Martinez," Wayland continued, "was there when your wife died, Mr. Cutter. You may not have seen her. She had also gone for the device with me. In fact, I had argued with her that you could get to it first, or your wife could. We had but to wait for you to return with it. But she got greedy. She even tried to have you killed. Imagine that?"

"He's lying," she said.

Cutter turned toward her. "Were you there?"

"Of course she was," Wayland said.

"Shut up!" Cutter held up a finger and did not look the man's way. "Were you there?" he repeated as his entire world began to collapse around him.

"I was." She shifted on her feet, closer. "I admit it. But we never made it into the mine. I had just arrived, and we were preparing to—"

"She lies so well, doesn't she?" Wayland said. "She wants it all for herself. She always did. I was the one who argued with Moray about bringing you back for this assignment, Mr. Cutter. It was I who believed in you. I knew you could find it. When I was informed she would be involved as well, I made certain that you and your team were too. I figured that you would put everything together and realize who she really was and what her intentions actually were and shoot her yourself. But I guess I was wrong."

"He's lying," Dr. Martinez said. "He wants it for himself. He knows what it can do."

"Yes, she is right," Wayland said mockingly. "I do want it for myself. And this time, I expect it not to be destroyed. So please, hand it over. *Now.*"

"Wait," Cutter said. "Tell me what it is first. Why do you want it so much?"

"Why do I want it?" Wayland said. He twirled the end of his gun in smaller and smaller circles and finally pointed it at Cutter and stepped forward.

"Maybe I should just shoot you. But with all you have been through for me, you deserve an explanation. It is really quite simple, Mr. Cutter. I'll make it easy and get right to the point. Human life has little value any longer. We have spread like locusts—like a disease…a plague. Human beings have become a common pestilence. The more we reproduce, the more we destroy. The more we destroy, the less remains to be consumed by those who actually deserve to live. It's just the axiomatic truth of our times. Imagine a planet devoid of all but the smartest and most productive people, Mr. Cutter. Wouldn't that be a wondrous thing?"

Cutter scoffed. "Been tried. And that doesn't explain what the hell that thing can do. You'll just create more of those zombie things, and they will come after you, eventually."

"Ah, but you are wrong, Mr. Cutter. You've seen too many of those ghastly zombie movies. There has been too much useless fiction in your life, I suppose. No, zombies are not actually real, and neither are these creatures. Think of them more like automatons that desire to quickly infect others and then die—rot away, so to speak. That's the fallacy presented by all those zombie stories. The creatures in them never just rot away into oblivion. The stories just go on and on. Silly and unscientific, if you ask me." He stopped to take a breath. "If you had bothered to read your own wife's writing on the subject, she had discovered this truth. Which is why she had gone after the device herself. She wished only to study it and ultimately destroy it so it could never be used by others again."

*That's not exactly what she told me.* She had wanted to retrieve it for study but not to destroy it. *Had she ever meant to destroy it?* It would have been so easy to have done so in the beginning when they had arrived in Ecuador. *Drop the whole damn mountain on top of it and bury it forever.* And if she had done that in the first place, she would still be alive.

"I do not believe you," Cutter said. "You sound like some type of evil villain in one of those bad movies, going on and on about how much of a genius you are."

Wayland chuckled. "Am I now?"

"Yeah. Think about it. Just pure melodrama. Now, Kahn? You saw Star Trek, right? The guy in that movie was a great villain. 'From hell's heart I stab at thee.' See, great line. I get that. You are nothing but a two-bit hustler."

Wayland raised his gun and aimed it at Cutter. He puffed out through his lips. "That was Melville, Mr. Cutter. Moby Dick." He shook his head, stopped, and steadied his aim. "I suggest you choose your next wisecrack carefully, for it may be your last."

"Well, how about a little honesty then?"

"And what is that supposed to mean?"

"You might want to check behind you."

Wayland laughed heartily. "There's nothing behind me, Mr. Cutter. Though, I appreciate the joke. Oldest trick in the book."

Jackson Cutter shrugged a questioning apology. Wayland took one step forward and glanced over each shoulder. Then he frowned as if he half expected something to be there.

Cutter shrugged. "Guess I was wrong."

Wayland grinned wide. "I guess I could ask you to get on the elevator and go back into the mine, but I'm certain you know it would be a one-way trip. You see this?" He held up a small device about the size of a TV remote.

Cutter recognized the device.

Wayland made a show of hovering one finger over the button on the remote. "The explosives are on a time delay and set for five minutes. I could ask you to wait around for them to go off, but that would give you a chance to escape and would be too…Ian Fleming-like. So, I figure we'll just shoot you and toss your bodies down the shaft before I trigger the explosives. They'll be no wiggling out of this one."

Cutter smiled.

"Why are you smiling?" Wayland asked. He suddenly seemed nervous and checked over his shoulders again.

"Nothing. Forget it. Want to make a deal?"

Wayland shook his head no. "It is far too late for that, I'm afraid."

"So be it."

Wayland spoke directly to Dr. Martinez. "Please, be a dear and hand it over. I am asking nicely, but I promise you that I won't ask nicely again."

"No," she said.

"Kill her and take the case," Wayland said to the man standing next to him.

The guy raised his rifle to fire, making the mistake of taking his aim off Cutter for a brief second. Cutter went for Betty, hoping he was right about it being loaded.

In one smooth motion, he let go of Gauge, grabbed Betty, drew, and fired when the barrel came in line with the man. The guy stumbled backward from the blow that hit him square in the chest, opening up a fist-sized hole there and causing him to stagger back on his heels. He glanced down, blinked, and then fell over dead on his back.

Cutter aimed at Wayland and squeezed the trigger once more.

Nothing happened.

Then he noticed the slide on the big Desert Eagle had locked open—out of ammunition. He still had his Glock and figured he still had at least one more shot left in it.

*Maybe.*

Before he could get to it, though, hot lead slammed into his right shoulder, and he jerked backward and dropped Betty on top of the crumpled forms of Morgan and Gauge, who had fallen when he'd gone for Gauge's gun. Cutter dropped to his knees, and his hand shot to his injured shoulder. He grimaced in pain and tried to go for his Glock, but couldn't reach it.

Wayland watched him for a second then aimed his gun at Dr. Martinez and held it steady. "Final chance, my dear. Come with me and I'll save you from all this. I could use your expertise with what I have planned."

"No," she said.

Wayland fired again. The bullet struck Dr. Martinez, and she staggered forward. He fired again, and she fell to her knees, letting go of the case, and catching herself on her right hand. The metal case slid to a stop.

"Kill them," Wayland ordered the man next to him. The guy raised one of the MP5Ks that Cutter had left behind and took aim.

But he was never able to cut loose with it because Wayland suddenly screamed out in pain.

The man with the submachine gun spun and jerked the trigger, blasting the writhing shape on the ground that had slithered up behind Wayland and had taken a bite out of his calf. Then another creature attacked the man with the gun. The guy bent backward, and the MP5K went wild, spraying bullets in all directions. Cutter dropped to his belly and reached left-handed for his Glock and dragged it out and prepared to shoot the writhing man dead, using what might be his last bullet.

The creature that had first bitten Wayland had him occupied. He tried to pull away from it as the man with MP5K let up on the trigger and fell sideways and took them both to the dirt. The zombie lunged and bit down on the guy's throat. Blood sprayed from the wound like a busted hose, and the guy bucked in agony.

Wayland struggled to get his gun angled so he could fire at the creature, but he became caught up in the twisting and turning. Screaming in fear, he clawed at the dirt, pulling himself forward and away from the thing in panicked flight. His back arched and his arm outstretched and flailed, and the remote for the explosives he'd been holding flew from his hand.

Cutter drew a breath and started to pull himself to his feet along with Morgan and Gauge and race to stop the man. But John Wayland clawed his way forward by his fingernails and landed on the remote and collapsed there with his hand slapping on top of it. A small LED on the remote started blinking red.

If the guy had been telling the truth, they now had five minutes before the explosives went off. Cutter fixed the time in his mind and began the countdown. As he regained his feet, he saw movement coming from the other end of the tunnel, the end closest to the entrance, or the exit—*closest to safety.*

He hoped it was the cavalry, coming to rescue them.

Those faint hopes were quickly dashed. It was another, even larger group of those possessed miners, those zombie creatures—*a whole damn gigantic horde of them.*

# ~46~
## *IMPOSSIBLE ODDS*

By Cutter's estimation, most of the five minutes still remained before the explosives would go off. Based on the size of the horde, though, five minutes wasn't going to be nearly enough. The new horde was quickly becoming a teeming mass of arms and legs and terrible snarling faces. But he knew a little more about them now. They were still humans, essentially. It was just that damn artifact or device or whatever the hell it was that held them in thrall. If he could destroy it, they might—

It was such an obvious, stupid answer. He should have tried it earlier. He cursed himself and prepared to retrieve the case from Dr. Martinez and destroy the thing once and for all.

He took a step and nearly dropped to the ground. The pain in his shoulder was excruciating. He flinched and hunched over.

It had been just in the nick of time.

One of the same zombies that attacked Wayland had scrambled its way across the gritty mineshaft floor and was trying to bite at Cutter's ankle. He raised his booted foot and slammed it down hard on the thing's head, causing it to still.

Rolling his shoulder to test it, he found it would still move relatively well—*but it sure hurt like hell.* Fortunately, the bullet had passed through flesh only, and while it had done considerable damage, it had not done enough to completely disable him. Gauge had somehow also regained his feet and was wobbling there unsteadily. Morgan was the only one that appeared relatively unscathed by the unfolding chaos of the past hour.

"Get that gun," Cutter barked at her as he braced himself against Gauge to keep both of them vertical.

Morgan went for the gun without hesitation, scooping up the MP5K that had come to rest in front of the twin zombies. Cutter made his way over to Wayland's corpse and snatched up the man's pistol in his left hand. The gun turned out to be a relatively tiny .38 snub nose Chief's Special revolver. That was it. That was all the firepower they had to get through the zombies and to the exit.

*Not nearly enough.*

"Can you shut off those explosives?" he asked Morgan while steadying Gauge's large frame. Satisfied that the big man would remain vertical, he hurried to help Dr. Martinez regain her feet as well.

"Maybe," she said after some consideration.

He glanced both directions, wondering if he should buy her time to disarm the explosives, or just tell them to get the hell out of Dodge. Since none of them could fire a weapon, it was all going to be up to her either way.

And, without delay, he made another decision and another plan, knowing it would probably be his last, but he trusted her completely to carry it out. He knew she would deliver.

Indicating toward the sub-machine gun, he said, "You'll just have to clear us a path so we can get the hell out of here."

She did not appear overly optimistic.

"That's a heck of a lot of zombies, Jack. I've never fired one of these things before at anything other than paper."

"You're smart, Morgan. Figure it out. I trust you. Completely. Utterly. Without question. Got that?"

She nodded and picked up the MP5K and two extra magazines she found on the guy. She flipped the strap over her head and leveled the business end of the barrel at the approaching horde.

Cutter let her be and stumbled over to check on Dr. Martinez. She was injured and bleeding from where she'd been hit in the abdomen, but the damage did not appear immediately life-threatening.

"Stay with me, Doc," he said. "I plan to get us all out of here. You and I haven't even had our first date yet. It'd be a real shame to miss it."

She smiled at him as he lifted her to her feet. It hurt like hell to move even a fraction of an inch, but he forced himself to continue. He was certain the agony was nearly unbearable for her as well. Bending over while supporting her weight, he swept up the metal case containing the artifact, and they both hurried back to join Morgan as quickly as they could amble the ten-yard distance.

"Two minutes, maybe three left," he told Morgan, "so don't be picky about target selection. Just clear us a path we can get through." She obviously knew what he meant. When the timer expired, the entire mountain would come crashing down right on top of them and squish them like bugs on a windshield.

Dr. Martinez tripped, and all her weight fell on Cutter. His shoulder screamed in protest. She recovered, and he bent forward, gritting his teeth as he dragged her along beside him. He felt that the weight of the metal case was just a bit too much and almost let go of it because it was slowing them down.

"Don't," she said, as if she had read his mind. "We need to bring it back and study it. We need to prevent this from every happening again."

Nodding his agreement, he held on to the case. He knew she was right. Just as his wife had been right. They needed to know more about it. He understood that now. He was certain his wife had the best of intentions for keeping the artifact, and that was what she had died for. If they figured out the secret to the thing, perhaps countless lives could be saved if another was ever uncovered.

Destroying it would be a mistake. *A tragic mistake.*

The pain in his shoulder was growing worse. He could barely support the weight of Dr. Martinez any longer. To his surprise, Gauge came alongside, also stumbling, and Cutter half-wondered if Gauge had become a zombie himself. He had not spoken a word in some time. Then the big man stumbled forward to stand beside Morgan. He started whispering to her, but the rising noise coming from the moaning zombies blocked out whatever he was saying. Cutter just couldn't hear the conversation, but he was fairly certain what the big man was telling her. And, whatever it was, it had the desired effect. Morgan raised the tiny MP5K like she owned it. Her back stiffened, and she widened her stance and prepared to open fire. Cutter knew it was going to be loud, and without the earbuds in place, if he got too close to her, he'd go partially deaf for the next hour or so—*if I manage to live that long.*

Morgan opened up with a spray of hellfire. Lead belched from the barrel of the gun in rapid succession and tore into the heads of approaching zombies. Cutter could almost count the impacts as bullets knocked the zombies backward in a bloody spray that clouded the scene in a pink mist. Soon, he couldn't tell which were incapacitated zombies and which still remained a threat.

Three seconds later, the gun stopped. It had fired the entire magazine. Morgan quickly inspected the gun, and then raised it and tried to fire.

*Nothing.*

Gauge yelled something at her, and she fumbled another full magazine out of her pocket, struggled with the release, and swapped the full one with the empty one. She tried to fire again.

*Nothing.*

She checked the gun again as Gauge struggled to reach her. Right as he did, she figured out the issue and clicked the bolt forward and flicked the selector switch. Then she raised the gun and fired a single-shot, dropping the nearest zombie. She fired again, sweeping to the left. *Another dead zombie. Another.* Her selective firing was having the desired effect and working like a snowplow in a storm. She continued to advance and meet the enemy, putting lead in heads, and parting the horde right down the middle.

Then Cutter noticed something odd. The creatures were no longer coming at her directly. They were pushing each other aside to get to him. And it was then that he realized what they really wanted—the artifact. And that simple fact was something he knew he could use against them.

He pushed forward, pulling Dr. Martinez along beside him. He reached Gauge, and the big man looked at him with confusion.

Cutter mouthed, "Save her."

Gauge's eyes widened in surprise as he took the weight of Dr. Martinez against his own stumbling form and somehow, together, they were able to keep up with Morgan, who was clearing the way forward with single-shot head busters.

Scanning those remaining, Cutter realized that the host was too big to get through without significantly more firepower. If he continued with Morgan, Gauge, and Dr. Martinez, the entire horde would collapse around them as the things went for the artifact. And, as soon as Morgan ran out of ammunition, they would all be taken down, and turned into more of those things.

Stopping, Cutter fell back with the metal case containing the artifact in hand. He raised it and shook it mockingly at the horde as he retreated another step. He continued backing away on his heels, and the ocean of zombies spread out and closed off his only remaining path to safety.

But his final plan was working. The zombies were focusing on him, and that would let the others escape.

He kept backpedaling all the way to the top of the lift and stopped at the threshold of the elevator shaft. One glance up at the explosives strapped to the top of the metal girder assembly told him everything he needed to know. The detonators did not have any flashing lights or blinking LEDs. They just sat there, invisible timer ticking away.

His internal clock told him he had less than a minute remaining in his life. This was where he would make his final stand. Here he would die just as his wife had died, buried under millions of tons of rock. He'd die like Colonel Suvorov had died, only without a final cigarette. He was neither frightened by the prospect of death, nor overly saddened by where he might end up. Sharon had died so needlessly. At least he would die for a purpose. Maybe he'd even get to see her again.

And that was good. *I'm a lucky man.* He had the opportunity now to do one final good deed before he had to account for all his sins. While that might not completely square him with the man upstairs, it might be just enough to squeeze him past St. Peter.

In his mind, his score was settled—*paid in full.*

He glanced down the elevator shaft and then back at the approaching zombies and grinned broadly. As they closed in on him, he opened the case and let the artifact fall out of the padded interior.

He watched it fall away.

The silvery bar caught the light coming from the spotlight above and glinted all the colors of the rainbow as it went tumbling down into the abyss.

# ~47~
## MINDLESS ZOMBIES

Cutter ignored the artifact falling away and turned back to watch the zombies as they grew closer. That minute that was left to him was taking far longer than he would have it wished it to.

*I'm ready. Jesus, make up my dyin' bed.*

With an icy realization, he knew that the zombies would reach him before the explosives ever went off. But it would all be over soon enough. Even if they turned him into one of those things, the explosion would vaporize him, and the entire mountain would collapse and bury him and all of those terrible things along with him.

*Resurrection, my ass.*

The timer in his head told him he had thirty seconds remaining as the first of the zombies grew close enough to smell. They did not stink, per say, they mostly smelled of damp earth. Cutter held up his hands, palms first, with the insane idea that he would be able to stop them with the gesture, but they did not stop. They did not even slow.

But then they—

The eyes that had held such satanic evil before suddenly cleared and arms dropped to sides and mouths closed, and confusion broke out among the horde. It was as if the creatures had suddenly become human again. Some fell to their knees, some simply collapsed into heaps on the ground. A few raised their hands to their heads and broke out in wild screams. But most just stood there blinking as their eyes returned to normal.

One of the former zombies, what looked to be a stooping old man, led the way forward and stopped in front of Cutter. The old man stooped over in front of him grabbed him by the wrist and raised his left hand in the air. The man twisted the open palm back and forth as if he were examining it.

Cutter blinked back at the old miner in confusion. Then the man let go and Cutter's hand dropped to his side.

*Twenty seconds,* flashed in his mind.

Cutter realized then that he still had a chance to escape. With an increasing pace, he began pushing his way through the confused mass, moving faster and faster, using shoulders of the former zombies to push his way through their midst.

He stopped at the other side and spun around.

*"Come on!"* he shouted to the former zombies, who were merely teeming people now lost in the wheels of confusion. *"Come on! Let's all get the hell out of here!"*

But in a moment of dread, he realized that none of them spoke English. He started waving his arms, trying to get them to follow him, racking his brain to remember anything Colonel Suvorov had said to his men that got them to move.

He started jumping up and down and waving. None of the men were moving to follow him, nor were they paying him any attention whatsoever. They were too lost in surprise, staring at the backs of their hands, or their neighbors, jaws going slack.

He whistled and waved at them once more with both arms to come with him, ignoring the shooting pains coming from his battered body.

None followed.

He shouted and waved at them again, moving steadily backward on his feet toward the exit.

*Nothing?*

"Come on!" he yelled again.

*Fifteen seconds.*

With renewed vigor, he waved one final time.

A couple of the miners started in his direction.

*"Da!"* he shouted, remembering the one word he did know in Russian.

More began to follow him, but they were moving so slowly. *Too slowly.*

*"Da!"* he shouted again, trying to wave his arms. The joyful feeling that he was about to save them all kept the pain at bay.

They started moving faster, and he noticed something new as well. Their eyes were no longer normal. They had changed back to that same red satanic gaze they had before, and their lips had once again drawn back to expose their stained teeth.

The horde continued to move faster and faster toward him, and he spun on his heel and ran his hardest, no longer looking at what chased after him. All he could see was the door ahead that led out of the mine and into the light.

He ran with everything he had left in him. His heart raced, and his lungs were laboring to expand well beyond normal capacity. Life-giving blood pumped to every muscle and cell of his tortured body. He pushed harder, wanting nothing more than to escape before the explosion went off.

He wanted to live.

*Five seconds.*

He sprinted for the steel double doors just ahead. He heard the zombie horde gaining on him from behind. They were moving as fast as he was now. He was not going to be fast enough. He just didn't have it in him.

*Four seconds.*

The distance was just too great. He redoubled his efforts and a burst of pain shot through every corner of his body like he'd been struck by lightning.

*Three seconds.*

He wished again and again that he had never smoked, never drank, had taken better care of himself.

*Two seconds.*

The doorway was in sight. Morgan was standing there with the MP5K submachine gun, waving him through with one arm and getting ready to cover his retreat. They had made it. He would too. She backed away when he neared and propped open the door for him with her foot, leaving it wide open and ready.

*One second—*

He flung himself at the doorway like Superman taking flight—and flew through the threshold and smacked into the ground on the other side, skidding and painfully scraping away the skin on his hands and arms. He came to a stop and covered his head with his hands and clamped his eyes shut and anticipated the explosion.

Then—*nothing.*

Morgan grabbed him by the back of the shirt and yanked him away from the doorway he had flown through. It wouldn't close fully because his foot was somehow blocking it. He scrambled on his hands and knees away from the shadow of the entryway and into the dawning sunlight of the day.

*Was I wrong? Were the timers even set? Was Wayland full of shit?* He had just started to stand and brush the grit from his palms when the concussive wave from the explosion hit him like a sledgehammer from behind and flattened him against the concrete pathway leading to the mine entrance.

The massive initial explosion and secondary explosions of the collapsing mountain kept him flat on his stomach. He stayed low and pulled himself forward to be closer to Morgan and Gauge. From the corner of his eye, he spotted Dr. Martinez. She was also flat on her stomach. She was not moving. He tried to reach her but was hit with a heat that pressed against his back as flames pushed open the metal doors into the mine and an angry fireball roared out the doorway.

He remained on his belly for a few more seconds to recover as the world calmed around him. Then he rolled over. The earth still rumbled under him, but the bright sunlight warmed his face in a different kind of way from the flames, and the steam of his labored breathing created clouds of mist above him.

With what little he had left in him, he went to check on Dr. Martinez. When he got close to her, she turned her head and moaned something. He put a hand on her back and leaned nearer. His hearing was just about shot and would be for days. He waited for her to say something, but she just continued to groan.

Dull popping noises caused him to turn. He fell onto his backside and rubbed his face. His shoulder still hurt like hell, but all that fear juice pumping through his system had numbed away enough of the pain to make it tolerable.

Then he noticed all the soldiers and blinked away the confusion. At the doorway to what remained of the mine were soldiers. *A whole squad? Probably twenty or more.* They had pried opened the newly warped steel door he had come through and were tossing in bulky backpacks. Another line of soldiers stood about twenty feet off from the door. They were shooting anything that came through the threshold. Only a few of the remaining creatures actually tried to escape.

Cutter blinked a few more times. His eyes were not yet adjusted to the brightness of the day, but when his vision cleared, there was a man standing before him. The guy was blurred by the glare of the sun, but he recognized the man.

It was Anton Moray, the same guy who was paying them four-million dollars to retrieve the artifact. Moray said something, but Cutter could not understand him. The man repeated what he said, and Cutter watched the guy's lips move, but still could not quite make out what was being said.

"What?" Cutter said as he shook his head and stuck a finger in his ear to clear it. Everything sounded as if he were underwater.

Moray stepped closer and asked with the harsh tone of insistence, "Where is it?"

"It's gone," Cutter said. He might have even shouted it.

The man sucked in his lips and nodded. He appeared accustomed to absorbing and processing bad news without overreacting. He signaled to one of the soldiers, and the entire squad backed away from the entrance and another set of explosions went off.

Cutter covered his head and turned away. *All those people. Those men. Those former miners. They were all innocents, really.* He had seen them come back from the dead or undead or whatever the hell they had become. He was certain it had happened when the artifact had hit the bottom of the shaft and been destroyed. But the effects had only been temporary. Something seemed to have resumed control of those men again. *And the one old guy who let me go after looking at my hand? What was that all about?* Cutter had no idea, but he thanked the guy nonetheless. It was all so senseless. The killing. *Too much death.* He wondered if he had just kept the thing, maybe someone could have found a way to save all those people.

*Too late now.*

Morgan came over and helped him to his feet and stood next to him.

"I owe you an apology, Mr. Cutter," Moray said, still standing before him.

Cutter blinked and turned his left ear toward the man. It was working slightly better than his right. "Why?"

"I hired Mr. Wayland to oversee this operation. He failed me in so many ways. Once completed, he was expected to pay you and your team enough of a bonus that you would remain silent on what you had found here. I'm afraid I misunderstood his actual intentions. I am most disappointed in myself for allowing this to happen. So, if there is anything I can do for you, Mr. Cutter— anything at all—you have but to ask it of me."

Anton Moray thrust out his hand, and hesitantly, Cutter offered his. The man had a firm grip and a steely look to his eyes, and in that brief window of time, Cutter realized down to his core that he could work for the man again and forgive him as well—even if the guy did look like a chimpanzee in a suit.

Moray didn't linger. He spun and barked orders to the men around him, leaving Cutter standing beside Morgan Crow. Still a bit stunned by everything, he let her walk him over to where Gauge and Dr. Martinez were being looked after by a medic. The woman working on Dr. Martinez took one look at him and pointed to the grassy patch of dirt next to Gauge. The poor woman appeared as if she were handling far more than she had signed up for.

Cutter put his hand on his injured shoulder. The pain was returning in waves, and he winced to absorb it, but he did not cry out, nor would he. While he'd failed to retrieve the artifact, he realized he would have had to sacrifice something far more important to him to have kept it.

He glanced over at Dr. Martinez. Something in the back of his mind had him wondering all along what her game had been and whether or not she would betray him in the end. It probably would have been the expected thing, but he was sure glad she hadn't.

He glanced up at Morgan.

She asked him in what seemed almost a whisper, "So after all that, what do we call ourselves? I don't think we are a salvage and recovery team any longer. Maybe we call ourselves something cool like Zombie Team Alpha? Hashtag-ZTA maybe?"

"Yeah," Cutter replied, yawning and working his jaw back and forth, "I like that."

# ~48~
## *SPETSNAZ TOUGH (EPILOGUE)*

Yuri Stakhanov had known all along that he was a dead man walking. There was little left of the real him, and he had known it too well.

*Death will be a welcome change. It won't be long. But to the man with the white-gold ring—?*

It had taken everything inside of what remained of Yuri to keep from killing the brave man. It had been the shine of the ring, that faint glimmer of hope. It had reminded him of the one thing in his life that had mattered to him before he had begun his descent into hell—his beloved chocolate and the silver wrapper that had contained it.

And that same man had destroyed one of the Ancient Ones. Yuri admired the man with the ring for that. He wished he could have struck such a blow. Sadly, he'd only been able to resist the presence in his mind for a short period of time. He'd only been able to hold it back for a few moments due to his military experience. It had been difficult to do, but Yuri was tough.

*Spetsnaz tough.*

The alien mind inside of his head had screamed out when its mother had been destroyed. But the entity inside him had not given him more than a few moments of peace before it had smothered his own mind again with its desires. If anything, after he had let the man go, the alien mind had only redoubled its efforts to control him and kill the man who had destroyed one of the Ancient Ones. The alien inside of him still wanted to survive, and so he could not die either, much as he may have wished it to happen.

It had ultimately won the battle.

Everything he'd experienced over the past few days had been so horrible. He'd been present for it all. Every bit of pain had been amplified to torturous levels, and there was nothing he could do to resist it. He was not even allowed the brief respite of unconsciousness or sleep that such pain usually brought to most men. All he could do was watch the world through his own eyes as he did terrible things to others—terrible, terrible, unspeakable things.

All he wished for now was to die and be free of the pain. But he was not about to die. Not yet. Like his mind had been, his body was Spetsnaz tough as well. It had not broken as the bodies of many of his former co-laborers had. He knew that his own back was severed and pressed out of place along the spine, and his legs were nothing more than meat sacks containing shattered bones, and his left arm was dislocated and twisted grotesquely. Yet, his body persisted.

It survived.

His body had one good arm remaining, and with it, he scraped at the dirt in front of him as he clawed himself forward, centimeter by centimeter, all throughout the night.

When he had tried to fight the invading presence, that presence had stolen something from him. Something most precious that he'd been trying desperately to hide from it. Now the thing in his mind knew where his village was located and where his wife and family lived.

It was not too far away. In fact, Yuri could already see his home in the distance.

## THE END

# ABOUT THE AUTHOR

Steve R. Yeager is a part-time author who lives in Northern California with his wife, two kids, and a pair of crazy dogs. He has worked as a corporate software engineer for over 25 years and now spends much of spare time reading, writing, playing guitar, and shooting bows.

# CHECK OUT OTHER GREAT ZOMBIE NOVELS

## Z BURBIA
by Jake Bible

Whispering Pines is a classic, quiet, private American subdivision on the edge of Asheville, NC, set in the pristine Blue Ridge Mountains. Which is good since the zombie apocalypse has come to Western North Carolina and really put suburban living to the test!

Surrounded by a sea of the undead, the residents of Whispering Pines have adapted their bucolic life of block parties to scavenging parties, common area groundskeeping to immediate area warfare, neighborhood beautification to neighborhood fortification.

But, even in the best of times, suburban living has its ups and downs what with nosy neighbors, a strict Home Owners' Association, and a property management company that believes the words "strict interpretation" are holy words when applied to the HOA covenants. Now with the zombie apocalypse upon them even those innocuous, daily irritations quickly become dramatic struggles for personal identity, family security, and straight up survival.

## ZOMBIE RULES
by David Achord

Zach Gunderson's life sucked and then the zombie apocalypse began.

Rick, an aging Vietnam veteran, alcoholic, and prepper, convinces Zach that the apocalypse is on the horizon. The two of them take refuge at a remote farm. As the zombie plague rages, they face a terrifying fight for survival.

They soon learn however that the walking dead are not the only monsters.

# CHECK OUT OTHER GREAT ZOMBIE NOVELS

## 900 MILES
## by S. Johnathan Davis

John is a killer, but that wasn't his day job before the Apocalypse.

In a harrowing 900 mile race against time to get to his wife just as the dead begin to rise, John, a business man trapped in New York, soon learns that the zombies are the least of his worries, as he sees first-hand the horror of what man is capable of with no rules, no consequences and death at every turn.

Teaming up with an ex-army pilot named Kyle, they escape New York only to stumble across a man who says that he has the key to a rumored underground stronghold called Avalon..... Will they find safety? Will they make it to Johns wife before it's too late?

Get ready to follow John and Kyle in this fast paced thriller that mixes zombie horror with gladiator style arena action!

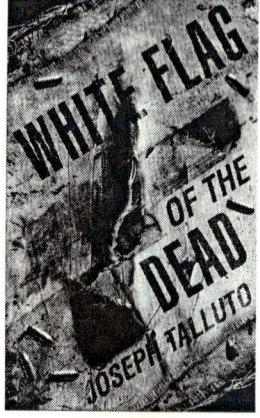

## WHITE FLAG OF THE DEAD
## by Joseph Talluto

Millions died when the Enillo Virus swept the earth. Millions more were lost when the victims of the plague refused to stay dead, instead rising to slaughter and feed on those left alive. For survivors like John Talon and his son Jake, they are faced with a choice: Do they submit to the dead, raising the white flag of surrender? Or do they find the will to fight, to try and hang on to the last shreds or humanity?

# CHECK OUT OTHER GREAT ZOMBIE NOVELS

## VACCINATION
by Phillip Tomasso

What if the H7N9 vaccination wasn't just a preventative measure against swine flu?

It seemed like the flu came out of nowhere and yet, in no time at all the government manufactured a vaccination. Were lab workers diligent, or could the virus itself have been man-made? Chase McKinney works as a dispatcher at 9-1-1. Taking emergency calls, it becomes immediately obvious that the entire city is infected with the walking dead. His first goal is to reach and save his two children.

Could the walls built by the U.S.A. to keep out illegal aliens, and the fact the Mexican government could not afford to vaccinate their citizens against the flu, make the southern border the only plausible destination for safety?

## ZOMBIE, INC
by Chris Dougherty

"WELCOME! To Zombie, Inc. The United Five State Republic's leading manufacturer of zombie defense systems! In business since 2027, Zombie, Inc. puts YOU first. YOUR safety is our MAIN GOAL! Our many home defense options - from Ze Fence® to Ze Popper® to Ze Shed® - fit every need and every budget. Use Scan Code "TELL ME MORE!" for your FREE, in-home*, no obligation consultation! *Schedule your appointment with the confidence that you will NEVER HAVE TO LEAVE YOUR HOME! It isn't safe out there and we know it better than most! Our sales staff is FULLY TRAINED to handle any and all adversarial encounters with the living and the undead". Twenty-five years after the deadly plague, the United Five State Republic's most successful company, Zombie, Inc., is in trouble. Will a simple case of dwindling supply and lessening demand be the end of them or will Zombie, Inc. find a way, however unpalatable, to survive?

# CHECK OUT OTHER GREAT ZOMBIE NOVELS

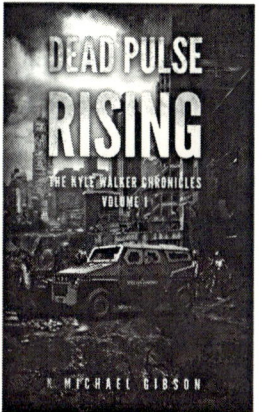

 SEVERED**PRESS**

⬤ facebook.com/severedpress

⬤ twitter.com/severedpress

# CHECK OUT OTHER GREAT ZOMBIE NOVELS

## RUN
## by Rich Restucci

The dead have risen, and they are hungry

Slow and plodding, they are Legion. The undead hunt the living. Stop and they will catch you. Hide and they will find you. If you have a heartbeat you do the only thing you can: You run.

Survivors escape to an island stronghold: A cop and his daughter, a computer nerd, a garbage man with a piece of rebar, and an escapee from a mental hospital with a life-saving secret. After reaching Alcatraz, the ever expanding group of survivors realize that the infected are not the only threat.

Caught between the viciousness of the undead, and the heartlessness of the living, what choice is there? Run.

## THE DEAD WALK THE EARTH
## by Luke Duffy

As the flames of war threaten to engulf the globe, a new threat emerges.

A 'deadly flu', the like of which no one has ever seen or imagined, relentlessly spreads, gripping the world by the throat and slowly squeezing the life from humanity.

Eight soldiers, accustomed to operating below the radar, carrying out the dirty work of a modern democracy, become trapped within the carnage of a new and terrifying world.

Deniable and completely expendable. That is how their government considers them, and as the dead begin to walk, Stan and his men must fight to survive.

 SEVEREDPRESS

facebook.com/severedpress

twitter.com/severedpress

# CHECK OUT OTHER GREAT ZOMBIE NOVELS

## DEAD ASCENT
## by Jason McPhearson

The dead have risen and they are hungry...

Grizzled war veteran turned game warden, Brayden James and a small group of survivors, fight their way through the rugged wilderness of southern Appalachia to an isolated cabin in the hope of finding sanctuary. Every terrifying step they make they are stalked by a growing mass of staggering corpses, and a raging forest fire, set by the government in hopes of containing the virus.

As all logical routes off the mountain are cut off from them, they seek the higher ground, but they soon realize there is little hope of escape when the dead walk and the world burns.

## CHAOS THEORY
## by Rich Restucci

The world has fallen to a relentless enemy beyond reason or mercy. With no remorse they rend the planet with tooth and nail.

One man stands against the scourge of death that consumes all.

Teamed with a genius survivalist and a teenage girl, he must flee the teeming dead, the evils of humans left unchecked, and those that would seek to use him. His best weapon to stave off the horrors of this new world? His wit.

CPSIA information can be obtained at www.ICGtesting.com
Printed in the USA
LVOW11s2249070916

503670LV00002B/150/P